NEVER GONNA DIG YOU UP

AN UNUSUALITIES NOVEL

KEL BRUEM

Copyright © 2024 by Kel Bruem

Cover design by Arash Jahani

Cover font design by B.L. Brown

All rights reserved. No part of this publication may be reproduced, stored or transmitted in any form or by any means, electronic, mechanical, photocopying, recording, scanning, or otherwise without written permission from the publisher. It is illegal to copy this book, post it to a website, or distribute it by any other means without permission.

This novel is entirely a work of fiction. The names, characters and incidents portrayed in it are the work of the author's imagination. Any resemblance to actual persons, living or dead, events or localities is entirely coincidental.

Designations used by companies to distinguish their products are often claimed as trademarks. All brand names and product names used in this book and on its cover are trade names, service marks, trademarks and registered trademarks of their respective owners. The publishers and the book are not associated with any product or vendor mentioned in this book. None of the companies referenced within the book have endorsed the book.

For Kourtney

Billy's OG ride-or-die

CONTENTS

Chapter One

Huxley Manor

The wind loved the manor, though it was probably the only one who did. It loved the whistle of its rage through the cracks in the ill-set stone, loved the push of the walls against its ever-present gusts, loved the bending groan of the trees as it encouraged their branches to whip far across their hedged captors.

For centuries, it had only been the wind and the manor, hissing and pushing and whispering to one another in solitude. It had been only the wind who noticed the moss growing further and further up the walls, who cheered on the climb of the ivy as it twisted its way up the front columns. No one else noticed the shriek of rust as it clamped shut the front gate or the muffled crash of support beams inside as they fell upon a carpet of rotted wooden flooring.

The manor was a forgotten place, a lonely place—a place that invited local rumors but deterred any curious visitors with a twist of their nerves, a fluttering in their stomach, a chill across the back of their neck that urged them *stay away, stay away, stay away.*

Some said it was cursed. They weren't entirely wrong.

The manor sat in total stillness, letting the constant wet of the English countryside seep deeper and deeper until the very foundation was soggy. It did nothing to ward off the moss, the weeds, the scuttling vermin burrowing within its walls. It practically urged on increasing holes in its roof, as if its imminent collapse would bring a formerly unknown relief.

It was not like other gothic monuments, wary of villains, welcoming of heroes, protective of ingenues. This manor had no guts, no glory, no god.

The monster had made sure of that.

This manor had watched a great amount of violence and never so much as rattled a doorknob to intervene. And so, as if in self-flagellation, it let itself rot. It let the wind's affection continue one-sided and did its best to warn away the local villagers.

It did not deserve residency. Not after everyone left.

Not after what happened here.

But one morning, early enough that neither the sun nor the birds were stretching to greet the day, a shudder went through the earth. It was a strange thing, felt only by those with an affinity for strange happenings and, of course, the manor. Because the warning was meant for it.

He had returned. The very same child of Adam the manor failed to protect stepped foot upon his home soil for the first time in too many bygone decades, drawing ever closer still.

A shudder of anticipation creaked through what walls remained. Maybe the time had come. Maybe change was arriving with the not-quite-man.

Maybe things would be different soon.

Maybe.

The wind whistled through and around the manor, repeating the possibility over and over again.

Maybe.

All the manor could do was wait.

And hope.

Chapter Two

BILLY

"We'll be preparing for landing in just a few moments, sir."

I looked up from my book, a new translation of *Beowulf* that had my eyebrows perpetually arched, to see Charles, my private flight attendant, holding out a fresh glass of champagne.

I accepted it, letting the book flip closed as I savored a sweet sip. He nodded to my hardback.

"I've been wondering about that one, sir," he said. "Seems to have caused a stir."

"I didn't know you liked poetry," I said, gesturing to the seat across from me.

He waved me away, flashing me a rare half smile. I tried not to let the rejection simmer.

"I studied it as much as anyone else in college," he said, tucking the silver tray under his arm. "But I've always been a sucker for a good epic hero." He gave me a nod before stepping back into the flight galley and busying himself with whatever it was flight crew did to prepare for landing.

I liked Charles as much as anyone else I hired to keep my life running smooth. And just like everyone on that roster, Charles liked me as much as staff should like their clients. But still my past pushed through—the ache in my feet at standing, running, serving for hours. I remembered the pang of wishing so desperately for the luxury I knew I'd never have. Despite the continuous polite rejection, and the sting it carried. I continued offering seats, tastes, samples, complimentary passes. What I had was mine alone with no one to share it with, it seemed a waste to keep it solely to myself.

But Charles was a professional. He only ever chatted about polite topics like books, weather, and food—only ever long enough to smooth the delivery of the object or service before continuing with his work.

The usual rejection to chat stung more than usual, and I knew it was because of what was behind me, far across the ocean we'd just crossed.

I pushed *her* from my mind, eager to avoid yet another spiral into self-loathing because I'd once more chosen a woman who didn't choose me back. The emotional feat had me downing a slightly too big sip of my traditional landing champagne.

Modern flight was a marvel. I'd never have dreamed of it in my mortal lifetime, and I certainly wasn't going to take it for granted now that I was undead. My vampiric life's endless stretch across the decades meant enjoying the fruits of mortal ingenuity—including things like the Industrial Revolution, tech startups, the stock market, and planes. Now that I commanded a private jet and crew, I had taken to celebrating each gravity-defying takeoff, each impossibly safe landing like a turn-of-the-century political leader smashing a bottle of champagne across the bow of an ocean liner.

Except I didn't want to make Charles clean up all that glass, so I settled for a single flute at takeoff and landing. Not that it tasted like much—vampirism doesn't leave room for earthly pleasures. Most food and drink taste like ash to the unlucky ones. To the rest of us, we're lucky to get any texture, much less flavor. It's more like chewing on air than anything, but I've found that some of the more opinionated consumables have the most feedback—champagne has bubbles, mousse is soft and creamy, and potato chips are crisp and snappy.

Which is all a way of saying that I promised my former soul I would indulge as much as possible on my long journey to wealth and luxury. I have no intention of depriving myself simply because the supernatural rules apply.

Usually, the champagne was Laurent Perrier Grand Siècle. Not the *most* expensive I could flaunt, but a delight to drink and of a good enough pedigree that each bottle was consistently enjoyable. I made a mental note to tell Charles to take the rest of the bottle with him to his hotel. There was no telling when we'd take off next.

I let a sigh push out of my chest as I watched the runway lights flash out into the dark. This part of the country was dark and quiet, nearly swallowed by the dark expanse of ocean breaking against the shore. The dark window reflected my pale face back to me—there were the red eyes, the porcelain skin that came with my curse, but also the shockingly white-blonde hair I'd had through both my lives. It was a point of pride for me to keep it clean, well-groomed, and on trend, as it was the only part of myself to bridge that divide.

Also, I was vain.

"There you are," I murmured to what bits of dark coastline I could make out around my reflection. It was the closest thing to home I had, this soggy expanse of meadows and cliffs rising to meet a thick, misty forest that separated the county line from the rest of England. The thought turned my stomach to bile, and I fought the urge to slam the last half of my glass. It wouldn't help.

But that was the whole fight, wasn't it? Don't let the memories swallow me, don't let who I was destroy who I *am*.

I'd let the place rot on purpose, my own version of a curse. But time had dragged on long enough, and the county was threatening to overrule my deed for fear of public safety. It only took one group of drunk teens nearly dying while tripping around in the dark to drag me out of my New York penthouse and across the ocean. They wouldn't be the last curious crew to wander through, and the local government was in a tizzy over the possible liabilities.

I hoped it'd be a simple matter of hiring the right crew to renovate, reconstruct, and reinvigorate the place into a money-making enterprise, depositing into my account monthly without further thought. I'd come prepared to grease whatever palms would make the process move as quickly as possible.

You could never really go home again, and I was banking on that, praying to the very deity who had turned their back on me so many centuries ago that time erased any prestige the manor held over the village. Maybe we could be done with its legacy once and for all, replacing it with a luxury hospitality "experience."

But I knew prayers never did any good, and time, like a woman, could be a cruel, self-serving mistress.

***

The plane door opened onto an empty tarmac, the smell of wet cement and jet fuel rising to meet me. Thanking Charles, I reminded him to take whatever was left from the flight so it wouldn't go to waste and braced myself for my next few steps. I hadn't returned to England since my last *necessary* visit nearly 150 years ago—a cool 50 years after my turning. There was no way to know what would happen now.

During our last conversation in Boston, a fellow vampire, Patrick, warned me strong forces may be at play when I returned. Most vampire ex-pats got along fine by keeping their home grave dirt nearby, and I had had my bedroom floors filled with earth from this very county before laying the wood floor and tile over the top of it. But the surge of power, the connection to the earth that I never returned to, that I never let claim my bones or my ash, would be much stronger here. *I* would be much stronger here.

I only remember my early years as a vampire in flashes. They aren't memories I strive to keep. Bloodlust is a foul, primal thing, and I don't plan on returning to its grip.

I steadied myself, prying my fingers off the railing of the stairs, and took my first step back onto English country.

A small shudder crawled up my body, tingling my bones and pounding in my chest before evaporating. The manor flashed in my mind's eye, decrepit, moldering, waiting.

"Well," I said to myself, looking around for the car I had booked to take me to the only hotel in the village that wasn't someone's spare room. "This will be fun."

My eyes landed on a wreck of a minivan, a single headlight flickering weakly across the wet cement. I looked again, sure there had been some mistake. But no—this was the only vehicle other than the plane behind me.

Just as I was about to turn back to the safety of the plane's leather seats and Charles's attention, a tall man in a cap appeared, waving from over the open driver side door of the minivan.

"You're going to Clotswold by Litchfield, right?"

I nodded, dumbstruck. There was *no fucking way* this ride cost me £200.

The man leapt from the car and pulled open the passenger side door, gesturing grandly inside. "Your carriage, monsieur."

"Sir?" Charles questioned from over my shoulder. He was holding my cabin bag in one hand, my suitcase handle in the other.

"It's okay," I said, feeling a small headache build behind my eyes. "They do things differently in the country. That's all. Nothing to worry about."

Charles followed me to the minivan. I heard him sniff disapprovingly as we got closer, noticing the cracked windshield, the scratches along the sides, and enough dents to make it look as if it rolled down a ravine and back up again.

As I climbed into the back seat, I noticed one of the side view mirrors dangling by a few sparking cords. The driver hummed a country song, the lyrics of which drifted through my memory—something about dust on a bottle but the drink being good. I didn't think it was a coincidence.

Once Charles loaded my bags, the trunk hatch barely thunking shut, I settled into the rattling ambience of the van. Backfire like an indoor shotgun kicked off what was sure to be a long ride to the hotel. I was already composing my complaint as the driver maneuvered the junk heap onto the country road, the wet crunch of gravel loud and grating against my now much bigger headache.

I'd been surprised to see a luxury offering like Clotswold in a village like Ashbourne. They'd only recently begun to see an influx of tourism, largely American, as the internet made the world smaller, and people started seeking destinations farther and farther from the beaten path. I'd been so grateful I wouldn't have to navigate my abnormal sleeping habits with a nosy bed-and-breakfast host I'd booked immediately. Maybe I should've been more suspicious of such lavish accommodations in such a remote place.

"What brings you to Ashbourne?" the driver asked. His eyes were too dark on his young face, and no expression met them even as he smiled. The flash of his fangs gave me some comfort before answering his question.

"Estate business," I said, flashing a fang back. The driver chuckled, and I watched his shoulders drop from around his ears. He settled into his seat, considerably more at ease, driving the screeching minivan with a single practiced hand.

"The old manor, then," he said. He had a soft accent—somewhere from the American northeast I couldn't quite place. Old, then, this one.

"Does this girl convert with fins?" I asked, directly avoiding his not-question.

"If we can break the curse of our kind to cross water, then getting a minivan to England from Florida isn't so complicated," he said, directly avoiding my actual question.

"Tricky language for a hotel driver," I said.

He held my gaze in the mirror in silence before letting loose a monstrous sigh.

"My last job was exhausting. Witches getting their *juices* all over the backseat, fighting off old gods, driving through actual hell. The Madame offered me a quieter assignment helping with her latest investment opportunity, and I'm not too proud to say I practically leapt for joy."

"The Madame? As in—"

"The same." He nodded.

Madame Laveau, New Orleans's most famous and reputable vampire voodoo witch. She commanded a legacy nest of vampires, golems, and other undead soldiers. If she had something to do with this driver's employment, then—

"Since when do vampire queens invest in hotels?"

"Ah, that's a fun one," he said, both fangs gleaming in the dark this time. The minivan's single headlight did little to cut the impressive dark around us, but the driver had long since stopped watching the road. "A little nest of fanglings turned up in the village with no sire to guide them. I'm hazy on the order of things, but I guess their new schedules lined up well with the night desk. They accidentally ate the managers—you remember how it is with bloodlust—and to cover it up, they've had to say they were promoted. Which..." He let out an affectionate cackle. "There's no way that's true, but humans will believe anything.

"Anyway, The Madame got wind and saw an opportunity to expand her reach and earn a little something at the same time."

I stared hard at the driver, trying to process what he was telling me. The headache had grown to a pounding and my vision blurred. I reached into my plane bag and pulled out a blood bag.

"If you get that on my seats—"

I held up a finger to silence the driver and bit into the top, sucking gratefully on the chilled, gelatinous substance. Once the blood hit my system, I felt the clarity follow. My headache subsided as I shoved the empty bag into a side pocket of my carry-on. Crossing the ocean last time had nearly killed me. I'd learned my lesson about bringing graveyard dirt with me when traveling—why was I still hurting?

"So, this is a vampire hotel?" It sounded stupid as I said it, but the driver simply nodded.

"Goblins have Vegas, the fae have Ireland, and the merfolk are starting corporate ocean liners. Madame thought it was time we earned some international income of our own."

"I suppose that makes sense." It was the only response I could manage as another blinding headache slammed through me. This one was twice the intensity and pain as the first. I put a hand over my eyes and tried to will it away, tried to give the blood more time to settle within me, for my body to take in its power fully. It had barely been a few moments. I didn't need to panic.

"You alright?" the driver asked as he guided the minivan along the twisting road. I clamped my eyes shut against the image of the single headlight swinging sickeningly in the dark. "I'd say you look a little pale, but..."

"Pull over." I gripped the edge of my seat as the whole world flipped, threatening to crack my head wide open.

"Don't you *dare* throw up back there."

"Then *pull. Over,*" I snarled. The minivan slid to a daredevil stop, the back-end fishtailing into the muddy moor stretching out before us. The driver slid the door open, and I barely made it past him before hot chunks of curdled blood crawled up my throat. They hit the grass with a wet squelching thud, the sound enough to inspire another round of vomiting.

Dirt. I need dirt. It was the only thought pounding through my skull, pushing past the waves of blinding pain behind my eyes. Somewhere far away, a voice was trying to reach me. It would never get through. I was alone in my panic and pain, and I had to get the dirt that would absolve me.

Without thinking, I dug my hands into the mud, bringing handfuls to my mouth. I sunk my fangs into the small mound in my palms as if it were a delicate, juicy—

"*Sir,*" the driver whispered. I paused, mouth full of life-saving dirt. The driver stared, a mixture of fear and disgust on his face. "Alright?"

I spit the dirt out, coming back to my senses. The headache had subsided to a dull throb, and the world was still again. I looked down at myself, my shirt covered in blood, mud, and sweat. My fingernails were caked with dirt, and my hands shook as I slowly convinced them to drop their earthy treasure.

"No," I said, shaking my head. "I am definitely not."

Chapter Three

Leslee

"Bullshit, Tyler. That's bullshit and you know it," I hissed into the phone.

"Les, don't be like this."

"Don't be like what? Pissed that you've taken all the credit for my work and left me nothing? Excuse me if I don't hire a brass band and go cha-chaing through the square." Rage pulsed through me, threatening to shoot out of my hands and around the room. If I wasn't careful, I was going to cast a hex while I was the only one in the room. I glanced over to see my window herb garden practically quivering and my box planters full of zinnias were straining against the recycled wood to lean away from me.

"I thought you'd be happy for me," Tyler whined.

"Oh, I am." I seethed. "I'm happy that you'll never have to see me again. I'm happy you'll have to explain to the Queen Madame herself why your work is suddenly so sub-fucking-par. I'm happy you'll get yourself fired, which is far less than you deserve."

"What...no...Les—" I hung up on his sputtering, flinging my phone and a screamed hex across the room. There was the shattering of glass and a dull thud from the wet lawn out front. The red disappeared from my vision as I took a few shuddering breaths to calm myself, pushing my magic back into its healthy circular flow through my body. I needed to pull it back out of my hands before I lost control and broke something else.

"That fucking wanker isn't worth my time," I exhaled. "And all I've spoken shall be true." I ended another round of breathing with that mantra, finally able to get my head together.

So, what, my business partner and best friend had absolutely fucked me over? The dreams we'd worked for together were suddenly shattered, much like my own goddamned windowpane. I still had the cottage. I still had Ashbourne. I still had chances I could make for myself.

"Ugh, but this still sucks." I dropped my shoulders before flinging open the front door. It groaned on its hinges, catching in the usual place on the uneven stone floor. I gave it a hearty shoulder shove, opting for something a little more physical than the usual magical fix because, damn it, I could.

Tyler and I grew up together, here in the village. He wasn't magically inclined like I was, but that never stopped us from tearing the town apart with whatever scheme he cooked up. Once my powers manifested, he just saw another opportunity for mischief.

Of course, once we were older, he saw them as a chance to earn a way out—that's what he called it. My powers and his focus were our escape route. I needed his ability to complete tasks without getting sidetracked, and he needed my ability to make a flower grow from the side of a rockface.

Soon enough, our little gardening enterprise flourished, and we were hiring staff to take on clients in the farther reaches of the county, and even into the next few. I was spending more and more days trundling around in the truck with Tyler, meeting clients, tending to problem gardens, and generally thriving in a line of work that fed me as much as it paid me.

I think Tyler grew greedy with the first wedding. The client was an elderly woman with a trembling voice and a perpetually upturned nose. She wanted shrubs in the shape of her granddaughter and the bridegroom to celebrate their wedding. This kind of work would've been extravagant for a normal team, but Tyler promised, so I delivered. The shrubs were *so* annoyed with me. They didn't like the woman, or her family, and it took weeks of coaxing to get them to even start forming a foot.

But we did it. And then our phones wouldn't stop ringing.

The wealthy woman was apparently a duchess or something, and she'd told all her friends about us. We answered more and more requests, each more outlandish than the last, each taking more and more of my power.

Tyler didn't seem to care that I was coming back from each job drained and exhausted. He spent our profits on expensive cars and watches, posing on the internet like a would-be gangster with hand signs and exaggerated scowls—a bloody chav, I realized now. He talked a lot about "hustling" but I didn't see him do anything other than make promises he couldn't keep without me.

And when I complained, he wouldn't hear it.

"It's part of the job, Les."

"You love this, Les."

"Don't worry, Les, it won't always be like this."

The Royal Gardening Championships arrived, and I didn't want to do it. I'd dreamed of entering my whole life, but faced with the opportunity, I felt nothing. I was burnt-out to the very ends of my curls. But Tyler entered us anyway.

I told him I wouldn't do it. I was too tired. I wanted out.

"Please, Les," he pleaded, those bright blue eyes sparkling with unshed tears. "This'll be the last job we ever have to do. It'll be all managing and delegating after this, I promise. I'll get you a fleet of plant people to do your bidding."

I shouldn't have caved, sitting in the pub where our parents still met for cards once a week—where I'd run interference while he made out with boys visiting from college. All those memories whispered from beneath the floorboards that I couldn't say no—not to Tyler.

And then, when it was all said and done, he'd accepted the award, taken the title of Queen's Gardener in his name—and *only* his name.

He'd stolen all our hard work. No. He'd stolen *my* work.

Once outside, I felt the usual pull of my garden. I'd poured my heart and soul and every ounce of magic I had into this garden. This wasn't just my home—it was a part of me. I felt the reaching comfort of every root and stem and leaf as I stepped into its embrace. *This* was my craft. This was what I'd been born to do, and it was more than my powers. Even without magic, I knew the best dirt for each floral variety, the best time to re-pot a particularly sensitive sapling, the best direction to trim a hedge so it shaped *exactly* the way you wished. It was witchery honed by craft—not the other way around.

That's what I had over Tyler and his fancy connections, his smooth talking, his charm. I was a frizzy-haired, freckled, short weirdo with bug-eyed glasses and too many charm necklaces to be discreet.

"It doesn't matter," I said to the garden. "I have you guys. You have me. And we will figure out our next step."

The aspen in the corner—Spen, I called it—shuddered a whisper of leaves in response. I sidestepped to it and patted its white bark a few times tenderly.

"Thank you dear. I know you believe in us."

The evening was wet and moody—properly English for the time of year—and I suddenly remembered my very expensive cell phone soaking in the grass.

"Out of work, now. Can't replace that anymore," I sighed to myself. Following the curve of the cottage around to the kitchen window, framed by the now-anxious box planters and several twining strands of ivy, I pocketed my phone, not bothering to glance at the screen. There were most likely several missed calls from Tyler, as well as some new cracks in the glass. I didn't want to know.

I turned my attention instead to the zinnias drooping over the edge of their planter boxes. Even the ivy shrunk back at my temper tantrum—a feat given how tenacious it usually was. I spread my arms wide in apology, focusing a soothing energy into my center and pushing it out to the flowers.

"I'm sorry, friends," I whispered. "That was probably very stressful for you. Mummy didn't mean it for you."

Slowly, their rich red petals stretched out, their stems strengthened, and they preened. I turned my attention to the ivy strands, whispering the same apology, offering the same gentle energy. The leaves shuddered and perked up. I don't think I imagined the stretch of a few tendrils even further up the wall than before.

I had to be more careful with my temper. For all the release it offered, I'd be spending twice the time tending my babies.

And now I was on my own. I was going to need all the time I could get. I watched the flowers rustle knowingly as a wave of panic crashed through me. Pushing it back, I windmilled my arms through the air as if I were physically swimming through it.

"Can't keep me down," I chanted to myself. "Can't keep a bad witch down. Can't keep a hot bitch low. We climb like English ivy—determined, resilient, and overwhelming." My pinwheel dance devolved into rump shaking, and I'm pretty sure if leaves could cover their eyes they would.

"Right," I laughed to myself, finally feeling a little better. Moving my body in free, goofy ways always had that effect. "Guess we need to go drum up new business. We can't all be so bold as to lie to the Queen, gods bless her. Some of us have to do proper work. Right, Spen?" I waved to the ever-quivering aspen as I did a mock military march back into the house to start on my portfolio.

Tyler may have accepted the position of Royal Gardener, but it was still my project that earned him the title—I could still show it as mine even if I hadn't technically "won" the assignment. I had hundreds of proud photos to sort through and a rusty website to update.

But first: *tea.*

***

It was 7:45 PM before I realized I hadn't even opened my laptop. I looked around, annoyed and mildly confused at the now-empty pot of tea I had chugged and the writhing mass of cactuses I had begun charming to sing Christmas carols.

I put a finger to my lips and blew out a low whistle.

"Sorry gents," I said, dispelling the magic between us and watching all the spiky little babies settle back into their pots with visible relief. "I'll have to leave us here. This was *not* what I was supposed to be doing."

How had I got here?

"First it was tea," I said to myself, ticking the steps down on my fingers. "Then I remembered the string of pearls could move pots if I wanted to keep it as happy as it has been and, well, why shouldn't we attend to it now while we're thinking about it?" I twirled in a small, slow circle, the many stones I wore on cords around my neck bumping and clinking against each other. Naturally, I had told myself if we were having a potting party, I should attend to whoever needed it so no one would be jealous and somehow that devolved into teaching cactuses Christmas carols.

"Not that we could show anyone even if we wanted to," I sighed. "Neighbors might not want a witch around at Yuletide. Even if it's more my holiday than theirs." The cactus directly to my right settled its thick trunk with a low whistle. "Right, right, it doesn't actually matter. My portfolio."

I glanced out the window, noting the hang of the crescent moon and the dotting of stars. "But it's a beautiful night for recharging," I said, arguing with both myself and the whiny cactus. "It'd be a shame to spend it in front of a screen. Besides, it's not like the perfect client is searching for landscapers right this moment. It can wait 'till morning."

Yes, it would be *much* better to stroll the stretch of peaty farmland between the end of the village and the woods beneath the singing starlight. I'd bring a basket and hunt for some particularly grotesque mushrooms. Oh yes, that *would* be wonderful for my soul and my heart—which was what every good hedge witch needed in spades. Everything after that would fall into place, I was sure of it.

And if it didn't fall, I'd pull it to me anyway.

Chapter Four

BILLY

"Do I need to remind you who paid your fare?" I snapped. The driver was standing square between me and the open mini-van door. Even with his arms crossed, he was a waif of a man. I could've flicked him hard and watched him fall over. But those dead eyes were boring through me and refusing to give any acknowledgement of the situation I now found myself in.

"I'll give you a full refund," he said firmly.

"And how exactly will I get into town, then?"

"Clearly, you don't mind dirt," he said, nodding at my hands. "Take the walk."

"Absolutely not." I paid for the ride and I would *get* the ride, never mind my current panic over losing my mind a second time.

I really didn't want to be alone. Maybe I could call Charles. I pushed the thought away as quick as it arrived, promising to wallow in self-pity over my lack of emergency contacts later—preferably from the comfort of 800 thread count sheets.

"I'll pay another £200." I pulled my wallet from my back pocket and thrust the bills at the driver. My hands were shaking so hard the money sounded like wind through the trees. I held the driver's unwavering gaze as he considered it. In the silence between us, I felt a sudden tug from the earth beneath me, as if someone had tied a string to my gut and hung a large stone from it. I dropped like dead weight to the ground, and before I could understand what was happening, I felt the earth slinking up around my feet and ankles.

I was being swallowed—*reclaimed.*

Frantic, I scrambled to grab my entire wallet and held it in the air above my head, snatching my wrist free before the dirt looped over it.

"*Anything*," I said, knowing full well it was a dangerous offer between unusual folk like us. "I will pay you *anything.*"

Strong hands lifted under my arms and pulled me upright. The driver stomped one dainty foot on the ground, and the crawling dirt subsided.

"You need to make things right with your burial dirt," he said matter-of-factly. "I've never seen it this bad."

"What does that mean?" I asked, suppressing a shudder that rolled through me as I glanced down at the now-still earth beneath us.

"Vampires defy the grave by living undead. The only time the grave comes for them is if they ask it to," he said.

"I didn't ask for this," I said, smothering the indignance that threatened to drown out all reason.

"No, surely not." He looked thoughtful—or as much as he could with those pinched black eyes. "Best to get to the hotel and make some calls."

My shoulders slumped loose, and I clasped his hands. My knees threatened to buckle with relief. I just wanted a hot shower, soft sheets, maybe something decadent from room service—a slice of sponge maybe, that would taste like chewing warm air.

"Thank you, uh..." I realized I hadn't learned his name yet.

"Dies-well," he said, plucking my wallet from my trembling fingers. "And don't thank me yet." He turned and reached into the minivan, grabbing my plane bag and handing it to me with little delicacy. "Bring along your mud. I don't want to pull over again if we can help it. There's something strange afoot."

I opened my mouth to protest getting my things muddy, but I snapped it shut so quickly I nicked my lip with a fang—something I hadn't done since I was freshly turned. He was right. The earth was calling to me in a way it never had before, and my best bet was to listen until I could figure out another plan of action.

I opened the bag and carefully placed my laptop, folio, and various chargers and cables onto the backseat of the minivan. I gave myself a moment to prepare—and mourn. The inside of my plane bag was satin-lined, delicately embroidered with my initials flush against the burnished leather exterior. I'd paid a fortune for it, and I considered it my good-luck charm against a vampire's most dangerous feat—air travel. It would never recover from being filled with the peaty, muddy mess I could already feel writhing at my feet.

Dies-well cleared his throat behind me, humming the Jeopardy tune under his breath.

"I'll take 'people who have no patience for 500,' Alex."

I bent down, fighting off a wave of nausea as I remembered the dirt beneath my fangs, the press of the silty mud against my tongue. Worse, I felt a strange exhilaration as I scooped my bare hands into the earth, lifting a trembling pile and unceremoniously dumping it with a wet squelch into my bag. And yet, there was something else here too, something I couldn't quite name as I repeated the process until my bag was half full. Something called to me from deep within the earth—gentler than what had snatched me moments before. Something that promised sweetness, kindness, care.

Rest, it seemed to say. *Rest easy, here.*

A gasp broke my trance, and I glanced up, horrified to see a flashlight illuminating my scrambling in the dirt.

"Excuse me." A woman's voice, shocked, disgusted, but also curious. "Are you alright?"

"My client is feeling like boiled owl; apologies, miss. Nothing serious."

I remained frozen, unsure if I should continue my task, throw up again at the mention of "boiled owl," or let the dirt swallow me whole. Dirt climbed my arms and my body decided for me. I involuntarily shuddered, shaking it off and rising to my feet.

"Did you just imply I'm hungover?" I shot Dies-well a look.

He shot one back. "Yes. A perfectly normal state to be in as a human and not at all related to the supernatural."

"That seems like unnecessary clarification," the woman said. I could see around the light she held—her phone, I realized—to take in her wild hair, curling into a massive bush that she tamed with a simple cloth head band. Round glasses framed her hazel eyes, narrowed into a suspicious squint, and beneath them a dusting of freckles gave her face an earnestness I found hard to look away from. She wore a long, flowing skirt that reminded me of a disastrous music festival I'd attended in the 60s and a loose blouse above it. A small horde of crystals and gems of various sizes hung from her neck, and they clanked and clinked whenever she moved.

"My client is embarrassingly dim," Dies-well whispered loud enough for me to hear, and I rolled my eyes.

"Pardon us," I said finally. "I wasn't feeling well with the twisting roads and needed a moment in the fresh air. I slipped in the mud, and that's when you found us." In demonstration, I offered the bottom of my shoe, pointing to the slick surface coated in mud. "Can I offer you a ride into town? It's dark and I'm sure Dies-well won't mind dropping you at home."

Dies-well made a face that I ignored.

Suspicion lifted slowly from the woman's face as she shook her head. "No, thank you," she said. "I have mushrooms to seek and miles to go before I sleep."

"Nicely said, Mrs. Frost."

"You know she turned him down at first?"

"Who did?"

"Elinor White, Robert Frost's wife—Mrs. Frost. He proposed when she was in college after he published his first poem, but she wanted to finish her own degree first."

"Huh."

"I know," she leaned forward conspiratorially. "Men do one thing right and think it earns them the earth."

A smile cracked my face before I could think about what she was implying.

"Americans especially," I said, earning a tinkling giggle from this strange woman. When I glanced at Dies-well, he pointed to my teeth, indicating something was in them, and I slammed my mouth shut, running an anxious tongue across my fang and nicking it in the process.

"Well, we'll be on our way then," I said around a mouthful of my own old blood. "You're sure you don't want a ride?"

She shook her head, crystals clanking and jangling. Her eyes remained on us as we said goodbye, surely not missing my leap into the van. I shuddered as I closed my now violated plane bag, grateful I avoided a riotous wreck of an interaction. She didn't seem the type to hide a pitchfork in her skirt, but I certainly didn't need rumors swirling before I'd even checked into the hotel.

"It's not a big deal," I muttered to myself. Hopefully that woman would go on her own strange way, and no one would hear anything after. She seemed unusual enough herself, perhaps folk wouldn't listen if she repeated the events of the evening.

Somewhat comforted, I settled into the seat, leaning back and closing my eyes as the headache pulsed a thunderous beat against my skull.

"Did you get anything from her?" Dies-well asked from the driver's seat.

"A nice factoid about Robert Frost."

Dies-well let out a sigh to rival a particularly disgusted windstorm. "And from her mind?"

I shifted in my seat, keeping my eyes closed. "I was told it's rude to read human minds uninvited."

"You are truly in sad shape."

"What did *you* get?" My stomach was starting to turn again. I cracked the window, letting in fresh air.

"Nothing."

"So, you agree it's rude."

"If you could refrain from being *such* a flopdoodle for a second, you'd notice that only witches and other magic wielders can avoid mindreading so easily."

"Maybe she's just *incredibly* stupid, and there weren't any thoughts to read." I thought again of her sharp gaze, the way she watched me scramble in the dirt as if memorizing my every move, the cock of her head as if listening to everything all at once. Stupidity was not the issue.

"You're impossible, and I'm ending this conversation."

I let Dies-well have the last word, sinking into the repeating whisper that continued to circle my mind, refusing to give me peace as we continued toward the faintly flickering lights of town.

Rest. Rest here.

What could be weighing me down that made that voice so alluring?

A gunshot ricocheting off the rafters. Blood pooling fast—too fast. The last bit of my heart cracking into shards.

And then, a century later but not so long at all...

"I don't want to be someone you regret."

Her bright eyes, sharp laugh. The gasp of her beneath me, fingers clutching my shirt so tightly I was sure she'd rip it from me.

Watching her with him. Tender, gentle, loving. She would never be that with me. That was not what we were to each other.

It was not what I deserved. Not after everything.

Cold, wet earth sucked around my fingertips, and I jolted awake from the clash of memories from my old and new lives, panic rising in my throat. Had I somehow ended up back in the mud? Worse, had I never actually left it?

I glanced around the quietly rattling minivan. Dies-well was still driving, careful and confident, humming something that sounded like Carole King. I was definitely in the backseat, the stained fabric rough against the back of my trousers, the floorboard rattling beneath my loafers.

But I was also *definitely* touching dirt so—

"Oh." The satchel gaped open beside me, my right hand two knuckles deep in the dirt. I let the sucking mud pull my hand a little deeper and gave in to the sigh that escaped my lips. It felt *good*. Even better, it quieted my racing mind, pushing the memories of Evelyn away, washing over the heartache with the promise of a long-awaited rest.

Evelyn.

She was supposed to be a human I helped in New York—a quick favor for a friend before sinking back into obscurity. Patrick called, asking if I'd help her find her lunatic mershark boyfriend, and the next thing I knew I couldn't look away from her sharp eyes, couldn't stop myself from offering to fly her back to Boston. I couldn't stay away even as she spent every waking hour seeking a way to break her boyfriend's curse. We'd ended up tangled in each other but seeking different things—she wanted distraction, I wanted devotion.

Once she was reunited with her boyfriend—so fresh from the ocean he reeked of chum—it was more than I could stand. I left that very hour back to New York, but Evelyn's presence lingered no matter the distance I put between us.

I opened my eyes and decided to take advantage of my renewed clear-headedness.

"What did you mean, I need to make things right with my burial dirt?" I asked.

Dies-well glanced at me in the rearview.

"That's a question a fangling would ask," he said.

"I didn't get much time with my sire," I said. I didn't want to say more and Dies-well didn't press.

"We are all dependent on our graveyard dirt to rest. It's what we return to during the day and when we travel, we must have it with us. It's restorative."

I nodded. I knew this much. But how can you cross something restorative? How do you make amends with something meant to give you rest? Dies-well wasn't offering anything further, humming lightly to himself.

"Very helpful." I rolled my eyes, already feeling the beginnings of a slight headache. I crammed my hand further into the dirt. Immediately, a cooling sensation washed over my body even as my stomach heated and boiled. A cold sweat trickled down my spine and the world spun, twisting and turning at the edges of my vision.

If I could get a grip for a moment, think things through, find a solution for what was happening to me. But who could I even ask?

I was vaguely aware of Dies-well talking in the front seat, but I couldn't make out what he was saying over the ringing in my ears.

"Fine," I whispered, and shoveled a fistful of mud into my mouth. I chewed, ignoring the gritty texture and the occasional wriggling sensation as I swallowed. I was an undead creature of the night—I'd eaten far worse than a worm or two.

The effect was immediate: the world stopped spinning, the headache vanished, my ears stopped ringing, and suddenly I could hear Dies-well as if he were speaking into a headset in my mind. My supernatural senses kicked back online, and I felt the way I *usually* did after feeding—the way I was supposed to have felt after the blood bag that now lay in a clotted pile of roadside vomit.

"...doubt she'll know but I don't have a problem asking since you did promise me anything." Dies-well took that moment to glance meaningfully into the rearview mirror at me, and I nodded, relief seeping into every part of my body.

Town lights flashed above the car as we took a turn. White-washed thatched cottages behind crumbling stone walls and sprawling gardens lined each side of the street, blending seamlessly into squat store-fronts with lead-glass windows that rattled as we passed. Iron lamps had long since swapped gas for electric, but the stained smoky glass still smothered the warm light. The only source of life was the pub on the far end of the main street, front door flung open to release the heat of bodies out into the chill, misty air. I heard cacophonous chatter, the distinct sound of violins and a guitar, a few drunken voices.

We vibrated over the cobblestone bridge that split the town center in half, and my stomach lurched as we left the tiny creek behind. We passed a few more cottages before the town seemed to just end—as if an invisible force prevented further development on a strict straight edge.

I forgot how suddenly Ashbourne sprung from the ground, with no creeping buildings or parking lots or developments outside the limits. The hard boundaries were the result of superstition and archaic zoning laws—both of which dragged me back to this forsaken place.

Which reminded me, I needed to call Rye.

I pulled out my phone, swallowed a smaller handful of dirt—just to be safe—and tapped Rye's number. She'd still be in the office if my time zones were right.

"You make it alright?" She had a thick Jersey accent, lengthening her vowels, softening her R's. I admired that she never bothered to smother it despite her status, education, and impressive hourly rate.

"I've had bumpier landings," I said, hoping my voice didn't sound like someone who was literally just sucked down into the dirt. "I wanted to get the status of the land claim case I sent you."

"I had to blow dust off some books, but I think you've got a case," she said. I heard papers rustling on her end, the tell-tale plastic exhale of a water bottle being sucked on. "But honestly, can't you just small-town it and talk to the council? Promise to be a good boy from now on?"

"You know I can't make that promise," I said, letting a smirk creep up my face. This dirt was really helping—I'd have to sit with that thought later.

"Yeah, yeah, you could never lie to councilmen about how many of their wives you'll seduce." I could hear her rolling her eyes. "But I'm sure you could promise your upcoming renovations will ensure no further accidents to minors."

"Well..."

"Billy, as your lawyer, I need you to tell me yes, even if you don't necessarily mean it."

"Then yes."

"Great," she sighed. "Call me when you're settled, and we can go over the details. Are they bringing you to your hotel in an actual carriage? It's so loud on your end."

"You know my love of authenticity," I said, but Rye had already hung up.

I loved her.

"We're here," Dies-well announced, throwing the minivan into park with a lurch.

I looked out the window at the sleek, modern, three-story building blazing LED streetlights out into the oppressive English dark. Perfectly square cement tiles led the way to the oversized, dark wood door with light green glass inlays and a softly polished chrome handle. Abnormally round bushes speckled the wood chips that framed the path, and as Dies-well opened the door, I heard soft orchestral music pumped through a hidden outdoor speaker.

"Finally," I muttered, clutching my bag of dirt. "Some peace."

Chapter Five

Leslee

I'd been halfway across the field when I felt the pull. I'd stopped, shifting my focus to a slow alarm being raised from near the road that ran along the far edge, perpendicular to the thicket. A shudder went through the tall grass as it parted for me, clearing a way for me to investigate.

"Alright," I'd said. "The mushrooms can wait."

That's how I'd ended up staring what I *thought* was a dead man in the face—he was ghostly pale, with shining eyes, and I didn't think I imagined the unnatural length of his teeth. He was handsome despite his rough shape. I could see a defined jaw from where he looked up at me from the ground and the flex of his back muscles as he straightened to stand. He was dressed well, spoke well, and clearly had the means to hire a driver.

I wondered at our strange conversation, but the hangover might've explained most of that. Maybe even the teeth. What had the driver called it? Feeling like boiled owl?

I made a note to explore potential hangover side effects as the sound of their minivan grew faint. Turning back toward the field, I was stopped by the quivering grass.

"Yes, babies," I said. "What do you want me to see?"

I aimed my phone light down, checking the ground where the man had been supposedly vomiting and cold fear slid down my spine.

It wasn't the raked dig marks in the mud the man had left as he scrambled to stand, but what sat next to it, dark and glistening in the moonlight—a pool of blood. I steeled myself and squatted down to get a better look.

A dark reddish-brown, it looked as though it had been there for a while but was also still *very* wet. I blanched, dipping a single finger into the mess that came away slightly warm. Congealed masses within the pool suggested clotting, but how could so much warm blood be such an oxygenated color? How could it clot itself?

"How hungover were you?" I muttered.

I stood, trying again to leave, but the grass shivered violently.

"Well, if we're not done here, then what's left?" I put my hands on my hips, listening to the grass vibrate, knocking shaft against shaft as far back as my cottage, the sound like a hundred whistling wings in the night.

"Ah, right."

I set my basket down and pushed my sleeves back, scooping handfuls of wet earth and smoothing it over the congealed blood until it was entirely covered. I placed both hands flat on the fresh earth and closed my eyes, tilting my face up to the moon and welcoming the fresh charge.

The grass shuddered a final time as the path that had opened closed, and the field began to wave and whisper again with the natural breeze.

I let loose a deep breath and picked my basket back up, letting it thud against my hip as I rested my hands on my waist and surveyed the spot a final time.

"A final rest for all those that have lived," I said to no one. "Whatever that pile used to be, it's at peace now."

I set out across the field at a quicker pace, unable to shake the sense that I'd stumbled across the beginning of a much bigger mess—one that I didn't particularly want to get involved with further.

The night air met me with a crisp whisper against my skin, the moon above raising the hairs on the back of my neck in just the tiniest charge. It was a slim crescent, not nearly as powerful as a fuller form, but sometimes I just wanted to feel the snap of connection to the natural world and not the overwhelming out-pour of power that comes with a full moon.

I adjusted the small woven basket on my arm and took a deep breath. The lush field spread out before me, the breeze rustling the tall grass, the peaty dirt wafting in the damp air. A few miles off—not quite the horizon, not quite in town—a thicket of trees raised thinning arms against the stars. Soon they would be bare, scratching at the sky, but for now they still had a type of thinning plumage, brown and golden leaves fluttering in the breeze. It was this thicket that held the ugly mushrooms I was seeking.

I reached my intention through the soles of my boots to connect with the whispering earth beneath me, reminding myself of the conduit I am between the forces of air and earth, sky and forest, wind and fire. I focused my breath to match the pulse of the moon as it tingled across my skin, pushing the energy back into the earth. What I help grow helps me grow, and so we feed each other.

The thought comforted me, and I focused on the truth of it wrapping around my body and pushing out to the singing starlight as I returned to my mushroom hunt.

Chapter Six

BILLY

The pristine modern lobby opened before me, all soft whites and clean lines with the same music as outside drifting from hidden speakers. I smelled the fresh cleaning materials and the lack of dust on any surface. Light flickered from fake candle bulbs in the chandeliers that hung low overhead and a few well-placed luxurious rugs helped dampen the echoing space between sweeping ceilings and marble floors.

I double checked that my bag of dirt was securely closed as I crossed the lobby to the check-in desk. It was empty, which I was a little surprised by—there should have been a night manager. That assurance was part of the reason I booked expensive accommodation. I never had to answer questions from a stoned or sleep-deprived teenager about why I was checking in at such an hour.

I rang the bell and glanced around, noticing the dusting of candy wrappers and empty soda cans littering the back side of the desk. Again, not an unheard of coping mechanism for someone working the night shift, but certainly not the standard I had expected for what I was paying. I thought again of Dies-well's minivan and tried to roll the tension from my neck.

I was in the middle of English nowhere. Things were different here than London or New York. I just had to keep reminding myself of that.

From somewhere deep in the back office, I heard a growing stampede of feet, as if the entire staff had been slacking off and was now sprinting to make amends.

"Finally," I muttered, straightening my shoulders and slinging my dirt bag over my shoulder. I hoped I looked mildly annoyed but not so imposing as to inspire fear from whatever clearly inexperienced hospitality staff was about to burst through the side door.

My stance immediately shifted to the defensive, and I practically flung up my arms in surprise as six gawky teens piled out of the office door. It was cartoonish, the way they scrambled over each other, clawing the door frame to be the first one behind the desk. A freckled ginger with a sweep of styled hair made it first, quickly straightening the black vest over his white button up and adjusting his nametag.

"Welcome to the Clotswold by Litchfield, sir." His red eyes glinted in the light, long fingers flitting over his clothing as he spoke. But it was the brilliant smile he offered in welcome that stopped me. Two long fangs glinted in the low light.

Right. This was a vampire investment opportunity inspired by a young nest with no sire. I glanced at the other five teenagers who had sprung free of the back office. They were all dressed alike in a simple black vest, white button down, and black slacks, arguing over who was going to help with my luggage—a job that *maybe* required two people if I didn't carry one of the bags myself. It certainly didn't need five.

There was a willowy kid with black hair falling in luxurious waves around his shoulders, hiding his face. He pointed a finger and whispered his argument to yet another freckled ginger—probably the brother to the one behind the desk, younger from the looks of it.

A thick-necked, ruddy-looking teen stood to the side, arms crossed, eyes glossed over. He would look more at home on a tractor than in a five-star lobby. A fifth excitable teen was practically levitating, floating from foot to foot in a delicate but nervous dance. He had an unfortunate bowl cut that meant his glossy black hair hung directly over his eyes, giving him the exaggerated look of a fanged mouth with no owner.

"Welcome, sir!" The final teen caught me staring and waved with a massive grin to match the one the ginger behind the desk was offering. His neatly styled brown hair was pushed back from his face in a generous wave, and his clothes were neatly pressed. I would've guessed he was the eldest were it not for the slight hunch in his shoulders stooping his posture a little too submissively.

Too stunned to respond, I turned back to the kid behind the desk and arched my eyebrows.

"You'll have to forgive my, uh, staff," he said, as if he were trying to find the right descriptor for the motley crew who would attend me. "We're all new to this, and I'm afraid you have the unfortunate honor of being our first guest. Makes you a guinea pig, I suppose."

This time I returned the easy smile he offered and nodded.

"Wouldn't be the first time," I said. I tapped a hand on the desk. "But this pig would love to freshen up."

"Right, of course!" The ginger kid—Alfred, according to his nametag—began clacking away on the computer. "You're staying for seven nights?"

I nodded. "With the potential to extend," I said. "I'm here about some business with the town council that might drag on."

"Not a problem, sir." Alfred nodded, continuing to clack on the computer. He squinted at the screen before turning to a drawer behind him and producing a massive, ornate brass key. Before he could hand it to me, the second ginger appeared and plucked it from his hands. He turned to me, offering the key in both outstretched palms, and bowed deeply.

"Your key, monsieur," he said with an appallingly fake French accent.

"Merci." I stifled a laugh and took the key, stifling yet another giggle at the fang hanging over the corner of his very serious mouth. His nametag said Frederick.

"Freddie, come on." Alfred rolled his eyes. "I told you that's so stupid."

"Sod off, Alf," Frederick snapped, never losing his ceremonial pose. "These rich blokes get off on a little French shit."

I arched my eyebrows and glanced around, disappointed that there wasn't a single other person in the room to confirm this was really happening. Behind me, I saw the levitating teen now perched cross-legged on the top of my luggage, watching the scene at the desk like it happened all the time. Or at least, I assumed that was what he was looking at from behind his bangs. The ruddy teen picked up my other suitcase and hefted it over his shoulder like a bale of hay.

"I think maybe we shouldn't cuss in front of the customers?" This came from the potentially-eldest, his shoulders sloping even further inward.

"We will invite the opinion of Sir Bent Dick when it is warranted." Freddie gave another exaggerated bow, this time toward the nervous teen.

"Yeah, Dick. And we call them 'guests', not customers," Alfie joined in.

The migraine was raging again, thinning my patience. My hands twitched at the clasp of my dirt bag. I was in fellow vampire company, but I didn't want to show any weakness in the middle of a fresh nest. They were clearly already restless and amped up with each other. There was no telling what would set them off to violence.

"It's alright," I said, chiming in above what was quickly turning into many voices whingeing at each other. "Guest, customer, rich bloke—whatever. I'd just like to get to my room if that's alright."

"Of course, sir," Alfie and Freddie said in unison before immediately glaring at each other.

"Ford and Lex—I mean, Bradford and Alexander will bring your bags up. Richard can lead the way." Alfie broke his glare and adjusted his shirt yet again. "Thank you for choosing Clotswold by Lichfield, and enjoy your—"

"Have a banging day!" Freddie cut him off.

The two began nudging each other and muttering at such a rapid pace it sounded like they were speaking in tongues. The migraine was behind my eyes now, thudding with a dull ache that threatened to sharpen if I listened any longer.

"Thank you," I said. I turned to the three vampires near my luggage, barely able to keep my teeth from clenching. "Shall we?"

"Yes sir, absolutely sir, this way, sir." The nervous kid gestured his arms out like a game show starlet showing off a prize. "I'm Richard, sir. Let me know if there's anything I can help you with, sir."

"Just the elevators," I said, losing my grip on my calm and following his gesturing.

"Oh, no, sir, sorry, sir. They're this way, sir." Richard pinwheeled his arms across the lobby in the opposite direction before jetting off. The ruddy vampire and his bowl cut friend followed silently. The bowl cut kid floated lightly off the ground and my bag followed behind him.

"Welcome." The reedy voice came from directly over my shoulder, so near my ear I could feel the heat of it and I jumped despite myself.

I glanced to see the long-haired vampire give me a sheepish half-smile before melting into the few shadows of the room.

I wasn't going to make it to my room in one piece at this rate. Pausing half-way across the lobby, I watched the teens in front of me bicker with each other while they waited for the elevator to open. I opened the satchel enough to slide my hand in and scarfed down a handful of dirt as quickly as I could, hoping no one had noticed.

"Man, you're a wreck."

I choked on the dirt, spraying a dusting across the carpet before I could get a hold of myself and finish swallowing.

Dies-well stood beside me, holding my wallet up next to his grinning face.

"What's the matter? Never seen a vampire before?" He handed me my wallet while I continued coughing up the last of the dirt that had tried to go down the wrong tube. "You act like you don't know we can move silently and disappear suddenly—which, maybe you can't." He considered this seriously for a moment, squinting hard at me. "Are you disabled?"

I snatched my wallet back, throat finally clear.

"I'm going through something at the moment," I snapped. "If you hadn't noticed."

"You're *welcome.*" He rolled his eyes. "Anyway, I've come to discuss payment."

"I paid you."

"You said you'd give me anything if I let you back in my van," he said, crossing his arms and popping a hip.

I pinched the bridge of my nose, desperate to crawl inside my dirt bag and maybe never come back out. "I did," I ground out. "And?"

"I want my van fixed."

"That's it?"

"Completely repaired—new paint job, new interior, replace the broken lights and re-attach the side mirror."

"Can't I just buy you a new car?"

"No." Dies-well glared at me, leaning down so that we were nearly nose-to-nose. "She's irreplaceable."

"Fine, whatever." I waved a hand at him, the room suddenly too bright, everyone's voice suddenly too loud. It was like I could hear the bugs in the walls scuttling as if they were wearing microphones on their feet and I couldn't turn down the volume. The room was beginning to spin. "Send me the bill."

"Sir!" Richard called from the now open elevator doors.

"WHAT?" I roared.

He flinched, and I saw something like anger flicker across the big, ruddy vamp's face.

"The elevator, sir," Richard said meekly.

"Right, yes," I said, crossing to them quickly and leaving Dies-well behind. "Sorry," I muttered, stepping into the cramped space with the three teens. The doors dinged shut and the elevator gave a sickening lurch before moving.

"This is Bradford," Richard said, gesturing as dramatically as he could in the space to the thick-necked vamp who still held my suitcase over his shoulder. Bradford gave a slight nod. "And this is Alexander." Richard's arms flicked to the opposite side.

"Pleasure," Alexander said. "Welcome to Clotswold." He had a soft Scottish accent.

"Whatever you need, we're here to help, sir," Richard continued. "Anything at all. We're at your side, morning, noon, and night. Although you probably won't need us morning or noon. Hopefully not because I think we'll all be sleeping, although if you *really* needed something, I'm sure one of us could—"

"Thank you, Richard," I said, cutting him off as gently as I was able. My legs were shaking and my knees felt weak as the elevator doors opened.

By some small miracle, my suite was directly to the right and I was able to open the door quickly, although I noticed I could hear the lock tumblers much clearer than normal. Was this part of the dirt issue? My powers fluctuating and cranking themselves like this? I could hear like I'd just been turned, but I had been startled twice by vampires sneaking up on me, so my other senses were clearly hay-wire.

With a sigh of relief, I walked into the massive, silent suite. The king bed sprawled invitingly to the left and to the right, a TV, a plush couch, and the double doors to what I assumed was the washroom and water closet. Grey textured wallpaper gave the sense that I'd stepped into a shaded glen, and the carpet was a deep, plush off-white. The furniture was all rich, dark wood with emerald-green upholstery, and several golden accent pillows and throws dotted the room. It was comfortable, inviting, and pristine all at once.

"Perfect," I said.

I dropped my dirt bag on the console table in the entry and shucked off my loafers.

"Please put the bags at the end of the bed," I said. "I'll sort them shortly."

I pulled a few bills from my wallet and distributed them to the eager, outstretched hands before practically shoving the three young vampires from my room. The door clicked shut, and I heard their joyful chatter pick back up before it disappeared down the hall.

I was finally, truly, left in peace this time.

But fuck me, this was going to be a ridiculous stay.

Chapter Seven

Leslee

Crossing the threshold of the trees sent a thrill through me—it always did. The whispering branches above me always sounded like "welcome home," and the soft underbrush felt like it was paving the way for me. I felt keyed in, connected, alive in a way I rarely felt elsewhere. It was a high I chased with every garden or landscaping project but one I knew I would never capture. It was too wild, too feral, too natural to ever be contained within boundaries or boxes. Just like my family.

My father had been the first (and the last) to tame the wildness that ran through my mother's side—the side that sang in my veins in response to every green thing nearby. I'd inherited his steadfast, stubborn nature, and it was that side that kept me tethered to Ashbourne, that kept my heart buried in the comfort of the human world while my mother's side sang temptation through the trees at every opportunity.

I fed both by keeping my cottage but allowing for wanderings at any and every whim—just like tonight. I breathed deep, the wet dirt and dark moss smelling like home. It was green and alive and full of song tonight, each passed branch, crunched leaf, rubbed shrub speaking to me through humming hymns.

There was no place like the woods at night. No place like *my* woods.

I had just spotted some particularly gnarly mushrooms—gangly, porous, gills flaring out dark and angry—when movement in the corner of my eye made me stop. A warning flared along my skin, and my hairs stood on end. Slowly, cautiously, every nerve singing, I turned to where the shadow had paused.

A large form, barely perceptible against the shadows, was waiting. I held my breath, squinting into the dark, trying to see if it was another villager or something more ominous, setting off my alarms. It twitched, and I saw, for just a second, the ghostly white outline of a tall, not-quite-human creature. "Hello?" I tested the tense air between us, hopeful a friendly offering would, if nothing else, scare it off. But nothing happened. The creature did not accept my greeting, although it didn't run from it either. I waited. It waited.

Finally, a cloud shifted, and just enough extra starlight sifted through the trees that I caught a full glimpse of the creature before it vanished a final time.

I clamped a hand over my mouth to stifle a scream, my basket crashing to the ground. I stepped back, trampling the prized mushrooms and trying to calm my trembling heart.

A monster. A huge, hair-less monster, bent and pale in the light, with gaping black hungry eyes and fearsome fangs that hung low past its bottom lip.

I picked up my basket and made a quick but steady pace out of the woods. It wasn't until I was in the open field and could see all sides that I heaved a few gasping breaths, placing a steadying hand over my fluttering heart. At that same moment, a chilling thought sent me sprinting back to my cottage and the safety of the village.

Not what it was hunting—*who*.

In only a few minutes, which felt like hours, I finally slammed the cottage door behind me. It was a hefty, ancient wooden thing, and I felt secure the moment the iron bolt slid home across it. I'd need to remember to check my wards in the morning when the light was good for recasting—and maybe even add new protections. I threw off my coat and waved at the logs in the stove, willing a flame to life. It sparked weakly as I passed, and I took a steadying breath before backtracking to the tiny ember.

"Thank you," I breathed into the stove. "For your warmth and your energy." The spark grew, licking happily at the dry logs beneath it. Soon enough, a comfortable fire was crackling, flames licking along the bottom of the kettle as I hooked it to boil.

I paced the length of the kitchen while I waited. Did I need to call someone? I had never joined a coven or added myself to any national witch registries—Mum had said not to bother with any of it, given that we weren't quite of their ilk. But now, I regretted not having a larger network to tap into.

I couldn't call Tyler. He'd tell me to stop imagining things. Or worse, he'd offer to help, and I'd be too rattled to reject him.

"Fucking Tyler," I muttered to myself.

I tried to calm my racing thoughts, tried to think through what could possibly be lurking around the village. Despite my family's legacy, Ashbourne wasn't a particularly supernatural place. The old Huxley house had been a hotbed for a while, but until those teens hurt themselves, it hadn't had any—

"Wait," I said to the air. "Hurt or *attacked*?" It would make sense—their wounds could've been bites and claw marks confused for punctures from untended broken floorboards and nails. I had been relocating weeds for the mother of one of the boys and overheard her mentioning over the phone that her son—Alex, I think—had been acting strange ever since he came back from the hospital. He was constantly aggravated and slept all day.

He blamed it on his night shift at the new hotel, but his mother pointed out his appetite had shifted suspiciously. Her once-growing boy was suddenly apathetic toward anything she cooked. Weirder still, she kept finding rogue bird feathers all over the house, as if a cat was leaving presents for its owner.

Maybe I could talk to the mother and find out if anything else was strange with Alex or his friends.

"Or I could ask himself." I tapped a thoughtful finger to my lips—it always made me *feel* smart, even if it didn't inspire anything. "But is that too brash?"

The kettle whistled, calling me forward with its promise of a comforting cuppa.

"You're right," I sighed, pouring steaming water into my favorite mug—the one with the ivy twining around the lip. "That's a problem for Morning Leslee."

***

Morning found me where it always did—on my knees in the garden, a light sheen of sweat sticking my normally frazzled hair to my brow. I was dead set on protecting the veggie beds for the winter and helping the perennials prepare for the coming frosts. It was getting colder and colder by the night, and I didn't want anyone caught out in the chill without a coat—so to speak.

My plan for the day was to kick off the wintering projects, work on my portfolio—I was actually going to do it this time—and then head to the hotel in the evening to catch the mysterious Alex at the start of his shift.

I enjoyed welcoming the dawn in the garden. It was a beautiful time to stretch and bask and recharge—in a completely different way from how I'd charged beneath the moonlight. I thought again of the strange pool of blood and the monster in the woods. That had taken more energy than I'd replenished, and I was feeling particularly stretched. Some time in the sun would do me good.

My cellphone vibrated in my apron pocket and I stopped to tear off my gardening gloves before tapping to answer. I hadn't so much as glanced at the number, but surely, this early, it'd be someone I knew.

"Hello, hello, and cheerio," I teased into the phone like I would if it were my sister or mum or Ty—well, like I would a very good friend.

"Erm, yes, is this Miss Hawthorne?" A mellow voice I almost recognized asked if I was me in a very professional manner.

Shit, shit, double shit.

"This is she," I said, pitching my voice up half an octave like I'd seen other professional ladies do. I tried to shove away the immediate thought that *this* was why Tyler was successful and I'd been—

"I hope you don't mind the hour," the voice said. It was a man with an accent from a region I couldn't quite place. If I didn't know any better, I'd say he was a local. Again, something nagged at the back of my mind. "Alex said you're usually up in your garden before the sun. I keep an unusual schedule, so I was hoping to catch you now."

"And you have," I said. "Who may I ask is calling?"

"My name is Billy Barlow. I unfortunately own Huxley Manor. I'm in town while it's repaired and approved by the council so we have no more...accidents."

I nodded, then remembered I was on the phone.

"Ah yes, mmhmmm," I said, drawing out the confirmation that I'd heard him. I thought Huxley Manor hadn't been owned in a century.

"Alex is helping me here at the Clotswold, and in need of a talented landscaper and gardener. He said you were exactly who I wanted to talk with—something about working with royalty."

His voice was serene but frank, as if his calm emanated from his very core. And the tones in the bass range were…well. I shook my head, remembering I was on the phone and he couldn't see me, but he was still certainly waiting for me to say something and stop gawking at his voice.

Could you gawk at a voice?

"Well, I *am* a plant specialist," I said. "But I'm afraid I haven't exactly worked with royalty."

He gave a soft chuckle, and something fluttered in my stomach. The nagging grew louder, but I shoved it away. "This isn't a delicate assignment," he said. "I doubt we'll need the finesse required for the royal grounds, but I will need someone who knows what they're doing and isn't afraid to get a little dirty."

"Oh, I'm positively filthy," I said gleefully.

The line was quiet for a moment, so I took the opening.

"I'm afraid I don't have a portfolio right at the moment, but I'd be happy to—"

"That won't be necessary," he cut me off, which I did not enjoy. The calm in his voice seemed to be fraying quickly, and my butterflies wondered if I'd fallen for a façade. "Time is of the essence, so I'm happy to work off local recommendations. Are you familiar with the manor grounds?"

"Somewhat," I said, leaning back and stretching my arms up. The sun chased the lightest traces of frost from the yard, and I was already regretting answering the phone. I was missing the juiciest morning energy for a *work* conversation.

"Why don't you come to Clotswold at 6:30 tonight? We can review your proposal, and I can give you more details as to what work is needed. Bring any members of your crew you think will be necessary."

"Oh, I don't—" The line went dead before I could object.

I sighed and untied the apron from my neck, slipping my phone into my jeans pocket.

"I don't have a crew," I told the vegetables I'd been preparing for winter. "Do you think he knows?" The leaves shuddered in unison, and I nodded, feeling a small smile creep across my face despite myself. "Of course, I can do it alone—I always have. Thank you, friends."

I hooked the apron on the back wall of the garden and went to find the perfect sunny spot for my morning stretches and recharge.

At least this new opportunity aligned nicely with my pre-existing plans. *And* I wouldn't have to make a stupid portfolio.

Chapter Eight

INTERLUDE

Ashbourne, 1823

A strange black carriage streaked through the countryside that evening. Its torches were lit to a full blaze, and its horses snorted steam as they turned down the oak-sheltered entrance to Huxley Manor, their thundering hooves sending a tremor through the earth to announce their arrival. The branches above shivered, twitching as if they could get away, and every creature with breath in its body held still as the carriage passed.

The house staff at the doors threw their hands across their faces as the carriage came to a screaming halt, rocks and dirt flying from its wheels. They were instructed to approach, but none dared move. Only the carriage's stalwart driver broke the stillness, stepping down from his perch. He was a squat, stoic man with no hair beneath his tall hat and no thoughts behind his glassy eyes. He pulled open the carriage door with an automatic gesture and stood stone still as first one elegant long leg and then the other appeared in the frame.

An impossibly tall man with deathly pale skin and crimson eyes stood from the carriage. He adjusted his pinstriped coat with a keen sneer and patted the edges of his perfectly arranged black curls before turning to the staff.

"Bring me Alexander Huxley," he said in a voice that brokered no argument. The house staff scattered as if hellhounds barked at their heels.

The strange man could hear crashing and scattering from inside the manor house as if he stood within its walls. His hearing, his age, his speed—all were gifts of his kind meant to offset the misery of the curse. A curse he was feeding with a specific kind of justice.

Before too long, the housekeeper exited the front door, approaching with a quickstep that set her key ring singing against her thigh. She curtsied deeply to the stranger.

"Master Huxley welcomes you to his home," she said, voice shaking. "He requests your company in the salon."

"Lead the way." The strange man gestured to her and took slow, measured steps to match her pace. He could see the rapid beat of her heart beneath her skin, could trace her quick pulse through her limbs with his eyes.

Just a little longer, he told his hunger. *Just a little longer until we feast.*

The grand entrance to the manor opened upon shining marble floors, gilded fixtures with cozy, flickering candles, and a sweeping staircase of polished mahogany, each step cushioned in rich carpeting.

The man followed the housekeeper to the right into a luxurious salon. The same carpet from the steps swept out beneath his feet. A brilliantly patterned wallpaper covered the room, full of swirling forest greens and greys. Tasteful oil paintings were displayed in baroque frames, strung tightly from their hooks. The far wall was covered in leatherbound books, neatly shelved by author, their repetitious shapes occasionally interrupted by a framed cameo or small painted portrait.

Standing in the middle of the room, flanked on either side by plush sofas and leaning against a monstrous black wood desk, was a balding man with a mean mouth and fierce eyes. His arms were crossed, and his mouth pulled tighter on his pinched face as his eyes assessed the stranger.

A small gurgling cry went up from near the entrance of the salon, and the stranger glanced down to see a small child with a stack of blocks. She gave a wide toothless smile and smacked her fat little hands onto the blocks, scattering them to the ground.

The strange man rushed to her side, immediately scooping up all the blocks and whispering under his breath as he stacked them neatly. When he was done, he pointed to the child and, to no one in particular, said, "Remove this distraction."

Three servants moved in unison to collect the little girl and her blocks.

The man continued to scowl.

"You must be wondering what business I could have with you, Mr. Huxley, at such an hour." The strange man clasped his hands behind his back and faced the manor lord. "I have come to even the balance of society in this county."

Mr. Huxley said nothing.

"I would explain what I mean by that, but it will do you no good, as you will be dead shortly. Meaning will have no weight for you then."

Chapter Nine

BILLY

The manor was exactly as I remembered it, although the grounds were wilder and the trees more menacing.

It seemed 150 years was not long enough to destroy the stalwart main house or the stone walls surrounding it. And although it had been a full 200 years since I'd stepped foot in the house itself, covered in blood, eyes turning redder by the second, I was sure no one else had entered since the housekeeper turned the lock and threw the key to the wilds.

I let my feet guide me, embracing the hypnotic pull of this first return. I passed the overgrown gardens, vines and tendrils poking from the hedge walls that had long since lost their shape. Monstrous rose bushes with curious weeds intertwined gave way to the front entrance of the house, looming stark and menacing against the neon pink sky.

But my feet did not take me to the front door. No. They knew another entrance—a path from an older life that no mortal left on earth would remember anymore. The thought pulled on my loneliness, sparking it to a dull ache in my gut.

I wandered around the side of the manor, noting the lack of broken windowpanes, torn clapboards, or sagging eaves. Was *this* the place the county demanded I restore on threat of reclamation?

Behind the main house, a smattering of smaller buildings spread out along the acreage—a garden shed, a gazebo, and the stables. It was the last that pulled me forward at a brisker pace. I could almost hear the familiar sound of whinnying, could almost smell the comfort of fresh hay and dirt. That had been my life—my joy—once. Something in me was compelled to see if, much like the manor, the stables survived the onslaught of time.

I started to run, immediately regretting my choice of footwear as my black Ferragamos hit the earth with a dull thud that vibrated up my bones. Hope flooded my chest, settling close to relief. Was this what it was to come home?

I reached the main stable doors and threw them back. Inside, the twilight painted everything a rosy golden pink, and dust swirled in the slanted light above each empty stall. But this time, the whinnying I had imagined came directly from the last stall to the left.

"There's no way," I whispered, moving cautiously toward the sound.

That had been The Colonel's stall. He and I had—

"Don't do that," I said to myself. It may have been a miracle that the manor was still standing untouched, but it was physically impossible for a horse from 200 years ago to do the same. There was no point revisiting glowing memories for a creature who was certainly no more than bones in the ground.

Except when I finally stood in front of the stall, the horse that swung its elegant neck to survey me was the identical chestnut brown, had the exact same black markings around the nose and eyes, the same paint splotch of white on his forelock. He dipped his head in the same bow I had taught him when we greeted each other and when I returned it, he gave me the exact soft nicker that The Colonel always had.

"This isn't possible," I said. It was a phrase I was constantly repeating despite my own impossible existence. You'd think 200 years later I'd be more open to the supernatural.

But even if this were some feat of modern genetics, I'd always assumed animals would be spooked by the presence of the undead. Cats certainly were. With all their sensitivities and emotional intelligence, wouldn't horses be the same?

And yet, The Colonel bent his head down over the stall and nudged my shoulder. I raised my hand to his nose and stroked the soft, velvety skin there. I ran a hand up along his head, scratching along the paint splotch. He leaned into my touch, stamping a foot happily.

A warmth I'd forgotten washed over me. In my first life, this connection had kept me going despite Huxley's cruelty—a man I called "Hurls" because he made me want to throw the next heaviest object out of rage.

Nothing else mattered if I could stay in the stables. Nothing could touch me so long as I focused on horses like The Colonel, on the joy of knowing them and caring for them and in receiving their love and trust in return—not even the dead-end fate I knew was sealed before me.

"I missed you," I whispered.

And then the ground fell out beneath me and I was falling, falling, falling into a deep dark black. The Colonel whinnied in distress, throwing his head before the earth closed above me.

Wet earth pressed in on all sides until my floundering was constricted. I could feel it wrapping around my limbs, holding me in place as it pushed against my mouth, ears, eyes.

A wet, wriggling sensation pulsed at my ears and panic seized me. I was about to become worm food.

I tried to open my mouth to cry out, but more dirt poured in, choking me alive.

I sat up in bed in a cold sweat, gasping for air I only needed for reassurance.

Panic clamped against my body, and I practiced my go-to meditation. I imagined a small ball of light, glowing a soft yellow—like the sun used to—slowly encircling each limb, beginning at the tip of my toes and working its way methodically up. The rule was that everything the light touched would be magically healed. It was my job to remind my body of that truth. If the light touched my leg, my calves had to relax. If the light touched my stomach, the butterflies had to go.

I closed my eyes and worked through the meditation in silence until my room phone rang, startling me and re-tensing my shoulders.

"Fucking fuck fuckity—someone better be dead," I said by way of answer, running an aggrieved hand across my face.

"Breakfast?" a reedy voice asked.

I glanced over at the light-blocking curtains in the room before realizing they were doing a very good job and launched myself at the nightstand clock instead.

"It's barely 4 p.m.," I sighed.

"Yes."

"Which one are you?"

"William."

"Fucking of course you are." Naturally the one teen out of six that called me to ask about an absurdly early breakfast was named William—the same name of the mershark Evelyn had abandoned me for after I let her use me for some incredibly hot sex so she could avoid her fear of losing him. It had been a connection so magnetic, so irresistible, I'd seen the pain coming and signed up anyway. I couldn't have been any more masochistic if I'd walked into the midday sun butt naked.

"Breakfast?" he asked again. Clearly, one Will ruining my life wasn't enough.

"It's too early, William. I'll take my breakfast at a civilized hour." I had to physically stop myself from slamming the phone back into its cradle. I laid back down, pulling the heavy duvet over my head and wriggling in the sheets. I'd chosen my favorite silk pajamas before bed—a gaudy red two-piece number I didn't let anyone see me in. They made a delightfully soft whooshing noise whenever I rolled over that reminded me of waves on the shore. The color was what I'd thought vampires should wear to bed because blood or whatever, and they were Versace Valentine's limited edition, so I wasn't going to *not* wear them.

I made the whooshing noise now and tried to will away the tell-tale thud of a migraine. I didn't want to start my day eating dirt. I could hold this off for a few more—

Brrrrrinnnng, Brrrrrinnnnng.

"NO" I yelled without removing the duvet from my face. The phone continued. "I'm sleeping!"

A knock on the door had me vaulting across the room so fast I was nearly levitating—a skill I usually left alone as it made me nauseous.

I swung the door open to the long-haired teenager from last night—the one who had snuck up on me—and I recognized the reedy voice from the phone as he asked again, "Breakfast?"

The migraine now spread across my face, thudding in a dull pulse.

"Fine." I stepped back to allow William in with his clearly urgent food order, but he hesitated at the threshold.

"Sir?"

"Right." I tried not to roll my eyes, remembering what it was like to be freshly turned when everything was stranger, stronger, scarier. "Please come in, William."

I didn't imagine the relief on his pinched face as his curtain of hair swung back over his features. He pushed the service cart into my room, stopping in front of the sitting area, and whisked off the silver tray cover, bowing deeply as he pointed a single finger to the white porcelain plate atop the white tablecloth-covered cart.

"Breakfast," he said with deep reverence.

"Thank you," I said, not bothering to glance at the tray. I waited for him to recover from his deep bow so I could tip him, and he'd leave.

"Is it to your liking, sir?" Another voice called from the hall. I turned to see the ever-nervous Richard standing at full military attention in my doorway.

"Is breakfast a two-person job?" I was more confused than annoyed now.

"For you, it is, sir. Not because you're difficult or anything, but you're our only guest *and* our first guest so Alfie really wants to make sure we get this right. And William is great, don't get me wrong, but he can sometimes be a little over-enthusiastic. We don't want him scaring you off with his melodramatic flair, so I came along to—"

"Breakfast is great, Richard," I said. "I'd like to eat in solitude, now, gentlemen." I gestured to the door and William excused himself. I would thank God if I thought he was paying any attention to us.

Then, both teens hovered in the doorway, anxious smiles spread across their faces, an eager glint in their eyes.

Right.

I pulled a few small notes from my wallet and pressed them into their outstretched hands. They repeated a stream of "thank yous," nodding and sidestepping until they were out of my line of sight, and I could safely close the door.

Breakfast was a warm blood bag propped precariously next to a few suspicious-looking scrambled eggs, and hard toast that had clearly been made several hours prior. I imagined William and Richard waking early enough to be dangerous for young vampires to prepare the meal and then anxiously wondering how early was too early to make a wakeup call.

The human food in addition to the blood bag meant they'd done their homework—they knew some vamps were still weak to the earthly experience of food. I'd need to stock the hotel with guests if I was to survive the week—there was no way a week alone with this crew would be anything other than kindness torture.

Unfortunately, both offerings turned my stomach as I recalled the bloody bile I'd left on the side of the road last night.

The coffee pot was hot at least, and I gratefully poured myself a cup before remembering who had made it. To be safe, I mixed in a generous helping of milk and sugar before grabbing my cell and tapping on Rye's number.

I was up, might as well get started.

"You're up early." There was light chatter and the clattering of silverware on plates in the background.

"You know me, always trying to get the worm before the next bird."

"Are you sick?"

"Probably," I said, sipping the coffee. It didn't suck, so there was that. "Tell me good news."

"I would if I had any." She took a sip of whatever she was drinking.

"You said we had a case."

"We do. But you have work to do before we present it."

"What do you mean?"

"The law states that if you haven't proven your dedication to the care and maintenance of the property to satisfaction, they can dub you a dangerous property owner—whatever that means—and revoke your ownership. The town annexes the land, and you're still on the hook for whatever repairs are needed in the form of fees and fines."

"I'm working on it."

"If you say so." She took another sip. "What's the deal out there anyway? I've never heard of a dangerous property owner law until now. And it's even weirder that it's old as hell. Like, turn of the 20th century kind of shit."

Alexander Huxley—Hurls, affectionately—the original owner of Huxley Manor. Of course it was all his fault. It had to be.

I set my coffee down and pressed my free hand against the side of my face. The migraine was traveling down into my shoulders.

"You know how it was with those old colonizers." I tried to keep my tone light. "Some English fucker probably did something nightmare-worthy and the village decided to do something about it."

"So are you the English fucker in this case?"

"Fuck off." I was about to hang up and leave Rye to it, but the never-ending to-do list of my day was giving me pause. I would be here for months if I tried to do it all myself—hiring, managing, executing, all while trying to stay on top of the legal requirements. "I think you should come out here."

"You know my travel fee."

"I'll double it." Anything to get away from this place. The memory of my nightmare—wet, wriggling dirt on all sides—made me shudder.

"I'm not coming all the way to rural England if this is a bullshit effort to get out of trouble. We can lie over the phone."

I closed my eyes against the flashing pain of the migraine and gritted my teeth.

"I'm actually going to fix the place, Rye. It'll be a tourist trap or a rental or something. Americans love that shit, and I wouldn't mind the extra income."

"You're really selling me on your love for the place."

"You don't have to love something to keep it from killing anyone else."

She was silent a moment—a rarity.

"That's an insane thing to say." Another pause. "I'll be on the first plane out today."

"I'll send Charles and the crew for you, my treat." Commercial would mean landing in Heathrow and having to negotiate several hours out to the village from there. I wanted to reduce lag as much as possible.

"Fuck yeah." She hung up in her usual way, and I practically threw the phone across the room as I stood and dove under the bed.

A mahogany tray the size of the mattress had been provided on small wheels for ease of use. I slid it out, immediately thrusting both hands wrist-deep into the dirt I'd spread there. I bent down, scooping up dirt into my mouth like a dog devouring a kill. Before I realized what I was doing, I was wriggling into the dirt, shoving it down the front of my pajamas, pouring it over my face, rolling on my back until I felt fully settled within it.

"Finally," I whispered as the headache immediately ceased. My limbs felt weak and heavy, as if I'd just stopped running a marathon with no cool down or recovery plan. My stomach was flipping, threatening to throw back up all the dirt and coffee I'd swallowed if I moved too suddenly.

I had too much to do to be this controlled by a pile of dirt. I'd need to find, contact, and hire contractors to survey the restoration work on the manor. I'd need to meet with the landscaper I'd spoken with earlier. I'd need to call Charles and have him ready the crew immediately.

I needed to go to the manor itself.

My dream washed back over me—the house, the stables, The Colonel. I closed my eyes, suddenly exhausted.

It was too early to be awake right now anyway.

Chapter Ten

Leslee

Sketchpad under my arm, pencil lost amid my curls, I set out into the evening light toward the Clotswold.

It was an anomaly in Ashbourne, with clean lines and a flat roof rising out of the sagging walls and thatched roofs of the village. The windows burned bright even this early in the day, and I thought about the council meeting where the village demanded the hotel use softer wattage indoors as no one could get any sleep with the place burning like the midday sun at all hours.

My boots crunched up the road, and I took a moment to indulge in swishing my outfit. I'd chosen my favorite black swing skirt and a buttoned-up white silk blouse that fit me perfectly. I let my curls run wild, and I'd opted for slightly fewer talismans for the meeting—no reason to come on quite so strong, but I certainly wouldn't be going in unprotected. I felt more like Business Leslee than I had in a long time.

Tyler had always insisted he take client meetings. He said I was too wild to attract new work, and I'd wondered how anyone asking for help with wild things would be put off by a wild woman, but I'd chosen to keep my head down and do the dirty work instead—that was the fun part anyway.

On the occasions I had joined Tyler in client meetings, I'd felt so unlike myself I wouldn't even speak, unsure of whose words would slip past my lips. Tyler usually wore some combination of a tailored suit with cufflinks, his grandfather's watch, and a smart tie. He'd trussed me up in slacks and a blazer, insisting I tame my hair back into braids. I'd been all Business, zero Leslee.

This outfit, though, I smiled to myself as I turned the corner, the hotel rising in all its bright-lit, square-windowed glory, was entirely Business Leslee. And this was *my* client, earned on *my* merit.

Oh yes, this would be a great first solo venture; I could feel it in my gut.

Alex swung the massive door open, hands pressed against the six-foot chrome handle glinting in the sunset.

"Miss Hawthorne." He smiled, the soft brogue of his voice tickling my name.

"Hi Alex, love," I said, returning the grin. "How's your mum?"

"Enjoying her garden as we speak," he said. "She loves whatever trick you pulled on her roses. Says she could sit with a cuppa and stare all day if she didn't have to work."

He fell into step alongside me, gesturing toward the sleek chrome elevator doors on the far end of the empty lobby.

"Things still slow here?" I asked.

He shrugged by way of an answer.

"And how are you doing? With the new hours and all?" I took the opportunity to search his face for any signs of fatigue or worry. It had the blissful smoothness of youth—almost too smooth, even. And although he certainly seemed pale under the warm lights surrounding us, he didn't look sick. A certain strength ran through him, as if he had only just discovered his possible powers.

But something was off—something I couldn't quite put my finger on.

"The hours aren't so bad once you get used to it," he said. "And me and the boys have a cracking time together. Professionally, of course." His face split into an eye-crinkling grin and it was then I noticed the unusual sharpness of his canines. Had they always been like that?

"Sounds like the dream," I said, flashing him my own quick smile as I stepped into the elevator.

He joined me, pressing a button and slipping his hands into his pocket as the door slid closed.

"Can I tell you something, Miss Hawthorne?" His voice dropped to a whisper, and he studied the floor display as if it might tell him a secret.

"Of course, love."

"I'm not sure it's a dream I want forever," he said. "And I'm afraid I don't have a choice."

Before I could ask what he meant, the doors slid open and Alex was ushering me to the first door to the right.

"Mr. Barlow is a right posh gentleman, but he's alright," he said. "I think he'll like you."

"Come in." Came from the other side of the door and I recognized a muffled version of the voice on the phone. Something low and hot within me clenched at the possibility of who was on the other side of the door. I shoved it aside.

"Alex," I said, catching him lightly by the arm before he turned to leave. "You always have a choice. And you can always come see me if you feel like you don't. I'll do what I can."

I couldn't quite see his eyes beneath his bushy bowl cut—really, I was going to have to speak with his mum about that hair—but his lower lip trembled slightly as he reached up to squeeze my hand.

"Thanks, Miss Hawthorne. I'll keep that in mind."

I glanced at the door, wondering how long I could keep the client waiting.

"And one more thing—" but when I turned back, Alex was gone and I was alone in the hall.

So far, this visit was only confirming that something very strange was happening in the village.

"Hello?" The voice came from the other side of the door, closer this time.

"Yes, sorry, coming." I gave myself one last deep breath then squared my shoulders, shoved down my nerves and curiosity, and turned the knob.

It didn't budge.

"Erm, it's locked," I called, pressing my face close to the door.

The door swung open, startling me, and I felt my center of gravity shift suddenly from the way I'd been leaning against a thing that now didn't exist. I tumbled, landing directly onto a hard body wrapped in crisp cotton. I looked up from where my hands slid across the chest against my will into the same set of startlingly red eyes that had peered up at me in the dark last night. The man from the roadside gazed down at me in confusion and concern. And what was that intoxicating smell? I couldn't decide if I wanted to sniff him like a hunting dog or rub myself all over him like a cat on a post.

"It's you," he said. The nagging voice from our phone call earlier shifted into a screaming pitch—*that* was what I knew him from. But oh man—hearing his voice was one thing. Feeling it rumble up through his chest against my palms was more than I was prepared for.

Thank the gods I wasn't wearing tights—the pressure between my legs would've been too much.

"Yes, sorry. I'm horribly clumsy." I pried myself off him, giving his shirt one final pat to smooth the wrinkles and picked my sketchbook off the floor. A hot blush flashed across my face, and I knew when I looked up, he'd see it, which made it worse. "Oh, and lovely to see you again. Glad you're feeling better. Assuming you are feeling better. Aren't you?"

He just nodded.

Business, Leslee. This is BUSINESSS. Tyler would never. The thought made my body cool and my flush dissipate as the man extended a well-manicured hand to me. He wore a signet ring on his pinky but I couldn't get a good look at it.

"Billy Barlow," he said. "Thank you for meeting with me and my apologies again about last night. I hope my prior illness won't impact our business together." He held out a hand that I shook, hoping I got the firmness correct for business-type people. "I appreciate your flexibility with my schedule—I'm working on a large negotiation in Singapore and I'm afraid it means I'm running on their hours."

His hands were soft, and I was sure he moisturized. Gods, why was I horny about moisturizer?

"Leslee Hawthorne," I said, pleased with how confident I sounded. Although, it was just my name. That couldn't be the hard part.

"Pleasure to officially meet you," he said, a soft smile crawling on his face. He gestured toward the sitting area. "Please, join me."

The coffee table in the center held a steaming tea service and fresh biscuits, a delightful smell wafting off all.

I chose one of the wing-back chairs facing the sofa. Behind it, I saw a luxurious king bed with tidy bedding and a mass of pillows. My heart pulled at the sight, wondering what it felt like to flop in the center, just for a moment. My cottage was lovely, but 200-year-old buildings weren't made to accommodate modern luxuries like mattresses any bigger than a twin.

Mr. Barlow poured two cups and offered me one with a biscuit tucked neatly on the edge of the saucer.

"So, Miss Hawthorne," he said. "I understand you've quite a talent with all things green."

"It's a family business," I said. "Generations back, all the women in my family have tended gardens, farms, hedge mazes, and the like. I couldn't stay away from the dirt, ever since I was little girl."

A strange look flickered across his face.

Right, no family anecdotes in business meetings.

"I'm glad to hear I'll be hiring from a long-standing family business," he said. "My plan is to leverage this renovation into an opportunity to broker goodwill in the village so things can run smoothly after I leave."

"What do you mean?"

"I am crafting the manor into a destination—tours, dinners, rentals. That sort of thing."

"I don't know that anyone would come all the way out here just for dinner," I said, something like a warning settling on my shoulders.

"Americans will. There's a market for destinations 'off the map' so-to-speak. You know how it is now—the internet ruins everything so it's like everything's already been seen." He settled back on the sofa, crossing a long leg over his knee. His ankles flashed above his loafers. "We'll have a strict no photography policy, cut the tours a discount for groups of 20 or more, and, if all goes well, offer an exclusive wedding and events package."

"If no one ever sees pictures, how will they know it's worth visiting?"

"That's a question for the publicity staff," he said.

"So, all these people coming through to see the manor, what will that do to our roads and traffic?"

"The attraction will bring in a lot of money for the town, I imagine some infrastructure updates are due."

"Ashbourne has had the same road running through it since people settled here," I said, slightly aghast. "You can't just tear that up to make room for tour buses."

He shrugged. "How the council decides to apply the increased profits to the village's well-being is their business. That's not what I'm being asked to do."

"You're also not being asked to put a bloody beacon on our map."

Swearing at a client was *definitely* not what Business Leslee should be doing, but I couldn't help myself—my hackles were up. I didn't trust what this stranger with a sexy voice and naked ankles was doing here. And the feeling that something was wrong wouldn't let go. If anything, it had gotten stronger since my interaction with Alex in the hall. It was starting to overwhelm me.

Mr. Barlow stared at me in silence for a moment, those unsettling red eyes holding my gaze. But I refused to break. I meant what I said, and Business Leslee didn't back down any more than Regular Leslee did—which meant not at all. Not when I knew something wasn't right.

Finally, he looked away, running a hand through his bright blonde hair. He wore it slicked back so that the ends perpetually looked like they'd had hands run through them. Despite myself, my fingertips found my legs and dug in.

I would not be feeling up this asshole's scalp.

"What exactly *are* you being asked to do?" I finally broke the silence, surprising even myself with the sharpness of my tone.

"I have to prove I'm not a dangerous property owner," he said. "And it's a poor investment to renovate a historic English manor and not invite the public to it. I'd be sinking money into a pit."

"Ashbourne is not a *pit.*"

"Miss Hawthorne," he sighed.

"Mr. Barlow."

"You can call me Billy," he said.

"No, thank you."

He quirked an eyebrow at me. "Are you still interested in the job? Time is of the essence so I'm willing to double whatever rate would bring you on."

My stomach flipped.

"I really don't want to go searching for a landscaper who will come all the way out here and complete the demanding hours required while charming the village council."

"I haven't charmed anyone."

He gave me a half-smile and looked up at me from under serious brows. "I know for a fact that's not true."

I rolled my eyes, blatantly ignoring the somersaults my stomach was flipping.

Double whatever rate I say.

"When do you need the work completed?"

"End of the week."

"Absolutely not." I laughed. "It's not possible."

"I'm a hearty believer in the impossible."

"I don't have a crew, Mr. Barlow; it would just be me out there, and I have no interest in working round the clock, especially not with what's wandering the woods lately."

Why the fuck did I say that? It just popped out of my mouth, carried on the edge of my shock at this man's audacity and a little bit of fear at still not understanding what I saw last night.

Mr. Barlow cocked his head to the side, spreading his arms up along the back of the sofa.

"What would you say is wandering the woods?"

"Something that vomits blood and claws the earth," I said, letting loose a sigh and pushing my glasses up to the top of my head. "But that doesn't matter right now. If you adjust your timeline to a reasonable one, I'll send an invoice with my rate along with a few sketches for the manor's acreage. But not if you want it done in fewer than seven days. I might not be the most businessy of business people but even I know that's a fool's mission."

I stood, clutching my sketchbook under my arm.

"A good evening to you, Mr. Barlow." When I looked down at him to nod my stiff farewell, I saw that his face had gone completely slack. His ivory skin looked paler still and his eyes were wide. His hands clung to the back of the sofa where before they'd been resting loosely.

Not my problem.

I faced the door, and when he finally spoke, I didn't let it slow me down.

"Two weeks," he said.

I waved over my shoulder, resisting the urge to use a vulgar gesture.

"A month."

I reached for the handle, turning it firmly and swinging the door open.

"3 months." I paused, risking a glance over my shoulder. He was standing now, body leaning toward me as if he would chase me down. Something pleasant danced down my spine. "Please, Miss Hawthorne.

Your price, your timeline, your estimate—whatever it is you need. Consider it done."

"I don't think this is how negotiations work." I was taken aback by his sudden desperation. He'd seemed so cool and confident when I walked in. Half a cup of tea and my blathering and now he was reduced to giving me whatever I wanted. Not exactly the stalwart negotiator Tyler had always insisted men were.

Maybe this isn't the only thing about business Tyler got wrong.

"It's not, usually," he said, slipping his hands into his pockets. "Consider this a unique circumstance."

"Why?"

He squinted at me in confusion.

"Why are you so desperate for me to do the work? With an offer like that, you could get anyone you wanted in the entire country—maybe the world. Why does it have to be me?"

"Maybe it's enough that I want it to be you."

We stared at each other in silence for a moment. I didn't know what to say to *that*.

"You've been in the States too long, Mr. Barlow," I said, trying to recover my senses. "You've gained a deeply American sense of honesty."

He let loose a soft huff of a laugh.

"So?"

I let my shoulders drop. "Three months," I said. "And you pay whatever I invoice, no questions asked."

"Deal."

"I'll send sketches before the end of the week."

I turned and clicked the door shut before he could stop me again. If he said anything else *forward,* I wasn't going to make it home, even if that would be the stupidest, least Business Leslee thing I could do.

What a strange, strange man.

Chapter Eleven

BILLY

The pain was gone.

I don't know *who* that woman was or *what* she did, but the minute she walked in the door, I went from shaking in pain, frantically wondering how long I could make it before I dove back under the bed for a mouthful of dirt, to totally and entirely at ease.

And I hadn't even noticed until she'd mentioned finding claw marks in the dirt—next to a pile of blood that was most likely my mess from the other night. I'd had to work to keep from leaping off the couch in joy and kissing her in celebration.

Not that I was usually that kind of celebrator, but she had a quirky kind of beauty that reminded me of a sexy art teacher. And she was clearly muscular and fit from her line of work. Not to be a cliché, but when she pushed her glasses up—in frustration at me, I didn't miss that part—I could see how pretty she was.

I'd had to plead with her to take the job. Whatever power she had over what was happening to me, I needed to better understand it before she vanished through that door, possibly forever. Giving a contractor anything they demanded in exchange for their services was the world's most dangerous negotiating tactic. Still, the clear-headedness I had once free from pain had immediately been replaced by panic that the pain would return.

I hadn't been able to do any of the things I needed since waking the second time. I'd been plagued by a blinding migraine and a heaviness in my limbs that only barely abated when I laid in the dirt beneath my bed, chewing on intermittent mouthfuls.

My stomach was a wreck, my teeth were gritty, and, at this rate, I was going to run out of clean pajamas. The hotel had a laundry service, but I dreaded the idea of handing over silk to fucking Bradford.

Worse yet, I still needed to charter the jet for Rye, request proposals from construction companies in the county, and arrange for a meeting with the city council to go over my plans.

I turned to snatch my phone off the sofa behind me and nearly doubled over. A headache slammed through me, as if someone had cracked an egg of pain over my scalp, and it was dripping down along my shoulders and into my spine.

Desperation fueled my movement as I swung my coat on, pocketed my phone and practically tripped out the door.

She couldn't have gone far in the few moments I'd stood gob smacked in my room, and yet, the hall, the elevator, *and* the lobby were empty.

"No, no, no, no," I breathed, my steps heavy and leaden as I tried to catch a glimpse of her wild brown halo of hair.

"Alright?" That reedy voice appeared over my shoulder. This time I was too weighed down to jump.

"No, William, I'm not." The long-haired teen stared at me vacantly.

"What's wrong?"

"Did you see where Miss Hawthorne went?" I ground out, the dirt in my teeth grinding back.

"Are you looking for Miss Hawthorne, sir?" Richard called from behind the desk. The pitch and volume of his voice was going to make me black out. The migraine pulsed and spiked in unpredictable ways—as if it was looking for a heart to follow and was confused as to my lack of living one.

All I could do was nod.

"She usually goes to the pub around this time. She likes their soup. If you're lucky, you'll be able to catch the band before they get too drunk to finish their set. Mr. Garlish loves the drink a little too much, even if his Missus keeps reminding him it's not professional to get so—"

I turned on my heel and walked away, too pained and desperate for polite goodbyes.

The village spread out beneath the gentle slope of the hill the hotel was perched on, all twinkling lights in the dark. For a split second, I was transported back to another life, another era, when the sparkling lights would've been torches against the dark, the lives inside chasing dreams that their prodigy would've considered quaint.

I pressed a hand against my non-existent heart and rubbed. It would've ached if it could.

Not a single soul was here to remember me. Not a single soul was here to be remembered. This would never have been a homecoming, but still, loneliness sunk deep into my bones and settled, threatening to pull me deeper than the very earth that kept physically trying to swallow me.

Another blinding flash of pain broke my self-pitying revery and I set off along the main road.

There was only one pub, so it was easy enough to find. I was nearly giddy as I felt the pain slowly subsiding the closer I got to the front entrance. By the time I walked in, ordered a pint, and sat down, I was practically clear-headed.

I noticed a familiar halo of bushy brown hair across the bustling room. I wasn't ready to make myself known, but at least I had some time to make a few calls before she called it a night.

I raised my pint to the back of her head and settled into my seat, tapping across my phone screen.

"A pleasant surprise, sir." Charles voice came through the line crisp and controlled.

"I'm sorry to cut your vacation short," I said, before explaining who Rye was and why I needed her here as expeditiously as possible.

"And again," I said, when we were nearly finished with the call. "I'm sorry to cut into your time off."

"Not meaning to offend anyone, sir, but this isn't exactly a stimulating place to have nothing to do," he said. "I'm glad for the distraction."

I grimaced into the phone and made a mental note to give Charles a proper holiday when this was done. We said our goodbyes and I took a moment to scan the pub. I was still headache-free, but I didn't want to be caught off-guard. Leslee had shifted her seat to face a small stage directly to my left where a few rag-tag musicians were setting up. Too late, I realized she'd seen me. A flutter of concern crossed her face, and she looked like she wanted to catch my eye.

"Nope," I muttered to myself, immediately looking away and back down to my phone. "Not ready yet."

An attempted search online told me only that the service in the village was abysmal. I gave up after reloading the page a fourth time. A cork board held various announcements, notices, and offers fluttering in the draft from the door—but to get to it, I'd have to cross directly in front of Leslee.

Ah, but what good are supernatural vampire powers if not for avoiding confrontation?

I waited until I could no longer feel her eyes on me and then stood, stepping into the characteristic fast sprint of my kind.

It was a split second before I slammed face-first into the cork board. Was I *that* out of practice?

Unfortunately, my attempts at stalking quickly across the room to look for a contractor were ruined by my lack of grace. Several locals stared as I rubbed my injured nose.

I pretended to be thoroughly engrossed in the fliers in front of me, pushing down my rising embarrassment.

"You don't strike me as the dancing type."

I jumped, despite myself, and turned to see Leslee leaning over my shoulder. She had a pint clutched in one hand, her free arm crossed over her chest. She arched an eyebrow at my confusion and reached over me to tap the flyer I'd been pretending to read.

"Learn to Waltz today—lessons for all ages, genders, and feet presentations," I read out loud. "What does that mean?"

"Angela doesn't want anyone to feel unrepresented," she said. "I tried explaining to her that's not what 'two left feet' actually means but she wouldn't hear it."

A soft laugh escaped me. "Wait until you see me dance—Angela will be more right than you know."

"She teaches in her flat with nine cats. She insists they be involved because they're nature's ballerinas."

"Ah, well," I pretended to be put out. "Cats don't care for me, I suppose that's that dream dashed."

"Is that why you're here? Dreams?"

I turned to get a better look at her face. Her mouth was settled in a curious half-smile, and her eyes were a warm honey amber in the low light.

"How'd you know?" *Did* she know? About the nightmares and how they kept pulling me under?

"Cause that's all that's on this board," she said. "Hopes, dreams, supplications—let me teach you, let me show you, let me sell you."

"So no local contractors, huh?"

The spark in her eyes flared to something more dangerous and the half-smile settled into a line across her face. Wordlessly, she reached across me again, further this time so that we were pushed together and I was enveloped in the sharp earthy smell of her—like a field full of morning dew. Her blouse whispered against me, and I had the entirely primal, irrational thought of what it would feel like to hook my fingers through the buttons of it and set them loose. I imagined the soft press of her skin beneath my hands, the flutter of her stomach as—

"Henry does wonderful work," she said and flicked a business card under my nose. I took it, silent, still half in a horny daydream that felt more like I'd been blindsided by a semi than fantasizing in a pub.

"Does this mean you forgive my intentions?"

"Absolutely not," she said. "But if you're going to bastardize my village history, I'd prefer locals get paid in the process."

Before I could say another word, she turned on her heel and returned to her seat, just as the first notes rang out from an expert violin.

I'd have to make my next set of calls outside—if this woman's power would let me.

There was a back exit to the pub that allowed me to avoid the embarrassment of picking my way across the room—in front of Leslee—and I stepped out into the crisp night. I waited a moment, shoulders tense, stomach knotted and was relieved to find that only a light fuzzy kind of exhaustion hit me instead of a full migraine. I'd have to take it.

I dialed the number on the card and hoped I wasn't interrupting Henry's dinner.

***

"Okay, thank you for taking my call. I look forward to working together." I hung up the phone and leaned against the wall of the pub. It'd been an hour of working through a tight lattice of local recommendations to find someone who would take the work at the pace I wanted with the understanding that pay would be high and hours would be long. Henry said no, but gave me the name of Jonathan, who also declined on account of his sciatica acting up in the cold months (which he needed to tell me about in great detail) and then he gave me the name and number for Joseph. Joseph hadn't answered but called me back in the middle of my follow-up with Charles, and I'd been so frantic I hung-up on Charles mid-sentence.

Joseph had a crew of "darling misfits," as he called them, who would take the work despite the dark winter weeks and intense hours. Of course, then Joseph needed to spend twenty minutes describing his crew to me in detail so I would recognize them all when they showed.

This wasn't necessary. I didn't care. I couldn't scare him off because I couldn't make yet another phone call. I had no idea how much longer I had with Leslee in the pub, and I really didn't want to end up stalking her home so I could continue business.

What *was* I going to do about this whole migraine-dirt-Leslee affair?

"A problem for tomorrow," I muttered, tapping open a text from Rye. She'd taken it upon herself to arrange a date with the village council and connect with Charles about her rapidly impending flight.

I sent a kissing face emoji and shoved my phone in my pocket.

I leaned my head back and closed my eyes. My limbs wiggled dangerously beneath me and my stomach flipped for the thousandth time. I was starting to wonder if I'd ever truly felt settled in my body or if that had all been a distant mirage where feeling normal was a trick of the light and nothing more.

What was I going to do? I couldn't just hover around Leslee for the next however long. And what would happen when I needed to leave? I still hadn't figured out what was wrong, exactly, never mind how to fix it.

"You have to make right with your dirt."

There were very few possibilities for what that might mean in the vampire world. And I didn't want to wait around for Dies-well to figure it out.

I was going to have to return to the manor—much sooner than I'd thought.

I pushed off the wall, giving myself a moment to steady on my feet, and set off from the pub. I gritted my teeth as the headache set back in, but tried to focus on the task at hand—and hopefully the payoff it would offer.

If this didn't fix things, I could always just rebury myself in my old grave and stay there.

There were worse fates.

Chapter Twelve

INTERLUDE

Ashbourne, 1823

"You dare—" Mr. Huxley uncrossed his arms and pushed off the desk.

"I believe you are familiar with the Blithes."

Mr. Huxley froze his would-be attack mid-stride. "I employ one of their daughters," he snapped. "What of it?"

"Their eldest," the stranger said. "Mary. An innocent young thing of barely fourteen who is the sole provider for her sick mother and disabled father. Her sister is only seven."

"What do I care—"

"You recently had Miss Mary Blithe beaten so severely that she was unable to work the next day due to the bruising—an offense which you found fireable."

"I'm not paying if they're not working."

"I see," the stranger gave Mr. Huxley a look that would freeze a midday blaze. "So I assume you won't be moved by the news that she was sent to a workhouse in London to pay her family's debts. Debts, Mr. Huxley, that I believe you are in charge of collecting."

"What is your point, Mr...?"

"Gabriel Amdis. And my point is that you have caused a domino of suffering that you insist is just and fair. You cannot be allowed to continue."

"I'd like to see you—" Mr. Huxley found himself unable to take another step forward. His limbs wouldn't obey and a sharp stinging pain rang through his chest when he tried to push against their resistance.

"Also on your long, long list of persons wronged is Joshua Avery, who you disfigured permanently in a fire for serving your tea too hot, and Alice Watson, who can no longer run after her three-year-old son because of the damage to her lungs sustained cleaning your hearth."

"It shouldn't take anyone that long to clear some ash," Mr. Huxley seethed. Gabriel was pleased to see a small flicker of fear on the man's face.

"You demanded you be able to eat off the bottom of the hearth," he continued. "And when it still wasn't clear enough after six hours, you shoved her face into the discarded pile of ash and held it there until she passed out."

"I will not stand here and endure a lecture on the way I run my property."

"You *will* stand there, Mr. Huxley, and you *will* endure it, as these are your last moments on this earth. I meant it when I said I would not explain my motives to you, but I *will* ensure you understand the crimes for which you are being tried."

"Who are you to judge me?" Mr. Huxley's eyes were wide now, swallowing much of his pinched little face. A trickle of sweat slid freely across his bald brow.

"Elizabeth Barnell," Gabriel said, sidestepping the question.

Mr. Huxley grew ghostly pale and began to shake from head to toe.

"You employed her with the express intent of seducing her, is that correct?"

Mr. Huxley stayed silent. Frothing spittle formed at the edges of his mouth, and a vein bulged from his neck.

"But she refused your advances every time, going so far as to threaten you with a fire iron if you tried to touch her again."

"She was a whore—" The slap rang out clearly across the silent parlor, a shocking crack of palm to cheek.

"She was a hardworking young woman with enough presence of self to know letting you knock her up would only worsen her already pitiful situation. And you were enraged by that."

"No," breathed Mr. Huxley.

"So enraged that you waited for her to leave for the day, followed her through the trees, shot her with your hunting rifle, and did something so horrific to her bleeding body that even a monster like myself refuses to say it out loud."

The two men stood in silence, the only sound the whispering wind pressing against the rattling glass and groaning columns, the only answer the soft crackle of the fire in the hearth. From the kitchen, a blissful child's giggle followed by a dutiful "shush." Upstairs, nameless footsteps creaked, attending to whatever evening business would keep the manor running with frictionless full-steam.

Still, neither man spoke. If the Manor itself could lean in to hear, they would've felt it doing so, each wall and eave and archway strained for what came next.

"If," Mr. Huxley finally whispered before clearing his throat and continuing. "*If* that were true, how could I trust your knowledge? You've clearly come to my home with wicked intentions. Surely, you're not above falsehoods."

"You may have thought you were careful, that no one followed you, no one heard, but I have my ways," Gabriel said. He made a swooping, twisting gesture with his wrist and Mr. Huxley found himself bent painfully backwards over the desk despite the man not touching him.

Gabriel's face changed as if he'd ripped off a mask of propriety to reveal the monster beneath. His eyes widened and filled solely with that intriguing crimson that colored his iris until it looked as if bloody veins popped within his sockets. His teeth lengthened and hung over his bottom lip like a snake, and his jaw unhinged, dropping unnaturally low. He leaned over Mr. Huxley with his open mouth just above his tortured neck. Gabriel's breath smelled like rotting meat, a sickly-sweet stench that overwhelmed Mr. Huxley.

"*WAIT*," Huxley cried out. "*PLEASE LET ME SAY GOODBYE TO MY DAUGHTER.*"

Gabriel pushed his jaw back into place—a movement that would've been comical if anyone else was under threat of devourment.

"No," he said simply, letting his jaw drop again.

"*PLEASE*," Mr. Huxley pleaded. "Do me this final human kindness. You don't want to end up as wicked as I've been, do you? Devoid of sympathy or compassion for others? This could be how it starts for you!"

Gabriel licked down the side of Mr. Huxley's face with an unsettling slurping sound. He cocked his head to the side as if he were considering his plea. He licked the other side and pulled his tongue back in. Reaching up a second time, he pushed his jaw back into place. His fangs retracted to a normal size and shape, though the eyes remained pupil-less and bloodied.

"Alright," he said. "But only because I need to find some cayenne and paprika. It could be the weakness in the Empire's armor that Englishmen taste this bland."

Mr. Huxley felt control return to his limbs, and he collapsed to his knees, clinging to Gabriel's pants.

"Oh, thank you, thank you, merciful sir," he gasped out, sobs wracking his body. "And please, please, *please*—a final request."

"Seeing your daughter is your final request," Gabriel said dismissively, kicking the clinging manor master off his pants as if he were a leper. He clamped a clawed hand to Mr. Huxley's shoulder and hauled him to his feet as easily as lifting a sheet to pin to the line. "Call for your daughter," he commanded.

"In the kitchen, sir," Mr. Huxley blubbered. "Where we keep our herbs and spices. Our housekeeper lets her play where it's warm."

Gabriel dragged the man out of the salon, down a narrow hall, and around a tight corner until a swinging door pushed open onto a sprawling, tidy kitchen. In the far corner, next to a cheerily lit stove, the housekeeper entertained the little girl with a beautiful doll and a horse to match.

"My baby!" Gabriel didn't miss the confusion on the housekeeper's face at Mr. Huxley's outburst.

"Spices first," Gabriel said, squeezing the man's shoulder hard enough to draw blood. He crumpled under his grip and pointed to various jars on the far counter. Gabriel pulled him to the counter, lifting each lid and sniffing curiously. Again, such a silence fell across the room, such a full tension in the air that it would not be amiss to suggest the Manor *was* listening. But was it waiting for Huxley's demise? Did it believe in justice? In any other story, while Gabriel snuffled through the limited spice rack like a mole in the dark, the house would've signaled its intent. The hearth would've growled approvingly, or a door to escape would've swung open at just the right moment. But despite the eaves drooping suspiciously, there was no other action from the Manor, the room, or those within it.

"Salt, bay leaves, fennel, garlic..." Gabriel muttered to himself, lifting and replacing lids. Finally, he lifted the lid Mr. Huxley had been listening for.

"Pepper—" Before Gabriel could react, Mr. Huxley reached out and smacked the jar over, sending the peppercorns skittering and zinging across the kitchen.

Gabriel roared, releasing Mr. Huxley and diving after the scattered spice.

"*DAMN AND BLAST, YOU USELESS VULTURE!*" he screamed, talons delicately collecting the peppercorn into piles of ten, but Mr. Huxley was already gone.

Chapter Thirteen

Leslee

"*Maybe it's enough that I want it to be you.*"

"Ugh." I let my disgust loose into the night as I walked away from the pub. The air grew colder, and my breath came out in puffs before me. I wrapped my arms around myself, rubbing them as I picked up the pace. What kind of English idiot doesn't bring a coat when she leaves the house?

With every step, Mr. Barlow's words echoed through me. And what was all that at the corkboard? I'd only wandered over to see if he was too drunk to stand after he smashed his face into the wall, but then I'd found any excuse to brush against him, any reason to inhale his probably very expensive cologne.

"This would be so much easier if my new client wasn't hot." I freed the secret, watching it evaporate with my breath.

And he was. I couldn't deny that—even if he was irritating and heartless and entirely too capitalistic for a village like this. He had those startling eyes and that cut jaw, and I remembered a little too clearly what his chest felt like under my hands.

"Ugh," I yelled again, uncrossing my arms long enough to shake my hands free of the memory—like that would work.

I hated to admit it, but I was missing Tyler. He would never have been charmed by a model-looking client with fancy shoes. He would never rub himself all over a potential customer like a horny cat.

Of course, Tyler would never say or do anything to protect anything other than his own interests—at least I was better at the whole "human" part of our job.

"My job," I corrected, kicking open my garden gate with a little more force than I meant. I slammed into the cottage, a low rage kindling in my gut as I thought more about Tyler and his priorities.

"Bastard," I snapped to my empty kitchen. The Christmas cacti on my kitchen floor all flinched, and I was too wound up to feel sorry. I reached above the fridge, smearing my fingers through dust until they latched onto my emergency whiskey. Dragging it down brought a shower of dust bunnies onto my formerly crisp white blouse.

"A tomorrow problem," I announced, pulling the cork out with my teeth. I poured a healthy dram into a teacup and threw it back. I winced at the taste but relished the burn as I leaned back against the counter, looking down at my spiny little plant friends.

"What am I gonna do?" I asked, knowing they wouldn't respond. Cacti were marvelous singers with the right encouragement but not much for conversation or advice.

I pushed my glasses up and rubbed my hands down my cheeks, smearing more dust. I glanced out the kitchen window at the field beneath the moon, the strange shadows in the trees beyond.

I hadn't been able to get much out of Alex—he'd seemed happy until we were in the elevator together. What was all that about him not having a choice?

I downed another dram of whiskey, feeling the heat pool in my core as I slipped my jacket back on.

I was going to get to the bottom of this strangeness before it swallowed me whole. It's not what Tyler would've done, but I didn't want to be Tyler. I wanted to be Business Leslee—successful, thriving, and not spooked by strange goings-on in her home village.

I heard a low hum rise from the cacti as I shut the cottage door behind me. A warning or a victory chorus?

There was only one way to find out.

The hotel lobby was empty, as usual. One of Alex's friends—the younger red head, Freddie, who I always remembered as being more aggressive than his older brother—stood behind the counter.

"Good evening, Miss Hawthorne." He gave me a respectful dip of his head, hands clasped behind his back. "I'm afraid Mr. Barlow isn't in at the moment. Would you like to leave a note?"

"No, Freddie, that's alright," I said. "I'm actually looking for Alex. Is he around?"

"He'll be in the stables."

"Excuse me the *what*?"

"The stables—ah, yes, they are quite new, I understand the confusion. If you'll follow me." Freddie darted around the desk and looped an arm through mine, hauling me through the lobby, away from the elevators, and down a hallway I hadn't noticed before.

"Since when does this place have stables? And what in the gods' names are they for?"

"Horses, miss."

I reached up and tweaked his ear. He yelped, untangling himself from me and reaching up to rub his ear.

"The Madame—uh, our investor thought it would be an attraction to have horse drawn carriage rides for guests. And Ashbourne has a notable pedigree in its horses."

"Frederick Wimple, you stop right now." I stamped my feet, throwing my hands on my hips in what I hoped was a fearsome pose. "You tell me what's really going on here, or I'll have your mum in here so fast—"

"*Don't.*" He glanced nervously away from me and toward the exit door he'd been leading me toward.

"Well, then?" I arched my eyebrows and waited a beat before continuing. "You think I missed that useless attempt at a coverup? Who is The Madame? How did you get a stable built in twelve hours? And why are you all being so damn *weird*?"

He stared down at his feet a moment before looking back up at me, a strange glint in his eye.

"If no one has told you yet, don't you think it's because you aren't important enough to know?"

The mouthy little monster.

Before either of us could think about it, I had his ear in my fist and was hauling him out the exit door.

"First, you're going to apologize for implying that one of your elders is *unimportant* and has therefore *earned* the confusion they are experiencing, you entitled little prat. Then, you're going to apologize for wasting my time as a guest of the hotel and Mr. Barlow."

I could see the stark black shadow of the stables rising behind the hotel. They *definitely* hadn't been there before. The only reason the hotel had been permitted was that there were no other structures near it to clash against its aesthetic choices. And I would've heard construction when I was here earlier—I would've seen trucks, workers, remnants of work. Something that indicated a structure was being erected.

As it was, it seemed like it'd sprung fully formed from the ground.

"Let *go*, you *witch*."

I let loose a seething hiss between my teeth and pulled Freddie with me toward the stables.

"I'll show you a witch if you're not careful. This is pure village auntie rage right now. I changed your diapers. I know your dick isn't big enough to behave the way you are."

"And when will you apologize?" he snapped back, face red, feet stumbling.

"For what?"

"For bringing up my mum—"

"I assume a woman who works herself to the bone to ensure you and Alfie have good schooling and a nice home should know how the light of her life mouths off. I'm sure whatever punishment she'll give you is worse than anything I can devise."

By now, we'd reached the massive open barn doors of the stables. I released Freddie and peered into the dark. Someone was hammering, but why were they working in the pitch black?

"Turn on the lights before I hex you and this whole place." He sulked over to the doors and reached inside. A loud "click" echoed, and then a row of electric lights flickered to life, giving off the low hum of current as they did.

Sure enough, Alex was at the far end of the stables, shirt sleeves rolled up, hammering away at something.

"My eyesight must be getting much worse than I thought," I said. But Freddie had disappeared in the split second I'd been looking at Alex. "And slower, apparently."

I called to Alex as I stepped into the empty stables, the smell of fresh hay sharp in the air. He paused his hammering to wave. Despite the hard work he seemed to be putting in, his face wasn't flush and there wasn't a bead of sweat anywhere. He looked positively refreshed.

"Hullo, Miss Hawthorne," he said in that soft brogue. "What brings you out so far from a warm hearth?"

"I wanted to follow-up on our chat from earlier today, Alex," I said, hoping I sounded less intense than I felt.

He tilted his head, shifting his shaggy hair into a bell curve half in the air.

"You said in the elevator you weren't sure you wanted 'this dream' forever, but you were afraid you didn't have a choice."

Alex stilled, an almost unnatural stillness—as if he wasn't even breathing.

"What did you mean by that?"

His silence reached out for me, pressing against my chest with his nervousness, his fear. I wanted to reach out and reassure him, but I worried he'd become a stray animal since I opened my mouth. I worried he would flee, and I would never get any closer to answers.

Venturing a conspiratorial lean, I whispered, "You can tell me. I just want to make sure you're okay. You and the boys are like family to us all in the village. We feel responsible for you."

Alex shook his head, so violently I flinched.

"I don't know what you're talking about, Miss."

"Alex, please." This time I couldn't stop myself from reaching for his shoulder. He was freezing through his thin work shirt and I worried about the conditions he was working in.

"Everything is fine, Miss Hawthorne."

"We both know it's not," I said. "We both know something wrong has happened here, and no one will say anything about it. Ever since that night at the manor—"

"*Please*, Miss Hawthorne," Alex hissed, cutting me off. "It's best you don't ask questions. Shouldnae have complained to you. I was tired, nothing more."

"Is someone threatening you? Is someone holding you here? The whole village will—"

"The whole village will string me up if they learn the full story."

"Your mum—"

"Mum especially," he spat. "I've been given a lot, same as anyone. It's a matter of making do now."

"If you insist," I said. But something in my gut whispered that Alex's refusal and fear were signs I was pressing close to the truth. "I'll leave you to it. But..." I pushed Alex's bowl cut away from his face before he could protest. "Even those with a rotten lot in life deserve a proper cut. Let me fix it up for you soon, yeah?"

Alex nodded, eyes wide as he met my gaze.

I released his long dark hair, letting it fall back in his face. I gave a weak half-smile, feeling pathetic for walking away so quickly. There must be something more I could do for him—for the other boys. Whatever was going on here shouldn't be shoved under a blanket of expectation and luxurious hotel rooms.

I waved goodbye and made my way out of the stables. It wasn't until I crossed the threshold back into the dark that the hammering picked back up again.

I made my way home by the back path, not eager to cross swords with Alfie a second time. The whole way, boots crunching on the gravel, hands twisting in my pockets, I couldn't get Alex's eyes out of my head.

They were a brilliant crimson, and I *know* they hadn't always been that color, but the longer I tried to remember what color they had been before, the less I was sure they hadn't always been crimson. It was like swimming after a fish made of sugar in an upstream race. The longer I pushed, the more the thought disappeared until I was left only with the vague nagging thought that I'd seen eyes like Alex's before and they'd been just as striking.

"Enough," I muttered to myself after finally shutting my cottage door. "Another tomorrow problem for Leslee."

Chapter Fourteen

BILLY

I paused before the manor gates, now little more than two parallel stacks of weathered stone with a few hunks of twisted metal rusting away on top. The once glorious oaks that framed the road to the entrance were now gnarled and bent, rotting in places where their trunks had been left untended. Their long weeping arms reached over the crumbling stone fence line to drape down to the main road with leafy fingers. The row of trees laced limbs as far back as I could see, swallowing what little moonlight peeked between the clouds.

It looked like I was walking into a tomb.

"Stop being dramatic," I said to the air, forcing myself to step forward.

If nothing had changed—and I was certain it hadn't—then the graveyard would be directly to the right along the fence line. It would be maybe ten minutes of brisk walking at worst, and I wouldn't have to go near the manor.

Yet.

I couldn't help glancing over my shoulder as I turned to follow the crumbling stone marking the property's boundary, the once proud limestone peeking shamefully from beneath ivy and moss. The manor looked over everything with wide glass eyes, its sunken frame threatening collapse at any moment. I wondered, not for the first time this visit, what those stupid teenagers had been thinking wandering in there.

I tried to shake the feeling that it was watching me—that I was walking into a trap—focusing instead on the task at hand.

Who was to stop the earth from swallowing me once and for all at my grave? Worse, when it inevitably reached for me, who would come looking for my corpse?

Charles was midair by now. Rye was awaiting her luxurious ride. Evelyn was with Will, and Patrick was asleep, tucked deep within his cavernous Boston home.

Leslee?

She thought I was a greedy bastard and would probably tap dance on my grave. I deserved it. I knew that.

Small grey shadows raised weak hands from the earth as I neared the graveyard. I passed names I knew only from their markers, walking through on many occasions in my former life. My shoulders were tight, my hands balled into fists as I followed a trail built into my subconscious toward a place I never dreamed I'd return. I kept expecting to see new markers, new names—even someone I had known—but the stones looked as untouched as when I'd been alive.

I stopped as I reached the bulky shape of the Huxley mausoleum. From a short distance, I could see the claw marks in the stone and the hasty brickwork covering the doors and windows.

The screams from that night echoed out to me—screams I hadn't thought of with any remorse since they rang through my ears in real time.

Screams I was surprised sent a chill through my memory.

I thought I was over this.

I shook it off, willing myself not to look closer at the hulking building. I continued to the left of the mausoleum and away from the gathering of graves. Beneath a lone oak, some distance from the graveyard, the stables just visible to the left and the twinkling windows of the village to the right, was a lone grave—lonelier still in that it held no gift from the living to the dead.

It would be empty. I knew that even as I approached and knelt before the marker, clasping my hands together in a moment of silence. I knew that even as I slipped my gloves off and sunk my bare hands into the soft earth, stifling a moan as the energy reached back up for me. I felt the dirt slither further, wrapping itself delicately up my wrists, my forearms, my elbows.

"Tell me what to do," I whispered. "Tell me how I've wronged you."

The dirt did not respond; it just continued its silent slink up my body, coating my shoulders, my chest, my back.

Maybe I hadn't wronged the dirt. Maybe the dirt had wronged me and this gentle caress was an offering of rest to make amends.

Stay, it seemed to whisper.

It was tempting—more tempting than I wanted to admit. I felt the exhaustion of 200 years alone wash over me, pulling down on my bones with an unmatched weight. If I could just rest, then the migraines would stop. I would be able to think clearly after a good, long sleep. I could handle these problems another day—maybe even some morning, if the world would permit my entrance into the sun.

How do you make amends to an earth you've refused to return to? How do you apologize to a natural cycle old as life itself when you've forsaken it?

I feared the answer, even as the earth gave a gentle tug that I couldn't help but obey.

The cheery chimes of "Banana Boat" rang out from my back pocket.

I sat up, shaking free from living dirt that sighed in disappointment as I reached back and answered my phone.

"Did you change my ringtone?"

"Your answering is imperative, and I cannot risk being ignored," Dies-well's familiar voice was jarring in the pressing silence of the graveyard—like hearing marimbas during a séance.

"Like I would ever leave your minivan hanging."

"I don't appreciate your flip," he said. "And anyway, while my girl's in the shop, I have intel."

"You've decided to take me up on the offer for a new car after all." I stood, noticing the grave dirt reach for me again as I stepped away.

"Not a chance, saddlegoose." Dies-well snorted. "No, I have a message from Madame Laveau about your dirt problem." There was rustling in the background and the distinct sound of a case opening.

"Let me see here," he said. I could practically hear him squinting. "She said, and I quote, 'Suggest to Master Barlow if he's so miserable, he ought to do us all a favor by taking a long walk at noon.'"

I stopped pacing, staring in stunned silence at the dilapidated pile of wood that used to be the stables. So much of my dream had been wrong.

When Dies-well didn't say anything, I gave in.

"Is that it?"

"*Is that it*?" Dies-well mocked me. "The Madame herself gives you advice, and you want to know, 'Is that it?'"

"So that *is* it."

"Use the blagard brain rotting under all that hair gel," he said.

"So I'm asking for this?" I throttled the urge to throw my phone.

"By being a mopey fopdoodle, yes."

"Thanks, Dies-well, you've been beyond helpful." I hung up the phone before he could say anything else that would inspire practicing for shotput.

I turned on my heel, rage coursing through me.

"You think I *want* this?" I yelled, my voice startling a flock of birds out of the trees. They cawed their disgust as they fled. "You think I wanted to come back here after everything? You think I wouldn't rather be back in my penthouse drinking champagne with a hot red head?"

I kicked the grass, swinging my arms, fully aware I looked like a lunatic toddler.

"Do you hear me? I have a penthouse in New York full of art and leather furniture and 800 thread count sheets. And I can fill it with women whenever I want! *WHENEVER I WANT!*"

A strange rumbling growl rattled from beneath my feet. The earth trembled, as if a tiny earthquake were erupting, sending dirt and grass flying into the air and plugging my mouth until I gagged. It pushed up my nostrils, pressed against my ears. I tried to throw up my arms to protect myself but I couldn't move. I was held in place by the same dirt I'd been so lovingly embraced by only moments before.

Fine, I thought. *Have it your way.*

And I let go.

Chapter Fifteen

Leslee

I'd never been to the Huxley Manor. I'd never had any cause to over the years, though curiosity had certainly tugged at me. Something about the crumbling entrance and watchful windows of the sagging building were enough to warn me off.

The memory of a village tends to be longer than most and every time I'd asked about the manor as a little girl, people would scowl and shake their head.

"Best to leave well enough alone," they'd say.

Of course, that didn't stop us kids from telling ghost stories about the place—unjustly murdered ghosts seeking vengeance, restless souls buried alive on the property, a fanged monster hunting in the night.

It was the last one I tried to shake off as I stared through the former gates of the manor. The barest hint of the morning sun crawled across the ground, and a soft frost twinkled in the early light. But the magic of the dawn seemed to stop as it reached the now defunct gates. Beyond, I could see no frost, no sun, no refracted promise glittering in the air. It was thickly twined branches so far back it looked like a void and not a pathway.

And worse, it was dead silent. Not a single bug stirred, not a bird chirped, not a squirrel chittered. Where were all the goings on of a busy, crisp fall morning?

I took a deep breath and stepped through the gates. A shiver ran through me, but it was more my nerves than any portal magic at work. I forced myself to close my eyes and clasped the selenite pendant I wore for the occasion. I took another deep breath and let loose a low hum, focusing on the presence of the selenite in my hand.

A wave washed over me and I could feel the magical topography of the place. It was certainly still of this plane and of this realm—I had not crossed any portals, like I'd guessed. But that's where the magic stopped making sense. Everything in front of me should've been green. It should've been thick, twisting green lines and verdant waves pulsing to show the ancient lives of the Oaks and underbrush. But instead, only the barest green veins flickered weakly in the dark.

I opened my eyes, hands shaking as I pulled off the smoky quartz ring I always wore on my left hand. It'd been a gift from my mother, and the swirling silver setting always reminded me of her lopsided smile. Palming the ring, I pressed my hand flat against the trunk of the nearest oak so that the quartz was between the bark and my skin.

"Awake, ancestor," I whispered, head bowed in reverence. "Your progeny requests your wisdom."

Nothing.

More silence stretched out to reach me, but I waited, body stilled, head bowed, barely breathing.

After a few moments, all I could think was *Please, please, please, something is wrong and no one else can see it. Please don't leave me alone in this.*

A low rumbling groan came from the depths of the trunk. I risked a glance and saw a shiver run through the Oak from roots to leaves. I felt it stretch, straining against the intertwined branches from its siblings, pushing its roots further beneath us as if it had only just been granted the clearance to do so.

Speak, little one. I felt it greet me more than heard it, the whispering leaves above me almost enough to be a voice but not quite. I turned into the trunk, pressing my other palm flat against its bark, feeling the rough texture bite into my palms.

"Thank you, ancestor," I said, voice low and reverent. Despite the solemness of the occasion, a thrill ran through me. I was doing it. I was really talking to a 200-year-old Oak on a mysterious abandoned property, and it was *talking back*. Sure, my cacti sang to me and my veggie garden gave me encouragement, but *this* was something else. "And welcome to the 21st century. I hope your rest was fruitful."

Not a true rest.

Huh. Weird.

I swallowed and began again. "Someone wants to restore this property," I said. "They wish to bring life back to the grounds, visitors back through the gates—"

A second, louder groaning rose from the ground, shaking beneath my feet. A loud crack came from the branches above me, as if one of them had snapped in half and could come hurtling down at any moment.

No one must enter.

"Why not?"

Evil grew here.

My stomach flipped and my scalp prickled with a chill. I thought of the creature in the woods, Alex's strange behavior, and the nagging thought that crimson eyes were something I should look closer at though I couldn't be sure why.

"What evil? What do you mean?"

We did not interfere. We pay our penance. We sleep until the earth is restored.

I could feel my connection to the ancestor weakening. Their voice in my head growing faint.

"Please, don't go yet. What if evil is back? What if it never left?"

The earth knows what it wants.

"That doesn't answer any of my questions. Ancestor, please." Frustration edged my voice, threatening to wash over any respect I was pushing into my words.

Evil is buried here, but it does not rest. Be careful, little one. And with that, the languid stretch I felt beneath me shrank. The hum of the bark grew silent as everything stilled once more.

I stepped back, shaken by my interaction. Sure, it was my first time speaking with an ancestor, but I hadn't expected it to be so cryptic and foreboding. I'd hoped for, "good to see you great-great-great-niece, here's exactly how to solve your problem, cheerio then!"

Which, in hindsight, was probably stupid.

"Good thing there's eleven more of you here," I said, closing the gap between me and the next oak tree to the right. I pressed the ring to the bark, repeating my plea from earlier. But this time, the silence simply stretched. "Alright, hide then."

I went to the next oak down the line and repeated the process, dropping the ring into the decomposing leaves and dirt when a booming voice screamed in my head *GET OUT*.

I scrambled to find the ring, pushing it back onto my trembling hand before sprinting toward the entrance. Safely on the other side of the gate, the sun flashed across me as if I'd flung open church doors and not simply walked from one side of a fence to the other. I pressed a hand to my fluttering heart and tried to get a grip on my panic.

I still needed to survey the grounds so I could start my sketches. Mr. Barlow had asked to meet again that night and I didn't have a single thing ready. What was I going to do, show up and apologize that the trees said his property was evil and I was going to have to excuse myself?

A fresh rustling on the other side of the fence let fear grip my heart anew. I waited, holding my breath, the ancestor's warnings flashing through my mind. As the sound grew closer, I could hear uneven footsteps and a soft groan every few paces. Whatever it was, it was hurting.

Well, I wasn't going to let ancient evil just strut back into town after so many centuries buried.

I squared my shoulders and braced myself in the entry, careful not to cross the fence line. I was suddenly very aware of my lack of weaponry. It was a damned good thing I spent all my time throwing bags of fertilizer and wrestling with shrubbery. I was not a petite woman, to say the least.

As a shadowy figure emerged from the dark of the trees, I didn't wait to confirm. I was all action, no thought. I swung, my fist connecting with a loud crack. Pain ricocheted in my wrist and up my arm, causing me to cry out in unison with the potential evildoer.

I stepped back to shake out my arm and get a good look at my target in the sun.

"Shit, Mr. Barlow!" I'd just punched my employer.

I sprinted forward, holding my hands out in apology, but he flinched back.

"Oh, you look awful." His eyes were bloodshot, his lips chapped and grey. His face was paler than usual, and his normally coifed hair stuck out at all angles. He looked like he'd been wandering the woods drunk all night.

Stranger still, every inch of him was coated in mud.

The earth knows what it wants. I shook off the thought and pulled out my hankie, offering it to Mr. Barlow.

He took it, staring at me as if I were the one who had appeared out of thin air next to a clearly haunted manor and not the other way around. Steam wafted off his shoulders, and I wondered how wet he must be for that reaction.

"Careful, or people might think you're an evil capitalist *and* a vampire." Given the tense circumstances, I don't know where I pulled that joke from or why I thought *now* was the time to crack one, but it was enough to finally get a response from the very dirty, haggard, shocked Mr. Barlow.

"*Why* would you say such a thing?" His voice was rough, as if he'd been screaming for some time. The sound made me touch my own throat in sympathy.

"Cause it looks like you're smoking." I pointed to his shoulder. To my surprise, he glanced over and his eyes widened in alarm. He immediately stepped back into the shadows of the manor grounds and I'm not sure I imagined the steam immediately dissipating.

"Miss Hawthorne," he said.

"Please, call me Leslee, now I've socked you in the jaw."

"Leslee, then," he said through clenched teeth. "Could I trouble you for your cellphone? I seem to have lost mine and will need to contact the hotel for a ride up the hill. I'm afraid I'm not capable of the walk in my current state."

"Oh please, allow me. It'll take no more than a minute to go get my car. It's the least I can do."

He nodded, swaying lightly on his feet. It was all the go-ahead I needed. I took off down the main road, mortification nipping at my heels.

It wasn't until I was slipping into the front seat of my car that a thought slammed into me at full speed—could it be mere coincidence that the ancestor warned me of evil buried on the manor grounds and moments later Billy appeared coated in mud?

It had to be, right?

Right?

Chapter Sixteen

BILLY

Someone shod that horse incorrectly.

The thought woke me from a literal dead sleep. I must've been dreaming of The Colonel again, because the sound of uneven horse hooves on pavement was echoing through my room. I sat up, running a hand over my face.

The sound came again and this time I knew I wasn't imagining it. I glanced at the clock to see it was yet again barely 4 p.m., which meant I probably shouldn't peel back the curtains to see the source of the noise.

Whatever creature was clip-clopping past the hotel, I would need to locate its owner and pummel them. Was the shoe on sideways? I couldn't imagine the kind of mistreatment a horse would receive that no one would even notice its steps were painfully wrong.

The phone rang on the nightstand.

"*GODDAMNIT WILLIAM.*" The horse's owner wasn't going to be the only person I pummeled if this fucking child didn't stop calling me for breakfast at absurd hours.

"*What,*" I snarled into the phone.

"Good evening sir," Freddie's voice came through the line crisp, clean, confident. "A Miss Rye Amato is here. She'd like to meet with you as soon as possible."

"Send her up." I hung up and groaned. I still hadn't showered from last night, and my sheets were covered in the mud I shook off in my sleep. My filthy clothes were strewn about the room, and all the curtains were drawn. It would look to Rye like I'd had a drug-fueled dig in the dirt and hadn't yet recovered.

Worse, only my clothes were on the floor, so there was no explaining away my actions with lechery.

A prompt knock at the door meant I needed to come up with a good excuse in the ten steps it would take me to answer it. My brain felt like it'd been ground up, tenderized, and left to rot in the sun.

"I guess it nearly was," I muttered, shoving out of bed and padding lightly to the door barefoot. If Leslee hadn't made that dumb joke about me smoking, she would've watched me burst into flames. It'd been close—*too close*. I was getting in over my head the longer I stayed in this cursed village.

By the time I twisted the knob, I resolved to pay whatever ridiculous fee the crews needed. I *would* be back on my jet with Charles, headed to New York and away from this place forever before the week was up.

"You look like shit," Rye said as she stepped past me into the room, leaving Bradford waiting in the hall expectantly. I closed the door in his face.

"What kind of shrooms are you doing?" Rye asked, glancing around the room, one eyebrow quirked. Cigarette smoke and the smell of nail polish wafted off her as she took off her coat and threw it on one of the chairs.

"What makes you think it's shrooms?" I asked.

"My cousin did them last summer, and she was convinced she was a squash that needed replanting. She also tried to bury herself fully clothed." Rye pointed at my discarded clothing from the night before. "Her apartment looked like this but worse."

Another quick knock at the door kicked off the start of a migraine that I was now learning to expect after a few precious moments of clear-headedness when I awoke.

"Apologies," I said. "The staff is—"

Rye had already pulled the door open and gestured comfortably to the sitting area. William pushed in the service cart topped with what looked like a toasted sandwich and a coffee service.

"Thanks, Will," Rye said, slipping him a small note and waving him out the door. "I hope you don't mind," she continued, pouring herself a cup and taking a grateful sip. "Jetlag's a bitch, and it looks like we both need a minute before digging into this case. You go freshen up; I'll get square with my stomach and my caffeine addiction."

"Have I told you I love you?"

She poured another cup and handed it to me.

"Yeah, yeah, you and every other rich guy in New York. Go shower, you smell like my Nona's vegetable beds."

***

I emerged from the shower to find loungewear hung on the back of the door for me. Once dressed, I stepped into a freshly cleaned hotel room, complete with turndown service and new candles lit on every surface. Soft jazz floated around the room from hidden speakers.

"Are you trying to seduce me, Miss Amato?"

Rye snorted into her coffee. "I called down and asked for them to tidy up when they had a moment, and all six of the little guys came up here and went to town. Took them like five minutes, *and* they set up what they called 'ambiance.'" She gave me a mock look over her mug before setting it down. "They think we're lovers."

"I've always said it's a shame we aren't."

"You wouldn't last ten minutes." She rolled her eyes before gesturing to the small coffee table in the sitting area, now completely covered in neat stacks of paper.

"Hope you're ready for a long night," she said.

"It'll go far too quickly in your company."

A faint smile flickered but didn't stay. I sat across from Rye and tried to focus while she fired off case law after case law, talking in her usual quick-draw pace. The migraine from earlier had not been soothed by my long hot shower, the coffee, or the comfortable clothing. In fact, the longer I tried to listen to Rye, the worse it got. After only a few minutes, I was squinting at the paperwork, willing the lines to stop wiggling long enough for me to read them.

"You good?" Rye finally asked after what felt like hours but must've been maybe twenty minutes.

I shook my head. "I'm having the worst time trying to think in this place," I said. "And I'm not sleeping well."

Rye nodded her head knowingly.

"Too quiet," she said. "Us city girls are too delicate for the big, bad silence out here."

"There's a pub in town..." I let my suggestion linger hoping Rye wouldn't ask for any further explanation—hoping Leslee would be there and my bet would pay off.

"You don't have to tell me twice," Rye said, standing and slipping into her coat. She finished packing up while I quickly changed into the only pair of jeans I owned, and a button-up. After Rye retired for the night, I was going to see who was in charge of the lame horse I'd heard earlier, and didn't want to dirty up my nice clothes any more than I already had.

Once at the pub, I felt the signature quirk of Leslee's particular magic as my headache eased, my shoulders dropped, and a pristine clarity whisked away any mental fog. Rye and I settled at the same table I'd chosen the night before, and this time, I was able to nod along as she explained our options.

"There's two ways about it," she said. Her blouse sleeves were rolled up in the warmth of the pub, and she tucked her cropped hair behind her ears. A tall, frothy pint sat at her elbow, condensation fogging the glass. "First, bulldoze everything and sell the land."

"Not an option, next."

Rye fixed me with a level stare.

"That's alright. I tell my nephew when he has big emotions that it's okay for men to be upset same as anyone else," she said, taking a meaningful sip of her beer and smacking her lips. "He's four."

"I want the highest return for all this fuckery," I said. I thought about Leslee's offense at my plans, at her horror at the pressure a new tourist destination would put on the village. "And the manor has been in my family for generations." The words slipped through before I could stop myself. "It's not as simple as razing it to the ground for the acreage." Not with Leslee. Nothing felt simple now, whatever her hold on me meant.

Rye held her hands up as if waving the thought off.

"I forget, you British types get all caught up in land rights and legacies," she said. "Who will pull the sword for your first son, yadda yadda."

I laughed, relieved at the joy that bloomed through me. "I always forget about that lesser known ending to King Arthur."

"Whatever," she said, sipping her beer again. "If you don't want to go that route, consider it kaput. Which means, you only have one option."

"Fix everything."

"Not just fix everything," she said, ticking the options off on her stiletto nails. "Restore structural integrity, ensure continued inspections and maintenance, *and* follow historical remodeling regulations."

"What's that last one?"

"The manor's a historic landmark so—"

"It's a *what*."

Rye arched an eyebrow at me.

"Sorry, I'm four today."

"Clearly." I let her sip her beer and stretch in her seat, waited as she glanced around the room before settling back on the table, arms crossed beneath her so that her weight rested on her elbows.

"As I was saying," she finally continued. "Because the manor is a historic landmark, you have to stay within certain restrictions during the construction process. Everything has to be restored or maintained as close to the original as possible."

"Who the fuck made that place a historic landmark?"

She thumbed through the papers for barely a second before sliding one across to me.

"Alexander Huxley," she said. "Must be a cousin of yours or something. Says his family has been in the village for 200 years and they have ties to the manor."

My stomach flipped and all noise in the room dulled to a hum. It was suddenly just me and that name on the page. It wasn't possible. After all these years...

"Alexander Huxley," I muttered, unclenching my jaw when I saw "the fourth" added in the appropriate field of the form.

"You recognize it?"

I shook my head. "Not immediately, no." Another lie. I didn't make it a habit to keep things from my lawyer—especially not one as sharp and full-service as Rye—but there were some things she was better off not knowing. My vampirism, the fact that I nearly mistook the name on the page for the manor owner I'd worked for two centuries ago, and how I took my eggs in the morning were just a few examples.

"Can we fight it?"

"The landmark status? We could, but it won't win you any goodwill with the town and you're going to want that to keep your ownership claim. No one likes the weirdo, rich, out-of-towner destroying treasured history."

"Believe me, it's not treasured."

Rye gave me another look, took another sip of her beer. "Your ancestor pull the sword out wrong?"

"It's more what they did with the sword once they had it." Alexander Huxley the First had not been a man renowned for his kindness. It figured the only villager left defending his honor was a direct descendent.

"You wouldn't be the first rich guy to come from a long line of dick bags," Rye said, polishing off her beer and looking at me through the bottom of the empty pint. "But it's on you to decide what to do with that kind of guilt. I'm just here to file your paperwork and argue the way you want."

"I value your input," I said. "I wouldn't work with you if I didn't."

"Okay, then sell it."

"Alright, I usually value your input, but today I have to decline."

Rye rolled her eyes. "I'm calling Huxley to request a hearing with the village council," she said.

"Why?"

"Cause you have to request it from the head councilman," she said, slipping into her coat. "Get some rest tonight. You're annoying when you're sleep deprived." She waved goodbye and disappeared out the door, allowing me a glance around the room.

A pleasant thrill slid down my spine when I locked eyes with Leslee. She gave me a half-smile and raised her pint in my direction. I took my own half-empty drink and crossed the room to her, not missing the appraising way her eyes ran over me. I tried not to shiver.

"You look...casual," she said. Her cheeks were flushed and her eyes reflected back the firelight from the hearth.

"I was going to tour the new stables this evening," I said.

She frowned, glancing down at her phone sitting face up on the table. I couldn't help but notice the screensaver was of a gorgeous English garden, and it was devoid of any notifications. No missed calls, no texts, not even a social media alert.

"At 8 p.m.?" she asked.

I shrugged. "Won't be any crowds." I nodded to her phone. "Is that your garden?"

"Oh yes, it is." She leaned forward, a fresh energy in her face I hadn't seen before. This was not a frustrated landscaper or a wary villager. This was a woman who really loved something and had just been given an opportunity to talk about it. I found myself returning her lean so that we were only a few inches apart as she spoke, describing to me her plans for the winter vegetables and the summer trellis and the spring floral boxes that were just beginning to doze off now in the cold weather.

Her curls glowed in the tavern light like a halo around her freckled face. Her hazel eyes were wide and animated, refracted further by the round-framed glasses she had yet to push up. I could see her pulse quick in her throat, pounding in her heart, pushing through every quivering piece of her. She was alive, radiant, enrapturing.

"You're beautiful," I said before I could stop myself.

She leaned back, face slack in surprise.

"What?"

"It's beautiful," I said louder, clearing my throat and taking a too-large gulp of beer. "Your garden. It's beautiful."

We both stared at each other a moment, and I watched several rapid-fire emotions play across her face before the guard returned. *There* was the Leslee I'd met in the suite—skeptical, appraising, unsure. I tried not to chew through my tongue in frustration at the glorious being that had just been shuttered away from me.

"Why do you keep coming here?" she asked. "They have beer at the hotel. And it's probably better than what James is pouring."

"I don't think well up there," I said. "It's too quiet." I was glad for the ready lie, although some small piece of me rioted at giving it to her.

"I've heard you city gents can be weird." Leslee leaned the rest of the way back in her seat, crossing her arms and dangling her half-finished beer from one hand. She crossed her legs and rolled one delicate ankle in the air as she did so. It was decorated in various silver tinkling decorations, and my mind flashed briefly with the image of them in the air over my shoulder. "Is that it?"

"Hmmm, what?"

"It's too quiet, so you come here," she repeated, giving me a curious look. "That's it?"

"And...I have a question for you," I said, floundering, not ready to give up the peace and clarity this woman somehow granted me. What could I possibly ask her that warranted coming in person and not calling her like a normal client would do?

"And?" she prompted after I was silent for a suspicious amount of time. I was clenching my jaw so hard I could feel my fangs grating along my lower gums. I was going to speak with a mouthful of blood in a moment.

"Will you go with me in the morning?" I blurted. "To the manor. I'm meeting the crew while they setup the work site."

"Worried you'll catch on fire again?"

"Oh no, we're going before the sun is up."

We both stared at each other a moment—me in slack-faced horror, hoping it passed for deadpan humor, her in startled confusion.

"You're not serious."

"I told you, Miss Hawthorne," I said. "The hours for this job are demanding. The crews will meet with me daily at 4 a.m. and continue until I sign off on their progress at 6 p.m."

She squinted at me like she could tell I was lying. I could only rely on the truth being dismissed as too strange.

"Why do you need me there?"

"To ensure we don't destroy anything you have plans for." *That* was smooth because it was mostly true.

She rolled her eyes so hard I was worried they'd land on the table. At this rate, I was going to have to learn to tumble in place to keep a conversation going with either Rye or Leslee.

"Fine," she said, polishing off her beer and setting it down. "But I won't be staying for your 'sign off' until past supper, that's insane."

"You have a longer contract duration than the work crews," I said. "You're welcome to keep whatever hours please you. But attend this first meeting with me."

"I'll see you in the morning," she said by way of goodbye and stormed past me.

That was the second woman to dismiss me after chugging her beer and leaving. I realized all too quickly that the rest of the pub customers were staring and whispering to each other.

"Well, that's my cue," I said, finishing my own beer and following the ladies' lead.

I had to see a vamp about a horse.

Chapter Seventeen

Leslee

The next morning, I was up before the sun—an unnatural rising for my family. We flourished under the sun and recharged by the moon. But those strange hours in-between—dusk and dawn and twilight—were best left to other more dangerous creatures.

But, my strange, handsome client had insisted I attend this 4 a.m. hoorah nonsense, and so, wrapped up in my good winter coat, boots pulled up my calves, gloved hands shoved in my pockets, I headed up the main road to the manor.

I supposed I could've driven, but I'd be lying if I said that was my preferred way of getting around. I preferred my own two feet on the ground, one step and then the other, surefooted in the dirt more than I could ever be behind a wheel. Besides, the crisp air gave me a chance to wake up before dealing with Mr. Barlow.

I paused to flip open the lid on the piping tea thermos I was carrying, taking a spluttering sip before continuing. Okay, so the crisp air *and* the caffeine. But something told me I'd need more than a few tea bags to get through this meeting.

I knew nothing about the contractors he'd hired for the work. Henry apparently hadn't been available, and all he knew was that he'd directed Mr. Barlow in the direction of someone else. I doubted it was that simple, which made the identity of the crew lead a mystery.

I didn't love that outcome, but hopefully we'd stay out of each other's way with minimal need for contact.

I still hadn't figured out how I was going to tame anything on the manor grounds much less replant, repot, and restructure several gardens on my own. Yes, I was a hedge witch with tree ancestors, but even that wasn't enough to make this task less daunting.

I took another sip of tea and readjusted my grip on my sketchpad. Inside were the plans I'd been putting off making for the manor's acreage. I'd finally had the mind to sit down after my second pub meeting with Mr. Barlow and put some thoughts down. They weren't luxurious or grand or award-winning, but they were executable on the timeline requested while maintaining the original roots of the current manor grounds. There would be all native plants, hedges in shapes that were easy to maintain while still attractive to the targeted tourist crowd, and I'd taken the liberty of planning a few scenic areas with stone benches and sculpture. More than that, the manor grounds would finally have the chance to shine through their mysterious reputation as clean, bright, and inviting without any pomp or circumstance.

Tyler would've said my plan was boring. I gave the Tyler in my head a mental vulgar gesture.

The manor grounds appeared on the horizon, tree limbs threatening in the dark as I approached the crumbling front gate. Too late, I realized Mr. Barlow hadn't told me where to meet him and the other crews. I could dawdle by the entrance and potentially miss the meeting, making it seem like I'd skipped on purpose, or I could strike out on my own, hopefully catching other signs of life nearby before panic set in.

I hesitated by the entrance, shifting my weight from foot to foot. I remembered all too clearly my conversation with the ancestors yesterday and the great booming voice that had commanded I leave. How had I been talked into returning so soon?

I sighed, blowing a curl out of my face. Tyler wouldn't be afraid to take this meeting. He would've mocked me for being so nervous and worrying so much about what the trees thought.

"Well, fuck that," I said, flinching at how loud my voice seemed in the silent dark. I crossed the entrance and made my way down the main path beneath the intertwined oaks.

"Forgive me, ancestors," I whispered to their shivering leaves. "I have to make my mortgage."

For the first time in my life, the trees gave no indication they could hear me. I hurried, picking up the pace and practically sprinting until I was nearly clear of the tunnel beneath the oaks.

And then I saw it—that same ghostly flash of white flesh, the gaunt eyes, and the hunched, ghastly form. But this time, it saw me too.

It froze, slowly turning pupilless red eyes to me as though unsure if I were predator or prey. I stopped dead, a startled gasp slipping past my lips. It cocked its head as if it heard me, but didn't move further. I could see the black pit of its mouth framed by four dangerous looking fangs, two each on top and bottom. It's wicked fingers curved into talons at the end, and I don't think I was imagining blood dripping from a few.

"What are you?" I breathed.

It answered with a blood-chilling scream as it lunged forward. It was nearly on top of me when a loud crack of wood rattled the air and there was the sound of impact on flapping flesh. A splash of starlight fell on my face, and a fluttering of leaves settled around my frozen form. It had happened so fast I wasn't sure it had happened at all.

I looked around, shaking where I stood, but did not see the creature. The branches above me resettled with a tired groan, the only sign that anything had changed from the moment I stepped into the dark grove.

"Thank you, ancestors," I said, nodding to the now-still branches as I hurried out of the trees' coverage.

I had no idea where the monster had gone, but I didn't want to wait to find out if it had the strength to return.

By some obscene luck, I saw the brilliant orange of hard hats and backhoes once I had a clear line of sight on the manor. I sprinted toward them, sure I was being watched as much as I was sure I was late.

As I grew closer to the murmuring group of men near the rumbling machinery, I could better see Mr. Barlow with a few others I didn't immediately recognize. A woman with a severe profile and a short, sharp haircut stood beside Mr. Barlow, a lit cigarette drifting smoke into the crisp air. I recognized the woman from the pub the night before.

"Morning, Miss Hawthorne," Mr. Barlow called without looking up from the construction plans spread out on a card table before him.

"Morning." Breath puffed out in front of my face like a steaming locomotive. I was sure I looked a hot mess, sweating under my layers, wide-eyed. As I took my place at the table, the woman with the cigarette reached across and pulled a massive oak leaf from my hair.

I nodded my thanks, mortified.

"Alright, now we have everyone," Mr. Barlow continued. "Thank you all for joining me so early. We have a lot to do and little time to do it. I've hired you all because you're willing to put in the time and effort to make this place not only safe for the community but somewhat enjoyable. I expect you to all work respectfully with one another—I don't have the time or energy to dispute whose ego is bigger. Anyone caught making life difficult for other teams will be replaced without hesitation."

An uncomfortable ripple went through the group. I held still. I knew I wasn't replaceable. I also knew I wouldn't be butting heads with anyone save Mr. Barlow himself.

Not that that would be so bad.

He rattled off instructions in a terse, rapid tone that made him look and sound the business magnate he must be to command the funds required for this project. I had only seen him haggard, desperate, and a little drunk so far. Something about the respect he commanded had me crossing my legs where I stood.

Finally, he fixed those startling crimson eyes on me.

"And this is Miss Hawthorne," he said. "I'm sure many of you know her and have employed her already. Anything she says for the grounds and its plant life, goes. Her authority is to be undisputed or you'll have me to answer to."

He nodded to me and I swear I hadn't seen him blink in actual minutes. It would've been unsettling if what he had just said hadn't been so *hot*.

No one had *ever* given me such authority. Most people thought I was too air-headed to complete a task on my own, and Tyler certainly thought I was too foolish to run anything.

"Which makes for a nice transition. Miss Hawthorne, would you like to give us the high-level of your plans for the acreage?"

I nearly froze, but Mr. Barlow gave me the subtlest of nods and I leapt into action. Business Leslee was strapped in and ready to take charge.

I laid out my sketches and explained to the crew the general aesthetic and goal of my plans. I listed key delivery dates, requested to borrow a few extra set of hands for statue installation, and made sure that any confused faces were addressed. By the time I was done, the sun was nearly up.

"What about those damned trees?" A squat man with a greasy neck lit a cigarette then spit loudly on the ground before taking a drag.

"I assume you mean the archway oaks." I breathed slowly through my nose, trying not to hiss at the stranger.

"Yes'm," he continued. "They're diseased and dangerous. They'll need to be cut down."

"They will be pruned and treated," I said, swallowing the seething anger pushing up from my gut. "They are more than 200 years old and have watched the village through the years. They are as much a part of this place as we are."

The man spit a second time. "We'll remember ya said that when the council wants ter know why someone've ended up under their split branches."

"Someone clearly wasn't listening at the outset," Mr. Barlow interjected. "Miss Hawthorne says the oaks stay, they stay. You'll be the only thing leaving if you disagree with her assessment."

The man didn't even flinch, just turned on his heel, flicking his cigarette into the wet grass as he walked away.

Part of me was humiliated. The other part was on fire.

"Any other respectful questions for Miss Hawthorne?" Mr. Barlow asked, scanning the crew. A few removed their hats as his gaze fell on them, turning to me and nodding as if I were an old-fashioned lady passing in the street. My cheeks flushed as the heat between my legs grew.

"Right then, let's get to work." He dismissed everyone with a clap of his hands. As the machinery around him screamed to life and men began calling to each other, I cleared the gap between us.

"That wasn't necessary," I snapped, unsure what to do with all the heat pulsing through my body. Yelling seemed as good a course as any. "I can handle myself."

"I don't doubt that, Miss Hawthorne," he said.

"I told you to call me fucking Leslee."

"Rye could you give us a moment?"

The woman held her hands up in peace and sauntered away, blowing a lazy puff into the air. I didn't miss the way his gaze lingered on her as she left—which just infuriated me further.

"You think you own everyone's attention?" I seethed. "You think you can just come in here with all your money, and your nice hair, and your handsome face and get everyone to do exactly what you want?"

"My what face?"

"I'm a professional and I don't need to be rescued like some cock-eyed damsel, are we clear?" At some point, I had moved so close to him to make my point that we were barely a breath apart. My chest was heaving, my head was spinning, and all I could smell was his incredibly expensive cologne.

"Crystal," he whispered, the heat of his breath ghosting on my lips. It only took one split-second glance at his mouth, and he was on me, sliding his fingers up into my hair and pressing firmly against my lips with such a force I let out a gasp of surprise. He took the opening, delicately sliding his tongue along mine before pulling away and nipping lightly at my bottom lip. Every nerve in my body sparked to life, and yet, something about the kiss felt strange—like our teeth were bumping but not quite so harsh. I couldn't put my finger on it. When he pulled away, delicately untangling himself from my hair I was so flabbergasted I initially didn't know what to do.

My knees were jelly, my stomach was fluttering, and my heart was pounding so loud it was all I could hear.

Then, it all came crashing through the lusty veil—the machines, the men shouting, the raucous crash of dirt being lifted and then falling.

My client had just kissed me in front of all my new project partners. Gods only knew what they'd assume that meant about the new unquestioned authority I'd been granted only moments ago.

"You fucking *asshole*," I hissed, letting my arm do what it wanted as I swung hard, punching Mr. Barlow for the second time is as many days.

Before I could devolve into a proper pummeling, I turned on my heel and stormed away. I heard him calling after me, heard his voice growing closer as he gave chase.

Owning up to this strange moment meant owning up to my frustration and attraction and humiliation all at once and honestly? It was too early for that. I picked up my skirt and ran.

Chapter Eighteen

BILLY

I watched Leslee sprint across the manor grounds, disappearing through the tunnel of trees. I had to catch her, had to apologize, or kiss her again—or explain myself.

But I couldn't run. Not right now. I was still sore from losing control of my speed and slamming into the pub corkboard. If I ran right now, nerves singing, chest clenching, I'd be on top of her in seconds.

I didn't know what I'd say.

I was usually so in control.

But this...

What was it about her? She was a swirling mess of fabric wrapped around pithy optimism and a green thumb. But when she'd come at me, enraged, everything about her sharpened. It was like I was seeing her in an entirely different light—wild, dangerous, dominant.

I lost it. I had to have her.

Once I was sure I wasn't trembling, I took off after Leslee. I could sense her ahead of me, her scent like fresh cut grass in the air.

This was different.

Two hundred years full of moments, and I'd never been caught up in one as I had with Leslee. No other moment had captured me, enchanted me, pulled me under in a sweep of hazel eyes and full lips.

Whatever was kindling between the two of us was something I'd never experienced before, something unknowable and strange. I couldn't let it be ruined by rogue urges.

I would have to explain myself. There was no other way forward. I would have to tell Leslee about the headaches, how she made them disappear, and hope she didn't think it was a backhanded romantic overture.

I would have to sort the rest out for myself later. At best, she'd forgive me and we'd continue working together while I sat on my hands and my feelings. At worst, I'd never see her again. In my wildest dreams, I'd get the chance to court her properly—not like the tongue-heavy demon I'd transformed into on the manor grounds. Maybe I'd take her for those dancing lessons we'd laughed at.

Either way, I had to try.

A warning rose on the back of my neck, but I pushed past it as I neared her cottage. Whatever else was giving chase, I would handle after.

I stopped at her garden gate just as she was half in the doorway.

"Leslee wait!"

Her eyes widened in shock and her jaw dropped. A light sheen glinted from her forehead, and her chest heaved from the run. Maybe I should've at least faked being out of breath.

"How the—*never mind!*" She slammed the door shut.

It wasn't until I was pounding on the door that I realized what the warning had been.

Sunlight streaked across the all-encompassing green of her garden, sending a glittering blaze over the early frost.

"*Shit shit shit shit*," I chanted, panic building in my core.

"*You cannot come in!*" she yelled through the door.

Damn it. Even if I accidentally broke the door down, I couldn't go in anyway.

"Leslee, please, let me come in and I'll explain!"

"Nice try, no!"

"I'm sorry! But you have to let me in. I won't touch you, just please, I can't be out here."

"THAT's the tactic you're taking? Are you serious?"

I could feel the sliver of shadow I was standing in beginning to warm. In just a moment, the sun would come round the corner of the bushes, and I would burst into flames.

Maybe I could take it. At least then I'd be free of the creeping dirt and the nightmares and the goddamn village council.

I let my shoulders slump. I knocked one last time.

"*FUCK. OFF.*"

"Okay," I said through the door. "But please know how sorry I am."

I leaned my forehead against the door, gritting my teeth and trying not to feel too sorry for myself as I realized there wouldn't really be anyone to tell about my blaze of glory. No one would mourn my final passing except maybe the people whose checks I signed.

I closed my eyes as heat bloomed across my shoulders and down my back. I knew there was a point in a flame where it burned so hot it was actually cool—the center of a destructive force so violent our bodies comprehended it purely as numbness.

I hoped for that numbness as the heat built.

I smelled smoke as the first flame caught, licking up my left side. And there, beneath the layers of resignation and cotton was pain. It was a screaming, relentless sensation, ripping across me in larger and larger waves until I couldn't contain the screams anymore.

I gripped the doorframe so hard I heard something snap, but I fought against the primal urge to save myself, to seek shelter or shade.

You deserve this, a voice in my head seethed. *You have done nothing but take and consume since your rebirth. A chance at an immortal life and you waste it in ski chateaus and luxury malls. You have nothing to show for your 200 years because you have built nothing in all that time. You're no better than the worst of the humans who put you in this damned position.*

This was the fate I'd chosen.

This was the hand I'd die by.

I let loose a final scream before a chilling darkness swept over me and I gave in to it.

Chapter Nineteen

INTERLUDE

Ashbourne, 1823

The Manor watched as the man sprinted out into the dark, the night air whipping across his face. He slammed into the shed where he'd last been cleaning his five-shot, sighing with relief at the sight of it, fully assembled and glinting in the moonlight. He checked that the Collier was loaded, stuffed extra cartridges into his pocket, and took off at a dead sprint for the stables.

A single light flickered in the dark signaling that the stable boy was still working. The Manor tensed as it watched, feeling the impatient stomp of horse hooves reverberate through the stables. Billy could tack a horse faster than any man alive. There was only one outcome for this night.

Inside the stables, oblivious to the night's dramas, Billy Barlow hummed to himself as he brushed The Colonel. The horse was massive—17 hands high with a barrel chest and a war horse temperament. But he loved Billy, and so he stood still while the young man brushed him, combed him, and picked burrs from his tail. He only flinched a little when Billy found the gash on his back right hoof.

"How did you do that, Colonel?" he asked, gently inspecting it further. "That looks nasty. We'll have to keep you here a few days while that heals up. Running around in the field will give you an infection, and we all know Hurls is looking for any excuse to chop you up into meat."

Everyone knew Billy was too talented, too handsome, too good with strong-willed or stubborn horses to stay at the country estate of a businessman. He should've been working at the races or for a reputable breeder. Hell, the housekeeper thought the King should hire him, god bless.

But Billy had the unfortunate luck of inheriting his family's debts and the man holding their contract—Mr. Huxley, also known with no affection as "Hurls"—was only interested in collecting the debt in the form of Billy's world-class horse care.

The Colonel whinnied in distress and stomped his feet, sending a spray of blood out of the wound and across Billy's face. The young man stood, wiping his face on his sleeve.

He was broad-shouldered and athletic, his body carved from riding, training, and caring for horses every hour of the day and night. His soft blonde hair hung around his shoulders and a few rogue freckles stood out across his nose. He had bright blue eyes and between that and his charming demeanor, Billy never wanted for company in the haystack each night.

But this night was different. None of the maids had been by to ask for his attention or to invite him to warm their beds. In fact, he hadn't so much as heard the bell ring for dinner as the sun slipped behind the fields and night crept over the manor.

Billy heard the tell-tale click of a rifle and stood slowly, from where he'd bent examining The Colonel's knee.

He came nose-to-nose with the end of a mean-looking gun, startled to find it in the cruel and capable hands of Hurls.

"Ready the horse," he barked as if giving orders to a small army and not a single horny stable hand. "Now."

Billy threw his hands in the air but didn't move.

"Do I look like I want to be *tested*?"

"Respectfully sir, you won't get far on The Colonel tonight," Billy said. "He's injured and needs rest or he'll be no use to you in a matter of days."

"He's of little use to me now," he snarled. "Ready him."

"Please, sir," Billy begged. "He's in pain. He needs rest and treatment not—"

"You care more for this horse than my imminent death!" Mr. Huxley screamed, cutting Billy off. He aimed the gun at the horse, and it threw its head in fear, whinnying at a high keen.

"*Sir, no! Don't!*"

Billy watched in horrified slow motion as the gun fired and connected with The Colonel's head. A spray of blood washed over the far stable wall and the horse collapsed, snorting slower and slower.

The Manor stilled, holding every creak and groan and whistle. In the silence that followed, the snap of Billy's heart sounded like a faint, desperate crack. The only thing keeping him going in the long, drudging slog to pay off the debts hanging over his head, that kept him from killing himself to escape those same debts, was the slain creature now at his feet.

He approached The Colonel's still twitching body, shaking from his very core, as fresh, hot rage rattled through him. He touched a trembling hand to The Colonel's paint-splotch forelock and closed his eyes. A final goodbye for a final friend.

Because Billy was going to kill Mr. Huxley and then probably himself.

But when Billy turned around, vengeance etched across his face, he saw a gruesome, fanged monster with its jaw unhinged like a snake hovering over Mr. Huxley's enraged, shaking form.

It descendedon him in the blink of an eye. A gunshot rang out as the monster clamped its mouth over the entirety of Mr. Huxley's neck. Too late, Billy realized, clutching his bleeding stomach, pain radiating through his body, that Mr. Huxley had kept his finger on the trigger. In his death throes, the gun went off.

Billy sank to his knees, confused, exhausted, delirious.

Was it good he was dying? Or now that Mr. Huxley had become a monster's supper, maybe it was a disappointment? The world wouldn't have let him walk out a free man. He was too low on the ladder for that.

He pulled himself across the stable floor, trying to block out the grotesque sounds of the monster slurping and sucking on Mr. Huxley's body. He stopped when he reached The Colonel, giving in to the weariness that soaked his body. He closed his eyes and released a rattling, wet cough.

He didn't know how long he floated there, someplace cold and faraway but not quite permanent. A sharp pain in his neck returned him to his physical body, and all of the hot, flashing pain assaulted him at once.

Billy jolted, reaching up to push away whatever was attacking him and finding a grown man wrapped around him instead.

He panicked, pushing with whatever strength was left in his body against the man, but he didn't budge. Finally, the man released him with a sickening slurping noise, pressing a firm hand against Billy's chest as he tried to rise.

"No, my friend, you must rest a moment. Do not get up just yet while I explain."

Billy looked up to see a sharply angled face framed by luxurious black curls. He had striking crimson eyes and seemed unnaturally tall if his lengthy torso was any indication.

"I have made a terrible mistake," the man said. "Mr. Huxley was supposed to be the only life taken tonight—a fair exchange given his evil presence in this world. But you, with a soft touch for animals and a kindness for wandering women, were not part of that deal."

Billy tried to look around but couldn't rise against the man's hand—even though the man seemed to exert no effort to keep him in place. His gaze finally landed on a pool of blood seeping out from under—

"Oh my god, Mr. Huxley," he gasped, voice rough with pain. "What happened? There was a monster and then—"

"I ate him," the man said simply.

"I can't imagine he tasted very good," Billy said, numb.

"He didn't," the man sighed. "I haven't had a *good* meal in maybe three hundred years. Avenging the innocent by consuming the wicked doesn't come with much of a flavor palate."

"Shouldn't that break your curse?"

"If only storybook rules applied," the man said, something wistful crossing his face. "But your time runs short. Here—" he reached down and bit a sizeable gash into his wrist, pressing against his forearm until blood cascaded out. "Drink this."

"*NO!*" Billy tried to move away, but the man pinned him a second time.

"You must, or you will die. This will grant you immortal life."

Billy had been ready to die mere seconds ago at the prospect of living a normal amount of time. He wasn't sure immortality was what he wanted.

"Think of the life you could have, young man—*any life* can be crafted when given enough time. And time will be all you have. You can be wealthy, educated, accomplished. You can invent, explore, create to your heart's content."

Billy looked at the bleeding wrist and arched an eyebrow.

"But I'll be like you," he said, understanding clicking into place.

"I'm afraid so," the man said. "It is the best I can offer to save your innocent life."

Billy looked over at The Colonel, who was now growing cold. He looked back to the pool of blood and the mangled corpse that had once been his employer.

"Why save me?"

"Because the world needs more good men in it," he said. "We can't afford to lose the few we have."

Billy considered this a moment but his thoughts didn't get far as lancing pain sang through his abdomen, pressing a groan from his mouth. He reached up instinctively and pulled the man's wrist down to his mouth, sucking lightly.

The blood wasn't as coppery as when Billy bit his own tongue or took a blow to the teeth. It tasted...older. It tasted how Billy imagined it would taste to leave a wound to scab for a few days and then lick it like a wild animal.

Before he could think further about it, a sudden frenzy took him. He sucked harder, gulping down the man's blood as if it were a fresh glass of water on the hottest day of the year, or a luxurious whiskey vintage in a crystal glass.

This was the only thing Billy would drink from now on, he decided, the only drink there could ever be after this. Nothing would ever compare. Nothing would erase the memory of it filling his stomach, his throat, his *soul.*

The man ripped his arm away, holding it out of Billy's floundering reach and wiping a dribble of blood from the edge of the already healing bite mark with the delicate edge of his finger.

"That's enough," he said. "Anymore and I won't recover for longer than I've already lost to this endeavor."

He stood, offering Billy a hand up. To his surprise, nothing hurt anymore. The pain in his stomach was gone, the wound on his neck no longer burned, and he felt a rush of fresh energy as though he'd just woken from a restful sleep.

Billy took the man's hand and stood.

"The first month will be overwhelming," he said. "And the first year after that will be even worse. You must do everything you can to control the feeding frenzy that will drive you to monstrous behavior. And you must *always* finish your kills."

"What do you mean finish?" Billy tried to take in everything the man was saying, his head spinning with the strange information, with the sudden onslaught of sound and smells around him. He could hear the Huxley baby cooing, but that wasn't possible—she would've been put to bed 50 meters away.

"I will not be here to guide you as your sire," the man said, ignoring Billy's question and pressing on hurriedly. "My mission is far too important to linger. But your final instruction is this: you must not stay in the village long enough for those around you to markedly age. People will grow suspicious when you do not age the same as them."

"You don't have to worry about that," Billy scoffed. "I'm leaving tonight."

The man nodded. "Then you must not return here until human memory has forgotten your face."

Billy nodded back. He wasn't sure if he should thank the man or be enraged at his interference with his final peace. He felt something in-between the two extremes but couldn't put his finger on what that would be called.

"I don't even know your name," he said.

"Gabriel Amdis," he said, extending a hand. Billy shook it.

"Billy Barlow."

"A pleasure, Billy," Gabriel said. "Best of luck."

And with that, the vampire strode out of the stable and out of Billy's life.

The Manor could've tracked the stranger's movements but loved Billy too much to try. He had died just then, and yet, here he was, standing in the middle of so much blood and carnage, a disgusted look crawling over his face as if he could smell the insides beginning to rot. The Manor couldn't look away.

Billy stumbled forward and paused before crossing the stable's threshold. He whipped around, staring in horror at the pile of flesh that had once been Mr. Huxley. He stood in disbelief, breathing heavily.

"Is that your heartbeat?" he asked. There was no answer. "It's not mine, as I can no longer feel it. But I can certainly *hear* yours. I should smash what's left of you and end it. That's what that bloke just told me to do."

He looked thoughtfully away from the carnage, eyes settling on the body of his beloved Colonel. Too late, the Manor realized what the tightening of his features meant, what the intention was behind those freshly reddening eyes. The Manor should shake the stables, shake itself, open a neighboring stall, knock something off the wall—*anything* to remind Billy of his humanity. Anything to knock him back to the side of good despite evil having already pulled him under.

The Manor should. But it couldn't. This wasn't that kind of story. This wasn't that kind of home.

"You should only receive the mercy you've dealt," Billy snarled, body shaking with rage. "And so I'll leave now, and hope you're too far gone to feel the last of the agony."

The Manor watched helplessly as the golden boy of the household strode out into the dark.

Chapter Twenty

Leslee

I threw open the door to Billy's screams. I was mad but not a monster. Whatever was torturing him couldn't be allowed to continue. He fell through my doorway, unconscious and wreathed in flames. I grabbed the horse blanket from the decorative hook on the wall and began slamming him mercilessly with it until he was only lightly smoking.

I pulled Billy further inside, dragging him along the floor and apologizing to his unconscious form when his nose caught on a knothole. I noticed a few rogue flames still licked his feet, and so I beat those, too.

That's when I realized that the part of Billy still on fire had been outside longer than the rest of him – it had been in the *sun.*

"You're a fucking *vampire*?" I dropped the blanket and slammed the door shut. Gods, this made so much more sense now. The weird eyes and the strange hours and the skulking around at 4 p.m.

Wait, his *eyes*.

"Oh, my gods, *ALEX IS A VAMPIRE TOO!*" I clutched the side of my head, tearing off my glasses as it all slammed home. "*YOU'RE ALL FUCKING VAMPIRES. OH, MY GODS!*"

I paced my kitchen, frantically talking to myself as if myself would talk back with any different offering than I could come up with.

"What am I gonna do? Do I even need to do something—fuck me, Leslee, of *course* you need to do something, they're all fucking vampires!"

But what was I supposed to do?

I glanced down at Billy's pitiful form, crumpled, charred, exhausted. I let loose a sigh, blowing a raspberry at the very end.

"Fine," I said. "I'll put him in my bed, universe, but I am *not* sleeping with him."

I dragged him along the floor into my room, giving a frustrated shriek when I saw how many godsforsaken windows I had open. Of course, I loved bright morning light first thing in the morning, but a vampire would not. And I didn't want my room to permanently smell like burnt flesh.

I slammed all the shutters and pulled the curtains, cursing under my breath as I did so. All that glorious dawn sun *wasted* because, naturally, I had to get pulled into the orbit of the undead.

Perfect first job without Tyler. He got the queen, and I got a monster.

It took several indelicate tries, but I finally managed to flop Billy's unconscious self into my bed and smothered him in blankets. That way, he'd be completely covered and safe even if the sun peeked through any cracks.

I didn't linger, forcing myself from the room and deciding that maybe it was finally time to call my mother.

I fluttered my fingers over the many items on the fridge door, pinned with touristy magnets and various clothespins with a little magic glued to the back. Finally, I found my mother's spindly handwriting on the torn corner of a napkin from the pub when she'd come to tell me she'd be taking a meditation sabbatical in the wilds. She was not to be disturbed unless it was absolutely an emergency:

"And snails don't count, dearheart," my mother had said over her pint, smiling her feral smile at me.

"I think seven fucking vampires count, Mum," I whispered, reading her instructions when it hit me. "Fucking fuck shit hell—*eight* vampires. Eight vampires, Mum." The ghoul in the woods—it had to be. There was no other explanation for the others being here, especially not the boys, who returned that night covered in unexplained gashes and bitemarks.

I took a deep, steadying breath and finished reading her instructions. They were simple enough—turn clockwise in the sun, burn an offering, speak love to an elm, and Mum would know to call.

Muttering my gratitude I snagged some of the drying mushrooms I'd collected the other night and stepped out into my garden. In the far corner, bathed in golden sunlight, was the elm tree Mum had always called her favorite. She'd designed the summons knowing I'd be able to do it at home with whatever was on hand—thank the gods.

I turned in the sun, arms out and open, then presented the mushrooms to the elm with a flourish. "You look ravishing today, my dear. Absolutely flourishing." The elm shuddered in joy and a bell chimed above my door. My phone vibrated in my pocket almost immediately.

"Hi, Mum."

"Leslee, dearheart," Mum was breathless as if she had run to whatever she was using to call me—it definitely wasn't a phone. They didn't have anything resembling technology where she was. "Is everything alright?"

"Not really," I said, beginning to pace the garden. I explained to Mum about the apparent vampire problem, catching her up on how I'd become entangled in the first place.

"That little twit," she hissed when I finished the part about Tyler. Warmth bloomed in my chest. Sometimes a girl just needed her mum to tell her that boy was a twit.

When I was finished, Mum sighed heavily.

"I'm coming home," she said.

"What about your sabbatical?"

"I've meditated so much I worry my brain has wandered off and left my body for a more spiritual place. Besides, I miss your father."

I pretended to vomit.

"Someday, you'll know love like ours, and you'll stop making that horrid noise."

I pretended to vomit again.

"I should be home the day after tomorrow."

"No, Mum, I can handle it." I didn't want her to swoop in and save the day. I was Business Leslee. I could do this. I needed to prove to myself I could do this. "Please, trust me. I just need a little guidance is all."

"If you're sure, dearheart." She sounded skeptical. "But if you're going to handle this, there are some things about our village you need to know."

I listened as she began a chilling story about cruelty, justice, and revenge.

***

I stumbled back into the cottage, dazed and overwhelmed. I set my phone down on the counter and flopped onto my sofa. I wished I could flop into my bed, but a certain charred vampire—a certain burnt-to-fuck *stable boy*—was occupying it.

Everything the ancestors said made sense now. The evil they witnessed, the things they warned me of. And the ghoul wandering the thicket, the one who had most likely turned Alex and his friends, was the former—or still current?—Mr. Huxley.

On one hand, things were severely more complicated than I'd thought. On the other, now I knew what to tell the ancestors when we began working to restore the acreage. I better understood how to untangle their grief and shame to let the sun back to their roots and the grass at their trunks. I no longer felt out of my depth in convincing the earth to grow there again.

After all, there was no better or more natural fertilizer than death. Nature needed it and demanded its price daily.

But that didn't make any of this easier to swallow. I was going to need several pints to wash this down.

With a quick glance at the bedroom door and then at my watch, I decided I could spare an hour or two at the pub before returning to my duties.

I had my hand on the knob, mouth and brain already drooling at the thought of a crisp, relaxing pint when I had the sudden worry that Billy would wake, not realize I was coming back, and just leave. Maybe he would be so fed up with me for making him catch on fire he'd fire me—there was a pun there, probably—and leave town, taking my first big job with him.

No, no, I definitely needed the opportunity to explain myself. Never mind that he was the one who kissed me. The memory washed over me, sending fresh heat through my gut. I pushed it away as I grabbed an envelope and scribbled a note on the back.

I tip- toed into the dark, silent bedroom, barely recognizing it as mine, and tucked the note where he would be sure to see it upon waking.

Then, I finally left the house, practically sprinting down the road toward the pub.

Yes, I was *absolutely* in need of a good few pints.

Chapter Twenty-One

BILLY

The mausoleum.

The thought slammed through me so violently it tore me from the clutches of sleep. I opened my eyes to darkness, a smothering, heavy heat holding me in place. I thrashed, trying to free myself from whatever strange confine I'd ended up in, rolling off whatever surface I was on, and slamming to the ground.

I finally pushed away the witchery engulfing me, gasping for air and blinking in a daze at the dark space.

Directly to my right was a bed on a simple iron frame. I stood, a little embarrassed, as I realized I had clearly fallen out of it and taken every piece of bedding with me. I gathered the blankets, piling them back on the bed, and tried to remember where I was.

Three perfectly square windows—two on the far side of the room, the third opposite them—were covered by velvet paisley curtains. Mobiles filled with hand-crafted butterflies, frogs, mushrooms, and birds hung from various places on the ceiling. Luxurious tapestries were draped above the headboard, giving the room a "palatial tent" feel. In the corner by the door, several large sketchpads leaned next to perfectly neat pencil boxes. The corner of a garden layout poked out from the back sketchpad, sparking recognition.

"Oh, right." I smacked a hand to my forehead. I'd let myself catch on fire outside Leslee's cottage. It was a safe assumption she hadn't let me self-immolate, and I was now inside her home.

The windows had the shutters pulled and the curtains drawn, but there were no tell-tale insistent peeks of sunlight that most places were subject to. Carefully, I cracked open the bedroom door, wary of any unwanted natural light.

The front of the cottage was silent save for the merry crackling of the wood stove in the kitchen. I could see from the several open windows that it was well past sundown—I must've slept the entire day.

I stepped into the front room, closing the bedroom door behind me. Her living room carried the same chaotic bohemian energy as the bedroom, with well-loved mismatched furniture crammed full of brightly colored cushions and wooly throws. Half-melted candles perched across the crammed bookshelves and the messy coffee table. In place of mobiles, drying plants of every shape and color hung from the ceiling, giving the effect of living within a forgotten flower vase.

The kitchen was the only tidy part of the house, with the scrubbed counters gleaming in the soft light of a single bulb above the sink. The stove gave off enough heat that I felt comfortable without the bulk of any blankets, and something was simmering on the back burner. The whole place smelled of citrus, cinnamon, cloves, and herbs.

An open book on the counter caught my attention.

The pages were filled with crooked print: notes on ingredients for some concoction, sketches of a tree's root system, and something that looked like a poem honoring a cactus.

I turned the page and was startled to see a spell diagram clearly labeled with components and locations and an all-caps highlighted note that read "DRAW STRAIGHT LINES OR ELSE."

I flipped to the front cover and saw the same handwriting in Sharpie across the composition notebook pattern:

HEDGEWITCH GRIMOIRE OF LESLEE HAWTHORNE

(MIND YOUR BUSINESS OR I'LL MIND IT FOR YOU)

A strange suspicion came over me as I stared at the stained cover, dirt sprinkling out from between the pages as my hands shook.

Of course, she was a witch. That explained *everything*—the outfits, the uncanny gardening abilities, her total and complete hold over all my senses.

I'd been literally bewitched.

But why?

I'd already agreed to pay her fees the same as all the other workers. She didn't stand to gain any more monetary successes from me than she could list on an invoice. She wasn't looking for a meal ticket out of town either—her impassioned speech about my plans for the manor had pinned her as a proud village resident. In fact, in almost every interaction, she seemed mistrustful of me and my motives as a stranger to the town.

"If only you knew," I muttered, setting down her grimoire exactly as I'd found it. Not even a moment later, I heard a high, clear voice singing and humming from outside. The song grew closer as the minstrel reached the gate, swore loudly, and then apparently crashed bodily through the gate based on the sounds of splitting wood.

The singing picked back up again, and I recognized an old Irish drinking song. I couldn't help the smile that split my face—she was getting the words entirely wrong but didn't seem to care, replacing each forgotten lyric with a different plant variety until she seemed to just be singing a list of plants.

Come guess me this riddle, what's ghost pipe, fig fiddle
What's mustard green, yarrow, and elders near stream
What black alders whistle, what's acer, beech, apple
Sweeter than blackthorn and stronger than ash

Corncockle, cow parsley, thrift, daisy, and kingcup
What's the elixir ramsons and wood anemone
And what helped Mr. Brunnell cornflower, chicory
Sure wasn't it lily from old sea kale, teasel

So we'll stick to the holly the best thing by golly
For sinkin' your sorrows and raisin' your joys
And bluebell honeysuckle lightning and thunder
Ragged robin, musk mallow whiskey me boys

The door swung open on the final note, and Leslee, face flushed and glasses pushed on top of her head, came whirling into the cottage.

She swayed unsteadily on her feet as she thrust an accusatory finger in my direction, face pulling down into an exaggerated frown.

"I know what you are." Her words were slurred, and a small hiccup escaped her down-turned mouth.

I clapped my hands together, giddy.

"Oh good, I've always wanted to do this bit." I struck what I hoped was a serious, brooding pose. "Say it," I said, dropping my voice an octave but working to make it breathy at the same time.

"A wampur." Her finger wiggled as if she could use it to help make herself focus. "Shaking tail breaking. Nope. Van-puh-reeee." She gave an exasperated sigh, blowing a raspberry at the end.

Holding up her finger as if asking for a momentary pause, she sidestepped me into the kitchen and picked up the grimoire, flipping through a few pages and squinting as if she couldn't quite make out the words.

"Your glasses are—"

"*Shhhhh.*"

She plucked a few leaves from one plant hanging above her and then another, crushing them in her fists before shaking them loose into a cup. She opened the fridge, nudging me where I stood with the door, and filled the glass with a small amount of apple juice from the fridge, and then pinched her nose before swallowing it like a shot—leaves and all.

She made a face as her throat bobbed and then stuck her tongue out when she was done.

"*Blech,*" she gasped. "That never gets easier." Miraculously, the slur was gone from her speech, and already her face seemed to be returning to its usual rosy glow where before she'd been beet-faced with alcohol.

She pointed at me a second time.

"Vampire," she said, triumphant. Pleased that she'd gotten out what she came to say, she came back to where I stood and reached over my head, pinning me in place.

She smelled like tobacco and sweat and woodsmoke—tell-tale signs she'd been at the pub for quite some time—but underneath it was her sharp, fresh scent, something floral and heady. I didn't miss the way her body lingered against mine as she settled back on her toes, a half-full whiskey bottle clutched in her hand.

"Didn't you just sober up?" I asked.

"Just long enough to make my point," she said, pulling the cork. "I'm choosing to take the night off from using my brain. Would you care to join me?" She looked me directly in the eye, her stare challenging and breath rank from whatever she had just chugged.

It didn't deter me from glancing down at her mouth.

Stop it, penis.

I nodded, feeling stupid.

She stepped away, grabbing two teacups with twining ivy around the rims and poured a generous amount into each.

"Please, make yourself comfortable," she said, gesturing to the overly cushioned sofa.

"I fear I already have," I said. She rolled her eyes as she shoved a teacup into my hands and took a long drink of her own. "Thank you, by the way."

She waved me off, flopping down onto the sofa. She took her glasses off her head, folding them and practically throwing them onto the coffee table.

"I'm not a monster," she said. "Unlike some people."

"No, just a witch."

She shrugged. "Not *just* a witch."

The challenge flared brighter in her gaze. I let her pull me in, crossing the room to sit beside her.

If this *was* an enchantment, why not enjoy it?

The couch was plush, perfectly worn-in. I'd forgotten what it felt like to sit on furniture that had lived a life before being pulled from a shipping crate or unloaded off a truck. The thick cushions threatened to swallow me whole.

"You are certainly more than meets the eye," I said. Smart, headstrong, dazzling in a way I couldn't seem to look away from. I felt her spell pull me forward so I let it, leaning closer to her as she watched me over the rim of her teacup. Her eyes softened,and she reached one hand up to the side of my neck, resting it there gently. Her hands were warm and rough, calloused from a hard day's work. I couldn't help the fleeting memory of my own calloused hands from a life far gone.

"Are you really just here to fix up the manor?" she asked, voice low enough to practically purr. She traced a pattern along my skin, and I had to resist the urge to rub against her like a cat.

"Yes," I said.

"Not to lead your brethren at the hotel?" Her fingers pushed up along the back of my scalp, and my eyes fluttered closed of their own accord. Warmth radiated through my body in a way it hadn't in a *very* long time. God, I loved magic.

"They're your problem," I finally managed. "Not mine."

She laughed, low and soft, the sound making my dick twitch. If she kept this up, I'd be helpless against whatever her next inquiry was—or her next demand.

The thought made my dick more than twitch, and I hoped the pillows were enough to hide how easily riled up this woman made me.

"So, I suppose you don't know anything about the big, pale monster in the woods." She practically cooed.

Everything in me froze.

The mausoleum.

The thought that had hauled me from a near-death experience came slamming back into me, dispelling all horny urges and magical finger enchantments. I took Leslee's hand, gently pulling it away. When she didn't automatically pull it back, I kept it, her pulse fluttering lightly between my palms.

"What did you say?" I asked. Confusion pulled her face tight.

"The ghoulish ghosty wandering around the woods with the big red eyes and incredibly long talons." She held up her free hand and wiggled it menacingly as if demonstrating. "If the kids at the hotel aren't your problem, as you say, then you probably also don't have anything to do with that thing."

A chill ran through me, and I fought the urge to shudder. My shoulders tensed up, and I feared the beginning of yet another incapacitating migraine. Before it could creep up on me, I pulled Leslee up from where she slouched into the cushions so that we both sat straight up, eye-to-eye.

"I need you to tell me everything about this 'monster,'" I said. "Start from the beginning."

She arched an eyebrow, finishing off her whiskey and setting the teacup down on the coffee table without looking.

"You were ready to jump me three seconds ago," she said. "The monster *must* be your problem for all that to disappear so quickly." She slipped her hand from mine and crossed her arms.

"It is, and it isn't," I said, choosing my words carefully. "I need to know more first."

Leslee waggled a finger in the air between us.

"Nuh-uh," she said. "I was finally getting something out of you, and you got distracted. Tell me why you want this monster so bad."

"I wouldn't have gotten distracted if your spell work was stronger," I snapped, frustrated. "Believe me, I would've rather let you seduce me than discuss what I think we're discussing."

"My *spell work?*" she spluttered. She put a hand to her chest, mouth agape, eyes fluttering. "You think...I don't need...my *spell work?*" She stood.

"Yeah," I said, feeling stupid despite the continued lack of headache. "I don't mind it; it was actually kind of nice. I—"

"You think I need magic to get laid?" she practically shrieked, face beet-red. She was lightly pacing the room now, a hand to her forehead. "You kissed *me*!"

"Yes, and I tried to apolo—"

"I am a hot item, Mr. Vampire Man." She stomped a foot down and jabbed a finger into her chest for emphasis. "I'll have you know love spells are *soooo* far out of my range of work I wouldn't even know what components to include."

My face would've burned hot if it could. Sometimes I missed being able to look properly ashamed—it saved a lot of explaining.

"Look," I held my hands out for peace. "Clearly, there's been a misunderstanding—"

"*You* misunderstood," she said.

"So..." I let that sink in for a moment, a half-smile stealing across my face despite myself. "You couldn't keep your hands off me then? If there wasn't any magic, that certainly seems like what was happening here."

Leslee was so red I feared for her blood pressure. Her mouth hung open, fluttering closed before opening again.

I ran a hand through my hair and smiled up at her from beneath the haze of my lashes, putting on an exaggerated pout for full effect.

"Not that I blame you," I said, lowering my voice to a comical pitch. "I am pretty irresistible."

"*Get out.*" She seethed, throwing a jagged arm at the doorway.

"Okay, okay, wait," I stood, putting my hands back out in supplication. "I'm sorry. Let's go back to the monster you saw."

The mausoleum.

Even if the nagging thought would let me leave, there was still the problem of only being clear-headed in Leslee's presence. And if there were a problem with the creature I locked up 150 years ago, I would need to not be bogged down by aggressive dirt and blinding headaches.

Her arm continued pointing, her face red, and her eyes bulging.

"Leslee, obviously, you don't need a spell to seduce me," I said. "You're a stunning, charming, ambitious woman with a unique magic all your own. And I'm sorry I kissed you like that. I just—I'm not myself lately."

Her arm continued pointing, but her shoulders loosened. She quirked an eyebrow.

"Partially because the dirt here keeps trying to swallow me, and if I don't let it, or if I don't swallow it in fistfuls, I get these insane headaches. They're blinding. I can't focus or think or get anything done other than swallow dirt. It's miserable—*I'm* miserable. And then you walked into the room, and all that evaporated in an instant." The words were tripping out of me, tumbling heavily through the air and landing with a self-pitying thud at her feet. "It's why I followed you to the pub those nights, and it's why I can't leave yet."

She crossed her arms and popped a hip, both eyebrows arched in skepticism.

"Being around you feels like magic, Leslee. It's so sudden and complete, the way you lift whatever it is that's trying to pull me under," I said, feeling more and more pathetic by the moment. "I chased after you to apologize and explain myself, but also because you're the only person in this insane place that makes things bearable. Then I woke up today, saw your grimoire and thought it all clicked into place."

She looked at me with something less guarded now, but her arms remained crossed. I didn't know what I wanted from her in that moment—to go back to the couch? For the callouses on her hands to run across my neck again? For her to promise just to be nearby so I could finish my business and get the fuck out?

No, it wasn't that last one. Not anymore.

"Can you understand now, why I assumed you were enchanting me?" I would end up on my knees in front of her if she kept up this silence. "Our time together has been the only clarity I've been granted since I got off the plane. I'm possessed by the need to be around you whether of my own will or not."

Finally, her arms uncrossed, and she threw her head back to the ceiling, releasing a long-suffering sigh.

"Godsdamn it," she moaned, tilting her face back to me, eyes bright, cheeks flushed. "I told the universe I wasn't going to sleep with you."

Chapter Twenty-Two

Leslee

It was well past midnight by the time Billy and I hashed through what each of us knew—about the monster, about the teens at the hotel, about each other. We were settled comfortably back on the couch, the empty bottle of whiskey the only thing keeping us from collapsing into each other. I let myself lean onto his shoulder some time ago, and he hadn't shifted.

The room was swimming with alcohol, exhaustion, and overwhelm. I needed time to process everything before I decided on a plan.

And there was still the matter of the manor grounds work to start.

"One more thing," Billy said, his shoulder shifting beneath me so that I raised my head. "You said you weren't 'just' a witch. What did you mean?"

"Mum's a druid," I muttered, nose leaning down to find his shoulder again. He smelled so *good*—musky but fresh. Like a very clean library made of all dark wood and brass. "It's probably why the dirt leaves you alone when I'm around."

"Well, that settles it then," he said. He gave my shoulders a squeeze before lifting me with him as he stood. He was stronger than I imagined a soft, rich man of his size and stature would be, and my drunk, sleepy brain wondered if he could throw me as easily as he could lift me. "You'll stay with me."

"'scuseme?" I slurred, squinting at him.

"Separate beds, of course," he said. "Nothing untoward unless you explicitly invite it. Think of it like the invitation rule for vampires but applied directly to your—"

"If you say pussy, I'll punch you."

"Personage," he finished, gulping.

"I told the universe, no fucking you." Were there several more of him all of a sudden? And why was all the light in the room so bright?

He nodded, face serious.

"No fucking me," he said. "We'll keep that promise to the universe."

"Don't be disappointed," I said, scowling and patted his chest. Oh *wow*, his chest. This dude was ripped. And for what? So he could conduct business calls with very good posture?

"Leslee..." I looked up at his face, a muscle in his jaw twitching, his eyes wide. I realized my hands were at his waistnow and I'd been dragging them along his chest like a horny drunk.

Oh no, I *was* a horny drunk.

"Sorry." I dropped my hands and swayed a little in place. "Okay, I'll help you. But only 'cause I am drunk and very sleepy. I get to change my mind if I want."

He nodded, a smile pulling at the corners of his mouth as he pulled his phone from his pocket. "Always."

One short phone call later and we were scooped up by a luxury van of some kind. I drifted in and out while Billy argued with the driver about cost of repairs and statutes of responsibility. The whiskey was doing a number on me at that point and I was slipping into its grip, enjoying the "brain-cation" I'd promised myself.

Tomorrow Leslee would have her hands full.

I don't remember how we got there, but soon enough we were in Billy's hotel room. He guided me to the bed and nodded repeatedly when I pointed yet another warning finger square at his nose.

"Not sleeping with you," I slurred and he repeated it back to me. Somehow my shoes were suddenly gone and holy *shit* the bed was amazingly comfortable. The last thing I remembered was the outline of Billy's shoulders against the low lamplight as he argued quietly with someone on the phone.

I caught the words "no more beds" before I drifted off to sleep.

***

I woke sometime later. My face was plastered to the pillow, and I could feel the dried drool clinging to my cheek as I rolled over. My head thumped unpleasantly,and my throat was tight. Blessedly, someone had left a glass of water and a small bottle of aspirin on the nightstand. A note was sketched next to them: "If it takes a universe's end, I'll wait."

My heart leapt into my throat, threatening to take the contents of my stomach with it. This was far too much earnestness first thing in the morning. I set the note face-down on the end table.

"I'll come back to you after tea," I whispered, voice hoarse.

A quick glance around the hotel room revealed I was entirely alone. Thick drapes hung over every window, blocking out any possible light, and I wondered if that had been planned for the current clientele.

Would more vampires be booking here specifically? I pressed a hand to my forehead as it continued to thump, trying not to answer that question or its implications just yet.

Tea. There definitely needed to be tea. I stood slowly and took in the rest of the room.

The walls were a deep forest green with stripes of shadowy grey that gave the effect of being deep in a glen. Gold metallic accents set off the dark wood furniture, and I recognized the sitting area next to a cheery fireplace where I'd met Billy for the first time—well, he'd been Mr. Barlow then. I wondered at what point I'd switched to his first name, just as I'd insisted he switch to mine.

We had just drunkenly shared the secrets of our unusual natures; it wasn't so strange, then, to be on a first-name basis. Maybe we'd have nicknames soon.

I let my stomach flutter at the thought and then released it. Billy was my client, and this sleeping arrangement was strictly to make our business easier on him. Never mind the thoughtful water, the heart-achingly romantic note, the press of him against me on the couch.

"Never mind, never mind, never mind," I whispered, willing the words into their own kind of ignorant magic.

I glanced over my shoulder and noticed the other side of the bed was distinctly unruffled, as if it hadn't been touched all night. I did *not* indulge the sinking feeling at realizing I'd slept alone. That had been the point—one I insisted on, even.

So why was I disappointed?

I shuffled to the hotel phone and was trying to figure out which number was room service when a soft snoring caught my attention.

I scanned the room again, sure I'd been alone and yet, there was *definitely* someone snoring in here.

I checked the sofa, the bathroom, the closet—all on tip-toes, holding my breath.

Finally, I realized the snoring sound was coming from the bed—but if no one was in it…

I ducked down, pushing back the bed skirt and coming nose-to-foot with Billy. From what I could see of his bottom half, he wore luxurious, cherry-red silk pajamas. But the stranger part still was that he was face-down in what looked like six inches of dirt.

I crawled as quietly as I could to the other side of the bed and pushed back the bed skirt. This time, I could see the top of his head, blond hair poking out in all directions. Sure enough, his entire face was shoved into the dirt. I wasn't sure how he was breathing, but as he let out a little snore, the dirt shifted around where his nose and mouth would be. I watched for a few seconds until a fit of giggles threatened to ruin the moment. Letting the bed skirt swing back for his privacy, I sprinted for the bathroom where I dissolved into hysterical laughter the minute the door was closed.

My client was a vampire—a handsome, kind, mysterious, capitalist, spoiled, rich-boy vampire. And he was sleeping face-down in the dirt like a drunk who didn't quite make it past the garden gate.

What a strange world we lived in.

"And you *love* it, Leslee Hawthorne," I whispered to the mirror, booping my own nose in the reflection.

I splashed water on my face and decided I'd navigate having a shower later. I hadn't packed a bag and had nothing to change into.

But everything else could be negotiated after tea.

Now that I finally had a grip on myself, I slipped back into the silent room and picked up the hotel phone. It rang on the other end for some time before I decided maybe the kitchen was busy.

I waited a few desperately long moments and tried again. Finally, a voice I didn't recognize answered.

"*What*," the voice snapped.

"Yes, good morning. Could I please have tea brought to room...uh..." I didn't know the room number and couldn't remember from my first visit. But Billy said he was the only guest. "To our room?" I ended weakly.

"Why?"

"Excuse me?"

"Why would I do that?"

I looked around the room, unsure if I had suddenly teleported to a place that didn't advertise and specialize in hospitality.

"Because I would like it? And I said please?" I was exasperated, and the aspirin was still a distant promise in my bloodstream.

"Not good enough." They hung up.

While I sat there staring at the receiver, stunned, a soft knock came at the door. I set the phone back in the cradle and tried to speed tiptoe across the room. I managed to swing the door open just as the second knock was sounding.

The expensively dressed woman with the cigarette from yesterday's job site stood in the hall. She somehow looked disheveled despite her sharp haircut aligning perfectly along her chin. Her makeup was tidy, and her clothes today were still stylish, although they looked considerably more comfortable than what I'd seen her in before. I imagined her strutting through an international airport someplace with large sunglasses and an easy air.

"Oh shit, sorry." She stepped back and looked like she would retreat, but I followed her into the hall, careful not to let the door close behind me.

"No worries," I called after her. "Can I help you?"

"I was looking for Billy," she said. "But I can see he's busy." She hooked one hand into her pocket and waved the other with a nervous half-smile.

"He's asleep, actually."

"Damn, still?" She looked at the smartwatch on her wrist, a gold chain glinted. "I know he keeps strange hours, but it's nearly noon."

I tried not to look as hungover as I felt at that news.

"Noon? And still not a drop of tea to be had, I'm afraid."

"You too, huh?" She turned toward me, rocking easily back on her heels. She wore pristine sneakers beneath her casual trousers and a slouchy t-shirt with a faded band logo on it that she had expertly tucked so that it didn't look slouchy at all. "I'm Rye," she said finally, extending a sharply manicured hand. I took it, trying not to stare at the dirt under my nails.

"Leslee."

Recognition flared in her eyes. "Right, the plant lady."

"Plant specialist," I corrected, and she nodded as if she had already struck out the prior name and written in the new one.

"Well, I'll tell you what, Leslee, I'm spending too much money on this goddamn hotel to not get a cup of coffee and a bagel before lunchtime. If they won't bring it to us, I say we go get it from them." Her voice carried the tone and tenor of a general rallying her troops in the dead of night, unable to rage how she wanted for fear of alerting the enemy.

I saluted as sharply as I could, given my current state. "I'll follow you anywhere, O captain, my captain."

She gave me a hungry, sharp smile that I both loved and feared and nodded toward the elevators.

Whoever this woman was to Billy, I was glad we were on the same side—for now.

Downstairs, we crossed the lobby and were disappointed to find no one at the front desk. Something nagged at the back of my mind and

I hoped it would present itself clearly once the aspirin finally started working.

"Figures," Rye sighed. She drummed long nails on the desk before setting her mouth in a line and nodding to me to follow. We set off down the back hallway that I had dragged Alfie down not so many nights ago. She stopped suddenly near the end of the hall and held a finger to her lips. The hotel was as silent as you would expect it to be given that only two guests—well, three now—were staying there, but I watched Rye tilt her head to the left.

"Ah-ha!" She pushed open a large door I hadn't seen set into the wall, revealing a gleaming commercial kitchen. "Empty, go-figure, but I think we can manage some coffee."

"Oh, tea, please. Coffee makes me jittery."

"More for me." She waved at me over her shoulder and began rummaging through shelves and cabinets.

I'd only made it through one section of the endless supply of pots and pans before the door swung open with a bang.

"*What do you think you're doing?*" screamed the voice from the phone. I dropped the kettle I'd found with a raucous clatter and turned to see a dour old man in the hotel uniform scowling at Rye. He was bald but for a few wisping hairs arcing toward the lights as if pulled there by a current, and his watery blue eyes sunk deep within his drooping face. His mouth pulled down in a permanent scowl, and he hunched when he walked with his hands at his middle as if a T-Rex had been diminished to this withered form. "Reginald" was printed on his nametag in aggressively large, all-caps black letters.

"Getting what I paid for," she said, not even pausing her search as the man stormed into the kitchen.

"This area is for staff only—"

"Then may I suggest you put some staff in it?"

I peered around the kitchen shelves to see Rye practically towering over the man despite him absolutely being physically taller than her. She had slipped her hands back into her pockets, and there was something about the feline shape of her shoulders, the set of her jaw, that made it easy for me to imagine she had killed a man for less than this slight.

To his credit, the strange man didn't back down, but his hands twisted together almost painfully.

"I *am* staff, and I'm here, and I'm saying you cannot be."

"If you had provided us with the tea and coffee service politely requested several hours ago, then we wouldn't be here at all."

Only then did the man seem to notice that I was also in the kitchen, which set off a renewed bluster.

"*Guests are not allowed—*"

"Do not raise your voice at her." Rye's tone was enough to silence the man entirely. He also seemed to be noticing the way she held herself and the murder it suggested. "Or I will have this hotel purchased tomorrow and fire you myself."

"You can't," he said. But his protest was pitiful—as if he wished she could, but it simply wasn't possible.

"I hope whatever makes you think that brings you comfort because I am not a woman to be stopped."

"Please," I interjected, watching the frail slouch of his shoulders droop even further. He would melt into a puddle at this rate, and I still hadn't had any tea. "We'd just like some morning beverages. The tea service here is so lovely, and it *is* included in the rate of the rooms, isn't it?"

The man glanced at Rye, then back at me, and gave the barest nod.

"Lovely. Then would it be so much to ask for that service? We're even happy to wait while it's all brewed. We understand we're the only guests here, so it'll take a moment."

Again, he looked to Rye and then back to me before nodding.

"Thank you so much!" I offered as brightly as I could. The poor thing was starting to look more and more like a kicked puppy than a blustering butler.

I looked to Rye and motioned toward the door.

"Shall we?"

"We'd like lunch as well," she said, leaning back out of the man's personal space, although it did nothing to make her less threatening. "Whatever the menu is for the day. And please don't worry—we *will* wait."

She didn't take her eyes off him until she stalked past the kitchen door and back into the hall. Then, as if a switch had been flipped, she nudged me with her shoulder, giving me a sly smile.

"So, Billy—how'd you end up in his room this morning, hmmm?"

"Oh uh, it's a...it has to do with...I got too drunk last night," I said, mind frantically scrambling for an answer that wouldn't imply anything worse. "I was falling all over myself—a little too much celebrating the big job, you know? Billy graciously watched over me."

"That's it?"

"Sure is."

"Well, I suppose it'll be easier to go over our plan for the city council meeting if you're with us." She checked her watch again. "If he ever gets up."

"Oh, he won't be up until the sun goes down," I chirped as I pressed the elevator call button. I realized too late that it was a stupid thing to say, but Rye only gave me a look before stepping through the sliding doors.

"In that case, I guess we better get to know each other."

Chapter Twenty-Three

BILLY

I was just rinsing the dirt out of my mouth when I heard the uneven hoofbeats again. Each ill-trod trot sounded through my whole being until it exited through the twitch in my left eye.

I was already in a foul mood. I'd spent the early morning hours chasing Alfie, Alex, Freddie, and Ford through every room in the hotel, looking for an extra bed. They'd insisted that there were no others over the phone, and I heard a chorus of joyous giggles before the line went silent.

Determined not to fuck up the progress I was making with Leslee—she'd forgiven me for catching on fire in her front yard, for fuck's sake—I decided to take matters into my own hands. Unfortunately, I didn't account for six freshly turned vampires against my ancient suffering ass.

For every room door I pried open, I was greeted by the imprint of a bedframe in the carpet and the fluttering drapes against the open window. In one room, I even saw Alex and Alfie leap into the night at the last second. When I reached the window to try and catch them, I saw Ford on the grass below, hefting the entire queen bed—frame and all—over his shoulder before marching off. I tried to get his attention and demand the bed, but he threw me a "V" with his free hand and kept walking.

I finally gave up when the sun threatened to rise. In all the chaos, I hadn't visited the mausoleum at the manor to address the strange thought that kept waking me *or* properly chewed out whoever was walking that horse about.

One problem was decidedly closer than the other—and easier.

I was opening the wardrobe to change when I heard the hoofbeats again, this time at a canter. Just the offbeat rhythm was painful enough I could only imagine what the horse was feeling. And who was forcing it to canter over cobblestones?

"That's it," I seethed, shoving open my window and dropping the three stories effortlessly to the back of the hotel.

A cobblestone road ran up from the backside of the village and met the freshly turned dirt where the new stables had been erected. I hadn't noticed how quickly the building had gone up in the time I'd been at the hotel, but I guessed that vampire speed and strength had something to do with it.

I spotted the horse idiot quickly as he led a beleaguered-looking chestnut up the road and toward the stables. Alex didn't bother brushing the hair from his eyes, giving his bowl cut the impression of a very big black mushroom engulfing his head as he bobbed alongside the horse in the dark. His shirt sleeves were pushed up, and a good amount of dirt was collecting along the edge of his pants. It seemed absurd to ask hospitality staff to train horses but I was starting to think this might be an absurd place.

I'd have some strong words for the new owner when this was all over.

I stalked over to Alex, careful to give the horse a wide berth so as not to startle it. I noticed the back left leg lagged behind the others, and the horse's ears were pinned back along its scalp.

"What are you doing?" I meant the words to be casual, but rage seeped out.

He didn't miss a step as he answered, "Boss wants horse-drawn carriages to bring guests to the hotel. We're famous for our horses, I guess."

"You guess?" I practically shrieked. The horse snorted and paused. Alex and I both took a long moment, settling our shoulders until he could encourage the horse forward again.

My best friend the migraine was working itself into a fervor, pinching behind my eyes and spreading tight hands along the base of my scalp.

"This village raised four generations of celebrated war horses and sold mares to the King of Spain," I said, biting off the end of each word.

Alex shrugged. "That was a long time ago."

But it wasn't. I glanced over at the chestnut he was forcing to limp along, taking in the familiar rich coloring, the graceful shape of its powerful neck, and the dappling of red through its mane.

This was and was not the same horse I'd cared for in my former life—the one that was simultaneously 150 years ago and still here today, rising out of the earth to try and swallow me whole.

The mausoleum.

"One problem at a time," I muttered. I watched Alex lead the horse to a stall, closing the gate before reaching over to undo the bridle.

"That's a good way to get slammed against the gate," I said. Was *anyone* going to train these kids?

He shrugged again. "He won't let me in with him," he said. "All I've been able to do is walk him back and forth between the pasture and here. He bites me for anything else."

"He's in pain," I said, throwing a wild arm towards the horse.

Alex stared at me blankly—or at least, I assumed he did, as I couldn't see his eyes.

"No, he's not," he said. "He wouldn't have walked all the way from the pasture the last few days if he was in pain."

"He would if he's descended from the horses trained here," I said. "And he is, right?"

More blank staring.

"Alex," I said, counting slowly as my brain pulsed against my skull. "Pay attention. I'm going to need you to get me a few things from the village."

I rattled off the tools and supplies I'd need to shoe the horse properly, adding a bag of carrots and a bottle of whiskey.

"Whiskey, sir?"

"So I don't kill you or whoever sold you this horse," I said. "Now go."

He vanished in the blink of an eye. I could hear his sprinting steps down the cobblestones.

The horse eyed me curiously from the back of the stall. One ear flicked forward as I clicked my teeth gently.

I eased open the gate, stepping inside one fraction at a time, carefully watching the horse's body language. Alex said he was biting, and I wasn't interested in adding that bruise to my current aches.

But the horse stayed where he was as I entered. His other ear even flicked forward as I closed the gate behind me.

"Hi, friend," I said in a low, calming voice. "I remember your great-great-grandfather. I don't imagine you remember me, though."

The horse took a few shuddering steps forward before pausing in front of me. He reached that long neck forward and rested his head over my shoulder, letting loose a snort that sounded more like a sigh. Carefully, I stroked his neck, feeling the coarse fur there.

"Once we get your shoes on right, we're going to give you a spa day," I said, picking out a small bur.

The horse nudged me none-too-gently, so I resumed petting him, enjoying the warmth and weight of his head on my shoulder. Horses had such a specific smell—musty and heady but not unenjoyable. I was transported back to when my only worry was keeping the troughs full of hay and the loft full of women.

After a few blissful minutes of horse snuggles, I heard someone clear their throat on the other side of the gate.

"Sir?" I shrugged out from under the horse, giving him a few reassuring pats on the nose.

"You got what I asked for?"

Alex nodded, hair jangling.

"Great, thank you," I said, reaching for the carrots. "Let's get started."

***

Not only was the shoe on crooked, it was the wrong size, and it was very clear he hadn't had a hoof trim in far too long—overdue by at least a month if my guess was close.

I'd decided to do things properly and worked up a sweat getting the old shoes off and the hooves trimmed down. I'd thrown my pajama shirt over the side of the gate and gone through half the bottle of whiskey, although neither action did anything to quell my rage.

I sent Alex out for an anvil and hammer so I could cold-shape the new shoes. When I heard someone clearing their throat behind me, I waved off to the side without turning around.

"Set it wherever, Alex. I'm almost done with this trim. And then we will have a lesson about cleaning hooves regularly."

"Billy?" Leslee's voice echoed in the barn, liltingly sweet and a little unsure.

I carefully set down the hoof I was working on and straightened to see the druidic witch staring at me, a bright flush along her cheeks, her mouth half open.

I should've known since the headache I'd been trying to drown with alcohol was now sliding down and away from my brain as if dispelled by magic.

I cleared my throat, realizing I was standing shirtless and barefoot in a horse stall, covered in dirt, hay, and sweat. I tried not to let my shoulders shrink in on themselves. And I really didn't want to put the sweaty silk shirt back on.

"What are you doing?" she asked.

"The horse's shoes were on wrong," I said. "It was driving me crazy."

"I've never heard of a hobbyist farrier."

"I used to work with horses."

"Looks like you still do."

I tapped the side of my head. "A vampire never forgets. It's the blessing and curse of living basically forever."

She stared another moment, something like disbelief on her face, but there was something else too, and I couldn't help remembering the comfortable way she had leaned into me on the couch last night, the way she'd brushed her body against mine in her kitchen.

Get it together, penis.

There wasn't hiding anything in silk pants.

Sure enough, I saw her gaze drop down my body at the same time my cock gave an answering twitch, and then she cleared her throat but didn't move her gaze. I didn't know whether to put myself on display or push the horse between us.

"Rye wants to meet," she said. Did she just lick her lips?

"I'll give you a ring..." I stumbled, body heating under her gaze. "Ah, give *her* a ring...a call...when I've done you—when I'm done."

Finally, blessedly, she looked back up to my face. The heat in her eyes and the slight drop of her jaw made me wish she'd looked back down.

I was going to fuck her in this stall if I didn't get a grip.

"You need to finish putting shoes on a horse before you'll take a business meeting?"

I could only nod.

Leslee considered me a moment, the stable lights bouncing off her voluminous hair, eyes bright and a little wicked behind her glasses.

"I'll tell her," she said. "Oh, and I haven't been able to track down another bed."

"The staff hasn't been very accommodating on that matter," I said, side-stepping the bed-chasing events of the night before.

"Oh, well," she sighed. "You don't sleep at the same time I do anyway—or apparently in the same place." She arched an eyebrow at me, and I realized with slow horror that she must have discovered me under the bed.

"I figured it was only right to allow you the bed, given your state." I didn't add that under normal circumstances I could sleep in a bed above my grave dirt, but, despite her nearness, I still hadn't been able to find peace until I was face-down in the tray under the bed. Apparently, her presence stopped the migraines but not the urge to feed on mud.

"I won't be in a state tonight," she said. We both seemed surprised by the offer in her voice, so much so that she took a few quick steps back and threw her hands up in a double wave—like a political candidate bidding farewell to her adoring public. "Ah, yes, well...I'll go tell Rye the good news."

"That you won't be in a state?" I called, smiling as she made her hasty retreat.

"That you've given up capitalism for horse feet."

I laughed, surprised at the way it bounced across the stable and came back to land at my feet, my joy a small but wondrous thing.

Chapter Twenty-Four

Leslee

"He was doing *what?*"

I was back in Rye's room, a luxurious blue and silver equivalent to Billy's.

We'd spent much of the day together, chatting amicably or working silently alongside one another. Lunch had eventually arrived, delivered by our grumpy new friend, Reginald, from the kitchen. It was a warm, hearty vegetable stew with crusty fresh bread and the requested tea and coffee service. Everything was delicious despite the rage it may have been prepared with—maybe spite made for the best seasoning.

I'd left in the late afternoon to stretch my legs and my mind, wandering the meadow behind my house for a while before eventually meandering back to the hotel. I stopped when I saw Alex standing anxiously outside the stables and had to see for myself when he told me Billy was inside.

"Rye, it was..." I took a deep, shuddering breath. "*Bloody sexy.*"

She stared at me, an unreadable expression on her face.

My client—the pompous, spoiled, gentle, caring vampire who was twisting my head all in knots—was standing shirtless in silk pants in a horse stall, a light sheen of sweat glistening off his hardened chest. His hair was pushed back from his face instead of the usual slicked, so the blond was soft and invited my fingers to push through it. And the horse that had been so shy and spooked all week was nudging his hand with his snout and standing happily beside him.

I'd been overcome in a way I had only read about in books. And when I'd caught him catching me staring at his dick, he'd seemed like he was enjoying the attention.

"Duh," Rye finally said, crossing her arms and arching her eyebrows at me. "He's hot, *and* he was helping an animal. Of course, you're gonna get all wet for him."

"Oh gods, don't say that." I leaned my face into my hands, horrified. "I told the universe I wouldn't sleep with him!"

"Sounds like the universe took that as a challenge."

"Rye, seriously, what do I do?"

"Don't stay in his room?" Her tone suggested I might be stupid.

"I kind of already made an agreement..."

"Okay, so," Rye pinched the bridge of her nose, squinting her eyes shut. "You're not sleeping with him even though you're sharing his room—because it's better for business or whatever." She waved her hands at me as I tried yet again to offer an explanation that didn't out me as a druidic hedge witch or Billy as a vampire. She hadn't bought anything I'd said and, judging from the sharp look in her eyes, didn't need it anyway. "And even though your loins are quivering, you're *not* going to hook up because you, what, told God you wouldn't?"

"The Universe," I corrected. She quirked an eyebrow and held my gaze. It made my heart stutter to try and hold her catlike stare, but I wouldn't back down in a promise to the Universe.

"You're like a crunchy nun."

"Gods, no," I snorted in disgust. "All that praying and drapery and celibacy. Not for me."

Rye and her eyebrow were still staring me down, waiting.

"Okay, look," I said, bracing myself. "Remember that guy Tyler I told you about?"

She nodded.

"I promised myself, if I trusted the Universe, I'd be fine without him, and wham, bam, here's a rich va—valiant man," that was close, "to hire me for a massive job. I told the Universe I wouldn't sleep with him and fuck this up."

Actually, I'd told the Universe that was very clearly throwing Billy at me, that I would let him rest in my bed after he caught fire in the sun but I wasn't going to sleep with him whatever it tried to pull. The Universe very clearly did not understand the intricacies of maintaining healthy client relationships.

I watched Rye, hoping she bought the lie.

She did not.

"Whatever you aren't telling me," she said, finally dropping the question from her face and refilling her cup from the still-warm coffee pot on the table. "It's your business. But it sounds to me like your options are to consummate your desires or suffer."

"Yeah." I leaned back into the plush sofa with a sigh. "I thought that might be the case."

We worked together for a few hours after that, occasionally chatting about the future of the manor house and helping one another puzzle through the intricacies of local, antiquated village law. Rye was nervous about the impending meeting with the village council, unsure how they would or wouldn't bend to her and Billy's efforts. I enjoyed having someone to bounce placement ideas off, appreciating Rye's keen eye for color.

Around dinner, I waved goodbye to Rye and headed off in search of Alex or one of the other boys.

In a hotel this size, there *had* to be another bed. There just had to be.

I found Alfie behind the front desk, the phone pressed to his ear. He was listening very seriously and scribbling rapidly, the pen barely a blur across the page. He glanced up as I approached and gave me a silent "one moment" gesture that seemed so adult and professional coming from someone with acne speckling his chin.

I glanced around the lobby while I waited, noticing for the first time the intricate pressed pattern along the edges of the ceiling. While the rest of the lobby was aggressive in its modernity, the pattern seemed ancient—almost like foreign runes that I couldn't quite identify.

"Miss Hawthorne?" I jumped, tearing my gaze away and finding Alfie staring. I guessed this wasn't the first time he'd said my name.

"Hi, Alfie, alright then?"

He nodded, flashing me a cheery, fanged smile. "Yes'm. You?"

"Well, I was hoping maybe you'd taken another look at the bed situation."

He shook his head solemnly, but I wasn't imagining the cheeky smirk that flashed across his face.

"Afraid not, miss. Is there an issue with the one in Mr. Barlow's room?"

"Only that it continues to be the only bed in the room."

He nodded as if sympathizing, and this time, the cheeky smirk was more pronounced.

"Alfred." I leaned across the counter, bracing my arms on the cold marble. "Are you having a laugh?"

He shook his head solemnly. "No, Miss."

I waited for his serious façade to crack, for a glimmer of mirth to shine through his bright eyes. Nothing.

"Alfie, I *know* there are other beds in this building, and Ford could bring one up to the room without breaking a sweat."

"I'm sorry, Miss, it's not possible."

"Alright then, *where* are all the beds then?"

"Repairs." This time, the slightest quiver around his mouth told me he was lying and greatly enjoying it.

"Repairs," I repeated, my jaw dropping low on its own.

"Alfie!" A joyful voice called from the side hall, nearly drowned by thundering footsteps. Ford, all broad shoulders and thick-necked muscle, came practically skipping into the lobby. His full weight crashed against the lobby desk, sending a pronounced shudder through the marble top. "Alfie, super bed is ready!"

"Cram it, Ford," Alfie hissed, and I watched realization scale Ford's chiseled features like a climber up a particularly challenging cliff.

"Aw, Alfie, Miss Hawthorne's alright," Ford said, giving me a truly award-winning smile. I remembered then his dad had done some time on London stages back in the day and his good looks hadn't faded. Bradford had certainly inherited at least that much from his folks. "Let her see, she'll understand."

"Yes, Alfie, let me see 'super bed,'" I practically purred. Alfie, looking sheepish, nodded and followed Ford as the giant skipped away. I trailed the two, curiosity a stronger force than annoyance.

Ford led us outside along the same path I'd taken with Freddie only a few days prior—had it really been so short a time?—but when we reached the stables, Ford continued passed the doors before darting to the side out of sight.

I could hear cheerful whoops and screams echoing across the starry night. As I followed Alfie around the side of the stables, a scene from a children's bedtime story bloomed beneath the moonlight.

At least twenty mattresses were stacked three thick to make a massive landing pad on the ground. A large ironwork structure blocked off the far side of the pile, multiple bedsheets tied together as a sail billowing in the chill air. A joyful yell came from above us and I caught the silhouette of a figure on the roof leaping into the air. I gasped, rushing forward, but Alfie caught me, holding me back with alarming strength for his lithe frame. As we watched, the figure landed on the mattress stack with a soft *thump*. The pillow tops dented around them so that they had to practically claw their way up and I was relieved to see Alex's grinning face pop up.

"Alright then, Miss Hawthorne?"

I nodded, dumbstruck as he bounded away, clearing the distance to the stable roof in a single leap.

Before he was barely clear of the landing pad, a second cry hit the air and another silhouette slid across the moon before landing with the same dull thump. This time Freddie poked his head up as he crawled from the mound.

"Aw, Alfie, come on," he groaned when he caught sight of the two of us. "You told?"

"No, no." I held up a hand as Alfie started to protest. "He's just doing his job. I demanded to see super bed."

"I don't think it's safe for you, Miss," Freddie said as he stood, dusting off his trousers. Someone landed behind him with a gleeful cackle. "But I 'spose if we restacked the mattresses..."

"No, no," I laughed, all irritation dissolving as William crawled out of the mattresses, long hair pushed away from his face just long enough for me to see the glint of red in his eyes before the curtain fell again. "I don't want to break anything, I have lots of digging in my future. You boys have fun."

"Wait, it's my turn, Miss Hawthorne! Watch me!" Ford called from the roof.

I waved, shouting back up at him. "Go for it!"

"Should we restack for him?"

"Nah, he'll be alright."

"I dunno, Alf, he's a lot of force..."

Before anyone could make a decision, Ford was in the air, his bulk blocking the light of the moon for just a moment before he fell in a swan dive. I could practically hear the air whistling around his form as he plummeted, and for one heart-stopping second, I wondered if I was about to see this young man die.

Instead, he hit the mattresses with enough force that he bounced, and when he rose, there was a blissful expression of peace on his face. He hit the billowing sheets on the frame behind him with a sharp snap before ricocheting back into the mattresses where he stayed down.

There was a brief moment of silence before the boys erupted into joyous roars, swarming Ford on the mattresses and jumping up and down together.

Swept up in their joy, I almost joined them before remembering I was *not* a teen vampire and didn't want to get trampled under their leaps.

I decided to leave them to their games, the thought of the cushy mattress in Billy's room too appealing for any other work to be done for the night. I turned to watch the boys a final time from the edge of the stables when I noticed a newcomer to their revelry.

Red silk flashed beneath the moonlight, and I realized Billy must've come out from where he was still working on horse things—whatever that entailed this many hours later. He gestured wildly at the mattresses and back toward the hotel. I couldn't hear what he said, but I didn't need to. The boys were still, looking properly chastised, until Alex saw I was watching. He gestured toward me and then back to Billy before all the boys started yelling and waving at me, calling my name.

Billy's gaze found me across the distance, and he gave a small wave, all his gestures quieted to that small motion—as if my presence made *him* feel sheepish as well. I returned the wave, a hearty laugh bubbling up in my chest and bouncing out through my teeth.

He looked like an irritated uncle who's woken up from a dead sleep to find his nephews had built the world's most irritating blanket fort with his imported antique furniture ...if his nephews could also leap from two stories up without fear of harm.

The boys gestured for me to come back, pointing at me and then at Billy in a plea for defense. I shook my head and turned back to the hotel, letting one of the remaining beds call me home, something warm cooking in my chest.

Back in the hotel room, I ran a scalding bath filled to the brim with fragrant, luxurious bubbles. I dimmed the bathroom lights and brought up my favorite playlist on my phone, humming as I piled my hair on top of my head. Settling in carefully, limb by limb, until my entire body was screaming pink with the heat and my muscles slowly unknotted, I let loose a satisfied sigh. It was lacking a few candles and maybe a crystal or two for charging the water, but for not having any of my home comforts the bath was exactly what I needed.

Now maybe I could clear my head of Billy and wake tomorrow ready to greet the sun at the job site. I'd done all I could for the planning parts—I needed to get my hands dirty.

But as soon as I tried to think through hedge placement and digging the needed lines for solar-powered watering systems, my mind drifted back to Billy in his red silk pajamas.

Billy shirtless and soft.

Billy barefoot and caring.

I groaned and slid deeper into the water, obscuring my vision with steam and bubbles.

"I'm not doing it, Universe," I said, wagging a finger in the air. "I don't care how hard you try. He is my *client*."

There was no response, unless you counted the gurgle of the overflow drain.

Gods damn it, why did he have to be so handsome? And thoughtful? And smell so good? I closed my eyes and could practically still smell him over the aromatic bath—something musky and expensive I couldn't name, but also a bright, sharp, clean smell like he'd just stepped from the shower, no matter where he was or what he was doing. He smelled like good sheets and top-shelf everything.

And I couldn't get the image of him with the horse out of my mind. All that effort, all that luxury, and yet there he was, silk pajamas coated in dirt and hay, white-blonde hair hazy around his face, just begging for me to twist my fingers in it and pull him closer.

Was it giving in to the Universe if I masturbated?

"It'll get him out of my system at least," I reasoned.

I let the water buoy me, lifting my hips, and slid my hand between my legs. The warm water lapped against my bare cunt, and I sighed, relaxing into the sensation as I slid a lazy finger up and down through my folds, then back up to circle my clit. My body pulsed in response, rising to meet the pleasure eagerly. I let my eyes half-close, imagining my hands were not my own, and reached up to twist a nipple as I flicked my clit with increasing speed.

I was just beginning to fall into the lusty fantasy of Billy running a fang across my breasts when I heard the room door open.

I froze.

"Leslee?"

Fuck me, Billy was back.

"Leslee, are you here?" His voice came closer, and I realized I hadn't closed the bathroom door all the way.

"I'm in here!" I called out, hand frozen on my clit, heartbeat thudding through my cunt like I wasn't about to be discovered.

Wait, why was that making me hornier?

"Oh, pardon." Billy's voice was just on the other side of the door. It wasn't flung wide, thank the gods, but it was cracked wide enough that I was sure he could see me in the mirror if he bothered to look.

And so what if he did?

There it was again, that thrilling heartbeat slamming through me and picking up pace as it whisked me away.

"I'm sorry about the whole bed fiasco," he continued. I leaned my head back and closed my eyes, giving in to my body's need. I returned to circling my clit before flicking over the delicate, sensitive hood. My body arched up in response, causing a splash of water I was sure would give me away.

So I did it again, nearly crying out in pleasure at the thrill, the sensation, the sound of this man's voice so close but so far away from me. I needed him closer—bearing down on me as we both gasped for the air the other exhaled.

"Those hooligans outside refuse to part with the contraption they've created, even if it means a little more propriety for you," he said, voice even and light, assuring me he wasn't peeping.

But gods, what if he was? What if he could see me now, twisting at my hard, peaked nipples, fingers finally pushing inside of my cunt to offer the delicious filling I so desperately needed? It wouldn't be enough. I needed him—his cock, his hands, his mouth. I needed him to push the door open and find me wet and ready for the taking.

"Leslee?" The door nudged, and a surge of pleasure swept through me.

I was close.

"Yes?" I gasped out.

Oh, gods, he had to know now what I was doing.

"You alright?"

I gripped the side of the tub for balance, sloshing more water over the side as I rode my hand as if it were his. If only he were asking me that question while he was inside me.

"Yes," I gasped again. "Just um...just finishing up in here."

"Oh, yes, right, I'll leave you to it."

"No!" I practically screamed.

"Pardon?"

"I..." I was so close to finishing, I was going to come with the next words he said. I needed to hear them. "Do you think I'm good?"

"What?"

I rocked against my hand, desperate, sloshing, gasping for air. Heat and pressure crept low within me, and they needed to be set loose.

"At my job," I gasped again. "Do you think I'm good at my job?"

I was being a manipulative, dirty little whore, and the whole thing was turning me on more than I had ever been in my entire life.

And my mother is a *fucking* wood nymph. Sex is not a foreign thing in my life.

"Well, yes," he said. "That's why I hired you."

"Could you say it?" I breathed, all fear of being discovered gone as white points appeared in my vision. If I didn't finish soon, I was going to die.

"Say what?" his voice grew concerned. "Are you sure you're alright?"

"Splendid," I thumbed my clit as I slid in a third finger, all other sound and thought narrowing to that glorious pressure. "Just having a small crisis."

"Oh well, I understand. Yes," he said. "I would say you're good."

"What's that?" *Sneaky, nasty, filthy slut. You'd do anything to hear it, even slip his cock in right now.*

"I said you're good, Leslee," he said, voice soft and careful. "You're very good."

I came with a silent cry, head thrown back, mouth wide and strained as I strangled any sound pressing out of me. I lifted myself over the edge of the tub to slam down on my rigid fingers for a final time before finally settling back into the water, trying and failing to slow my breathing. My heart was pounding so loud I was sure he could hear it through the door.

"Alright?" he asked again.

"Perfect," I sighed contentedly. "Thank you."

"Right, you're welcome." I heard his footsteps pad away before returning a moment later. "I'm going to call for dinner, are you hungry?"

"Starved," I said, stifling a giggle.

Chapter Twenty-Five

BILLY

It was all I could do to hide the massive erection tenting my pants when Leslee emerged from the bathroom in a puff of sweet-smelling steam. Her face was flushed and her skin was a rosy pink, all that blood pushed to the surface and pulsing happily along her curves. She wore the plain pajamas she'd brought for her stay, a simple flannel set buttoned chastely to her collar, but none of that mattered. I could easily imagine what lay beneath, given that I'd just glimpsed it.

I'd wondered if it'd been a trap, leaving the door cracked just enough that I could see her in the mirror, simpering, naked, breathless in the tub. But the longer I spoke to her, the more I realized she was masturbating to the *sound of my voice.*

I'd been on this godforsaken planet for too long to have never been this aroused.

And then I had to pretend I had no idea what was happening while she sat beside me in front of the dinner tray, warm and soft and aromatic.

I could barely stand watching her throat bob with a single swallow of tea before I excused myself to the bathroom, claiming I needed to wash the horse smell off before I could enjoy my meal.

The minute the shower turned on, I pumped myself hard and raw into my fist, making it a shuddering, painful three thrusts before I came in hot white ropes along the wall. I watched, shaking, as the water washed it down and swirling through the drain.

What is wrong with me?

We're both consenting adults, and despite telling the Universe she wasn't going to fuck me, there had to be a better answer than masturbating next to each other. At the thought of watching Leslee have at herself again, my dick twitched a second time.

I stepped from the shower, sliding into a plush robe and breathing in the steam for a moment.

Leslee had promised the Universe she wouldn't have sex with me, and it was a wish I would respect—whatever it meant. I hadn't written that morning note lightly. I *would* wait for the universe's end. I had all the time and then some. And I'd rather wait than push into regret.

Another loud refusal of temptation echoed in my memory—Evelyn's piercing gaze, the sharp cut of her chin in defiance, the desperate, almost feral way she ravaged my mouth when we kissed. And yet—I couldn't let Leslee regret me. I couldn't be a memory she looked back on with anything resembling pain because I would remember it for much longer than she would be alive.

I couldn't—and wouldn't—carry the weight of remembering something fondly that was soured by the knowledge the other party didn't do the same. Life was too long for that kind of emotional turmoil.

I wasn't going to end up an Anne Rice novel.

And yet, here I was, yet again staring contradictory refusal in the face.

I weighed my options, wondering if I should march into the room, drop the robe, and proposition Leslee right then and there. Or I could put on fresh pajamas, eat dinner. and go to bed in the hopes it would make the manor visit tomorrow easier.

The city council meeting was looming, my phone was ringing off the hook with problems with the demolition, and the call to the old mausoleum was haunting me. I would have to face the ghoul eventually, which meant staring down my lurking evils.

"And you spent the day playing with horses," I muttered, running a hand across my face.

"Because the world needs more good men in it. We can't afford to lose the few we have."

Before guilt could swallow me whole, I shifted my focus and stored the memory of Leslee away for a simpler period in my life. I'd change into my pajamas, have dinner, and treat this like the working relationship it was supposed to be.

Then I opened the bathroom door to Leslee sprawled across the bed, her landscaping sketches strewn over the comforter. She lay on her side with the curve of her hips on full display, and as my eyes ran over them, I noticed her pajama top was billowing open in the front, offering a full view of the creamy skin running between her breasts, hinting just barely at their pillowy mounds.

My mouth went dry.

"Do you have any preferences concerning perennials or annuals? Biennials can be quite dramatic depending on the bloom, and I was thinking you could use the timing as some kind of grand event, really bolster the tourism aspect."

The only thing that existed at that moment was the length of Leslee's sternum and the infuriating hidden acreage beyond it.

"Hullo, Billy?"

"Whatever the expert recommends," I said, stuttering out a cover and tearing my eyes away.

"Everything alright?" Her voice followed me from the bed to the sitting area where the dinner service I'd ordered had long since gone cold. I picked at a dinner roll absently.

"Oh yes, just grand," I muttered.

"Really? Cause you haven't looked me in the eyes since you ordered dinner."

Busted.

"If I tell you," I said, slowly turning around and finding her bright eyes fixed on me. "You cannot be offended."

"No," she scoffed. "Tell me, and I'll be what I am."

"Then I'm not telling you." I was being a child.

"Billy Barlow, you tell me right now." She stood from the bed, planting her hands on her hips like an angry schoolteacher.

"No, I won't." I stuck my tongue out. When she started toward me, I flung the dinner roll in mock defense, diving below the couch. She yelped in outrage, hurtling herself nimbly over the back of the couch and landing cat-like behind me.

I crawled away, comically dragging my knees on the carpet, a laugh rising unbidden and shaking my ribs. Her hand gripped my ankle, and I flopped dramatically, howling like a caged beast. She tugged, and I scooted toward her, surrendering on the floor. I closed my eyes and stuck my tongue out, letting my head loll to the side as if dead.

"Tell me what you're hiding," she hissed, poking her fingers into my ribs.

"You've caught me," I hummed, keeping my eyes closed. "I'm not ticklish. Now you know my big secret."

A sharp pain in my side made me sit straight up.

"But not immune to a good pinch, I see." Leslee leaned over me, holding her fingers together like pretend crab claws, a wicked grin across her face. This close, I could count the freckles on her face, like an intimate smattering of stars, and I found a hand reaching up on its own to stroke the soft skin of her cheek.

Her eyes fluttered at the touch, and I felt her body still.

"Oh, we are in a bit of trouble," she sighed.

"Does it have to be trouble?" I asked, tracing patterns along her neck the way she'd tempted me not so many nights ago. Unlike that moment, however, some of the pretense between us seemed to have melted, and she didn't fight the urge to lean into my touch.

"You're a client," she said, tilting her head back to give me better access. I leaned in, breathing her in, savoring the closeness of her warmth as I pressed a single kiss to her neck. "And you have to stay a client, or I'll never get this business off the ground."

"What does that have to do with anything?" I ventured a second kiss, lingering as she gave a short, sharp inhale.

"I won't make it far if I gain a reputation for fucking every client I take." Her voice was low and soft, rasping in her throat. The sound went straight to my already hard dick, and I thanked whatever being was above that I'd changed into looser pants.

"What makes you think I'd let you fuck anyone else?" I slid my hand along the base of her skull, bringing her mouth to mine and kissing it harder than I'd planned.

She sighed against my lips, sliding a curious tongue across mine just in time for a trio of sharp knocks to sound against the door.

"Billy, stop fucking around. We have to prepare for this council meeting."

Rye.

Before I could apologize, Leslee was across the room, adjusting her clothes and smoothing her hair. By the time I stood, she was under the blankets with her sketches in front of her, glasses perched on the end of her nose imperiously. The only sign anything had happened was the fresh flush across her chest that was dying as I watched.

"Do you know what time it is?" I asked, a little sharper than I meant when I opened the door.

"Duh," Rye said, strolling past me with her folio under one arm. "Smack in the middle of the hours you usually keep. And since you've decided to turn my work here into a massive game of hide and seek, I decided I'd rather seek out what you're hiding than continue waiting around."

"Hiding?" I nearly choked on the word, focusing on *not* glancing over at Leslee or the spot on the carpet where she had just been perched over me.

Rye waved her hand in a non-descript circle as she settled on the couch.

"Whatever all this is with you two," she said, flipping open her folio and clicking her pen open. Even at 2 a.m., she was all business.

Before I could respond, Rye held up a hand for silence, fixing me with a penetrating stare. "I don't want to know," she said. "I don't care. Leslee won't tell me either, so you two do whatever it is you're doing. But stop making me chase you around this empty hotel like a fucking Scooby Doo character, or I will—"

"Charge me overtime," I said, releasing a relieved sigh.

"—Quit," she finished, cocking her head to the side. The word made my knees buckle.

"Rye, you can't—"

"I handed over all my other current clients at the firm so I could drop what I was doing and come help you where I barely have a cell signal because you pay well and I like you," she said. "But my time is not to be wasted, Billy, favorite client or not."

I nodded, forcing my mouth shut. She was right. And what had I even been doing for the better part of the night? Re-shoeing a horse and yelling at teenagers about super bed.

And nearly fucking Leslee.

"I apologize for the runaround," I said, settling into the couch across from Rye. "I was distracted and won't allow it to continue."

I felt Leslee boring a hole into the back of my head.

"By a horse," I amended quickly, clearing my throat. "I was distracted by a horse."

Rye stared at me unblinking, face stone still, before she, too, cleared her throat and handed me a sheet of paper with a short agenda neatly scrawled across it.

"This is the planned agenda for Monday's meeting."

"Monday?"

"The council head has an 'unforeseen emergency' that lines up nicely with the camper I saw the head councilman hitch to the back of his car this afternoon. He's pushed us to Monday."

"So, we're here a few more days," I said, trying not to sound as elated as I felt, immediately imagining the excursions I could take Leslee on, the time we could have over the weekend unfettered by ghouls, plans, or work crews.

Why not stay, then?

Because I'd end up in the ground.

The thought fell low in my gut, sinking into my organs and settling. I knew I couldn't hide behind planned carriage rides and champagne forever. The ghoul would strike again, and old ghosts would rise to haunt me. No, I could not stay in this place any longer than was necessary.

I pulled my attention outward, looking over the proposal Rye slid across the table to me. Her voice filled the room, warm vowels and even tone blocking out the frantic past few hours as I sunk into familiar, controllable territory—city planning meetings.

***

By the time Rye and I finished our work for the evening, it was nearly four. Rye waved me goodnight around a massive yawn, clicking the door shut quietly behind her.

I leaned back, stretching my arms along the sofa and groaning at the stiffness in my neck. Leslee snored quietly behind me, reminding me that every light in the place was still on.

Groaning again, I stood, stretching my arms and back before padding around the room to click off each lamp until only the nightstand opposite Leslee's side of the bed remained. The soft yellow light cast a halo around the bed, glowing in her curls and illuminating the curve of her face in sleep. My fingers twitched to touch her skin, to trace along the edge of her jaw like a familiar lover might say a wordless goodnight.

But I was neither familiar nor her lover.

Careful not to disturb the mattress, I laid down next to her, closing my eyes and slipping into a daydream where we were just two people sharing a bed in anticipation of the coming dawn, not an immortal and a witch caught in an inescapable magnetic tango.

Why was I always landing in situations where I had to daydream an alternate reality? First, Evelyn, where the dream had been simply that I could lure her away from her cursed boyfriend. It was foolish to think roses and sex were enough to distract a woman from her true love, but I thought it anyway. And now, I was trying to pretend away my own curse—a force that pulled me here, threatening to bury me in the way my body sometimes cried out for after 200-too-many years above the ground.

If I weren't cursed as the undead, if I was just another member of the bourgeois with money to burn on mansion restoration, I wouldn't have to leave this place the first chance I had. I wouldn't have to fear being sucked down into the earth in front of Leslee, never to claw my way back out again. I wouldn't have to wish there was a way for us to continue discovering each other on an alternate timeline.

Maybe I wouldn't be so damnably tired. I could live a life where waking wasn't a reminder that my soul grew weary, thinking more and more of the silence of the grave as a reprieve.

Chapter Twenty-Six

Leslee

The hotel halls were darker than before, yawning open at every turn, defying the morning sunlight streaming through the floor-to-ceiling windows at the far end. My hair stood on end as I waited for the elevator to crawl up to our floor. How had I never noticed the scream of the metal pulleys and cogs before?

The usual chaos was silent downstairs, with each fangling in their deep sleep. I sighed in resignation as I turned the corner to the kitchen, knowing Reggie would shame me once more for asking for a basic cup of tea. Apprehension hung over me like a wool coat in the summer. Having to fight for my morning cuppa could *not* be long-term. I'd have to talk with Billy about all this if I was to stay through the renovations at the Manor.

As my mind turned to those haunted grounds, I didn't imagine the shadows creeping taller, reaching desperate tendrils to snake around my ankles, my thighs, my wrists. I tried to brush them off, but to my horror, they were as strong as jungle vines, thick and corded at their core, no matter how much dark mist I tried to dispel.

"Hello?" I called down the stretch of hall where the kitchen lay silent, where the outside grounds would still be covered in morning frost, where even the lone horse in his stable couldn't hear me. "Someone? I seem to have offended the hotel in some way."

The tendrils tightened, pulling me flush against the wall. The expensive textured wallpaper was rough on my cheek, the wall pushing the air from my lungs as I struggled against it.

Panic threatened to overwhelm me as all my attempts to thrash and wiggle were stifled.

"*Please! Anyone! Help me!*"

My cries were quickly choked by a slithering shadow vine plunging into my mouth, twisting down my throat until even my gasps were silenced.

I woke with a throttled cry, pressing frantic hands to my sweat-soaked neck and chest. I gasped in lungfuls of air, focusing on the slow exhales after, the expansion then contraction of my free, functioning lungs, the soft caress of the sheets around my legs.

"A dream," I said, my voice breaking the spell of the early morning silence, bringing me concretely to the present. "It was just a dream."

I showered and dressed quickly, trying to focus on the full Saturday of work ahead of me. I'd need to compare my estimations against true measurements on the manor grounds, put together my order for the rose bushes and delphiniums I hoped to start with and have a chat with the rattling aspens on the far side of the grounds for their input on potential new neighbors.

Relief swept over me as I stepped into a sun-flooded hall, waited for a swift and silent elevator, and was greeted by the sound of Reginald swearing loudly in the bubbling, steaming kitchen.

"Just a dream," I said again, pressing my hand to the kitchen door and swinging it open.

"*Guests cannot—*"

"Good morning, Reggie," I called in what I hoped was a kind and not at-all irritated voice.

The disgruntled day-shift employee was at the stove, sweating profusely as he stirred an unknown substance in a larger-than-life pot. It could've been a cauldron, but a closer look revealed it to be a massive stainless-steel stockpot, the sides bulging curiously. Fixing me with a glare, Reggie's lip curled as he pushed stray strands of stringy hair from his brow.

"*What* do you want?"

"The usual, if you please," I said.

"Can't."

"Are we going to do this every—"

Before I could finish, he lifted the lid of the stock pot, and the overwhelming stench of decaying flesh sent me flying back into the hall, one hand over my mouth, the other pressed to my stomach as if I could will my body not to vomit.

A moment later, Reggie poked his head through the door.

"Bit sensitive for a witch, innit?"

"What *is* that?"

"Ghoul bait. For Masters Alfred and Frederick."

"What on earth for?"

Reggie rolled his eyes as if the answer were obvious to any idiot. "For catching a ghoul."

Realization slowly dawned.

"They can't take that on themselves," I said, stepping further from the open kitchen door as the smell seeped into the hall.

"You know how boys are with their mothers."

"You mean—"

"I don't have all day to chat; this needs stirring." Reginald's sweaty, stringy head disappeared, leaving the kitchen door swinging at such a rate the smell wafted further and further into the hall. Slamming through the side exit near the stables and out into the fresh air, I decided I'd wander into town for my morning cuppa.

Following my feet and intuition, I wasn't surprised to find myself at Janice's door. The beleaguered mother of the notorious redheaded brothers swung the door open, chipped mug in one hand. Her eyes were bloodshot, and her brilliant orange hair was piled atop her head, stray wisps frizzing out to the ends. She looked a little like she'd stuck her finger in a socket.

"Leslee," she said, surprised and confused to see me. "Did we have plans?"

"Of course not," I heard myself chirp. "But what is the point of being friends and neighbors if we can't occasionally call on each other unannounced? Is there more tea?"

"Pots on the stove," she said, stepping aside to allow me in.

Her cottage was homey but tidy, the frayed edges of the couch and chairs covered with strategic blankets and doilies. The stains on the carpet were tucked beneath the coffee table and any other willing piece of furniture, so that only flashes of pattern winked out here and there. Framed school portraits of Alfie and Freddie through the years hung on the living room walls, and I felt a sharpness in my heart at the realization that they would never change again. Each year their portrait would look the same. What would they do when their mother grew suspicious?

"How're you? The boys?" I asked once I was settled at the wobbly kitchen table, stained mug full of stiffly brewed dark tea. I sipped and stifled a grimace, grateful at least that I had it, remembering the stench in the hotel kitchen.

"Funny you ask," Janice said, settling across from me after refreshing her own cup. "You're spending more time with them at that hotel than I am. They're never home, they only call at odd hours of the night, and when I do see them, they're..." She heaved a sigh. "I don't know, Leslee. They're strange. And especially so with this raccoon nonsense."

"Sorry?"

"I assume that's why you're here to 'drop in.' They did send you, didn't they?"

"I'm not exactly a raccoon expert."

"They said you might know what to plant to keep them away."

"What type of raccoon?"

It was her turn to look confused. "The usual type, I suppose."

Reginald had said he was making ghoul bait for Alfie and Freddie. That was a strong solution for a raccoon.

"Could you show me where?"

Janice led me out and around the side of her cottage, stopping before reaching the quaint vegetable boxes in the back. I pointed to them, but Janice shook her head.

"Bastard hasn't discovered those yet. Heaven help us when he does." She drew my attention instead to the white-washed wall just beneath a bedroom window. Claw marks gauged the wall, long and deep. It looked like the "raccoon" had pulled itself up along the wall to rest on the windowsill. A chill ran across my shoulders, sending goosebumps down my arms as I realized the creature had been peering into Janice's house.

"Honestly, I don't mind a little masked bloke or two wandering through, but the noise is unbearable. And they're right outside my bedroom window."

"Noise?"

"Leslee, it's awful." She looked near tears, gripping her tea with both hands now. "I know they're just vermin, and they're probably mating or calling to each other or whatever other nonsense, but I *swear* it sounds like screaming. Just tortured, awful screaming."

I wrapped my arms around my neighbor, rubbing a soothing hand along her shoulders as she leaned her forehead on my chest. "If I could get one night's sleep, I wouldn't be so dramatic. It's been like this for *days*," she sobbed.

"It's alright, love," I cooed, already running through what I had ready to pot at home that could sit in her window. "We'll get you some rosemary and bay leaf. The smell drives them off."

And they're protective. Those little spicy leaves won't let that ghoul anywhere near you.

I left promising to return later that day with plants for her window and some other natural wards for her vegetable boxes. My mind was whirling, heart pounding, feet practically tripping on the cobblestones I'd memorized in my rush to get home.

The ghoul was coming into town now. Soon, no one would be safe.

I had to do something.

***

"Noon on Monday," I repeated into the phone, jotting the delivery time in my planner. "Yes, I'll be there. See you then." I thanked the wholesale floral vendor and hung up. I was back at the hotel, working from the seating area in Billy's room after delivering the promised protective herbs to Janice and snapping a photo of the claw marks on my phone before heading to the manor to work for the day.

My body and soul hummed with the joy of hours spent focusing on my work. Not for the first time, I relished in the blessing of getting paid to do something I loved so dearly. And here I was, doing it *with-*

out Tyler. My measurements were spot on—nearly to the millimeter—and the aspens had been all too ready to talk my ear off with their preferences. Aspens were a chatty lot, given the opportunity. It was why they were always whispering in the wind, hoping anyone would listen. Naturally, this meant it had taken more time than I'd planned for, and it was now nearly sunset.

With the floral order in and the spindle bush delivery settled, the only thing left to do for the day was wait for Billy to wake up. I wanted his help tracking down the ghoul tonight.

All day, I couldn't stop thinking about Janice and her exhausted tears, about Alfie and Freddie trying to take on an ancient creature themselves. I couldn't leave my neighbors—people I'd grown up alongside and watched grow up—to fend for themselves. Not when I was better equipped and now, better acquainted to handle it.

Just in time, I heard Billy stirring beneath the bed.

Before I could think about it, I was up and crossing the room, hauling the dirt box out from under the bed with Billy still in it. It was heavy but not worse than hauling fertilizer to mark out new flower beds.

Billy blinked up at me, sleep still settled on his face. He was handsome, deliciously disheveled, and he'd decided to sleep shirtless, his grave dirt smudged across his chest. I wanted to lick it off, remembering the taste of him from the night before, the way his voice went straight to my pussy when he asked, *"What makes you think I'd let you fuck anyone else?"*

"Hullo?" He sat up slowly, running a hand through his hair and yawning. His fangs hung low in his mouth, and I had to stop myself from poking a curious finger to their tip.

"Morning," I said. "I'd like to go ghoul hunting tonight."

Chapter Twenty-Seven

BILLY

"I'd like to go ghoul hunting tonight."

I could barely register the words before Leslee was flinging clothing at me, unceremoniously rifling through my wardrobe. The Gucci shirt, the Hermes belt, and my treasured Burberry were flung aside in favor of a Ralph Lauren button-down in a plain, crisp cotton and the dirty jeans from the other night.

"Wait, Leslee!" I cried out in distress, but nothing would stop the whirlwind of woman touching everything I owned. "I have a system. You can't just—"

A waist-length quilted jacket caught me across the mouth before I could protest further.

"Do you own anything that *doesn't* need to be dry-cleaned?"

"These pants are dirty."

"Jeans aren't dirty after *one wear.*" She rolled her eyes, planting impatient hands on her hips. She was dressed practically—a loose linen shirt, an eggplant purple wool coat, and her ever-present swishing skirt, this one in all black. "And you can't hunt ghouls in business-people clothes."

"Oh?" I leaned back in my dirt, throwing her my best seductive look from under my disheveled hair. "Who says ghoul hunting happens with clothes on?"

I didn't miss the flush beneath her freckles before a second shirt smacked into me, the button catching the tip of my nose so that my eyes watered.

"Get dressed, please. We have a long night ahead of us."

"Alright, but don't say I didn't warn you." I stood, shedding my pajama pants. Leslee whirled around with a squeak, averting her eyes while I slipped easily into the jeans and shirt. I allowed myself one self-righteous cackle before letting her off. "Okay, it's safe. I'm dressed."

"I'm quick with a hex if I have to be, Mr. Barlow." She turned around, hands over her eyes, peeking through two fingers. She dropped her hands and shoulders in relief as I slid into the quilted jacket.

"Are we back to Mr. Barlow?" I asked, upset at the sudden switch.

"Only when you're being horribly inappropriate."

"Well, if that's my only punishment, I suppose I'll wear it with pride." I flashed her a grin, unable to stop myself. "Mr. Barlow, when I'm naughty. I could get into that." A sharp smack landed on my stomach, pushing an "oof" from me.

"Let's get provisions from the kitchen, and then we can be on our way."

"And where is it you're leading us this fine evening?"

"Alfie and Freddie's house."

I followed her to the elevator, where she punched the button four times, each harder than the last.

"Leslee—"

"It's harassing their mum—Janice," she said. "My neighbor."

I didn't have a snappy remark for that. Leslee's arms were crossed, her gaze trained on the carpet. I forgot that not everyone who lived here shared my 200-year-old disdain. To Leslee, especially, Ashbourne seemed special and worth protecting.

But was it worth dying over?

"Leslee," I said, catching her elbow as we entered the elevator. "This creature is dangerous. We know very little about it, and it could be more powerful than the two of us can handle."

"A good hunter is first and foremost a good observer." She turned toward me as I slid my hand up her strong bicep, feeling the muscle there, wishing her linen shirt wasn't barring my way to her skin.

"An expert hunter, are we," I said.

"When I find this thing, I'm going to make it sorry." She looked up at me, hazel eyes shining with unshed tears. "I'm going to make it wish it'd never been born."

"Or created." I offered the addendum without thinking. Leslee blinked at me, knitting her brows together. The elevator doors dinged as they slid open in the lobby, the usual classical music washing over us as we entered.

"Who would create such a monster?" She asked, striding across the marbled space with sure steps.

"Sometimes unusual creatures aren't as careful as they should be," I said. "That's how we end up with ghouls, thralls, and ghosts. The intended effect, whether as a meal, a servant, or a simple death, isn't always delivered despite all our powers."

"*You* could do something like *that?*" She threw an accusatory arm out toward the doors.

I held my hands up for peace, shaking my head emphatically. "No, no. I've never fed on anyone long enough—or rather *not* long enough—to not quite kill them. I've never turned anyone either. I stay away from all that."

"Good." Leslee sniffed. "Cause if you had *anything* to do with that monster outside, the one that turned these poor, sweet boys and ruined their lives and is now preying on my neighbors, I'd be forced to make you *very* sorry, Mr. Barlow."

I arched an eyebrow at how she said my last name, earning another smack.

The kitchen was silent—not even Reginald was lurking around. It felt like the calm before the fangling storm—the burners and pots waiting to be slammed, scorched, scraped, or otherwise violated by over-excited hands who didn't yet know their true strength.

Leslee opened the fridge and then the cabinets, laser-focused.

"How do you know where everything is?"

"I got tired of fighting Reginald for room service."

"I wish I had to fight for room service—Will calls me before I'm awake and tells me he has my dinner ready."

"I thought vampires didn't eat?" She stuffed a tote bag I hadn't noticed before with crackers, a hunk of cheese, and an expensive-looking package of ham slices. I swiped a bottle of champagne from the wine cooler, tucking it in her haul.

"They don't," I said. "Will brings me a blood bag and some very burnt toast."

"A classic English breakfast," Leslee gave me a half smile as she rifled through the silverware drawers.

"I still enjoy textures," I said, adding a few napkins to the picnic. I was rapidly romanticizing our ghoul hunting, tucking a few chocolates in with my bubble and white linen napkins. "It still tastes like nothing, but at least I get to pretend I remember what food tastes like while enjoying something crunchy or fluffy or bubbly." Incredibly, a crimson picnic blanket, checked with deep brown and black lines, was folded neatly on a back table, peeking out from behind an unused freezer. Before I could question who put it there—or if it was the hotel itself—I tucked it under my arm.

"That's very human of you." Leslee lifted the tote, grimacing at the weight. I slipped my arm through the strap, hefting it easily, cradling a protective hand under the bottom of the champagne.

"It's easier to bring the human parts with you on the road to vampirism than to squash them entirely," I said, offering the hedge witch my other arm. She took it, and I could've purred beneath the warmth of her hand on my bicep.

I let Leslee lead us out of the hotel and down into the village, walking at a good clip but never losing her touch on my arm. The air was crisp, the black night sky above clashing violently with the blood-red dregs of sunset on the horizon. We stopped in front of a quaint, white-washed, thatched-roof cottage identical to those on either side of it but for a cheery sign above the front door that marked it as "Alfie and Freddie Territory." The sign was written in a child's script, paint peeling and bubbling from withstanding so many wet seasons.

Before Leslee could knock, the door swung open, and an exhausted red-headed woman clutching a mug of tea practically leapt out to meet us.

"It was here, the damned vermin," the woman spat. "I chased it off with the broom, but it can't have got far."

"Janice, this is my friend Billy," Leslee said, gesturing between us by way of introduction.

"He's too fit to be a rat catcher." Janice squinted at me in the dim light.

"I take pride in my work," I said, dipping my head in acknowledgment. "Who says we can't look good for our tiny, plague-carrying friends?"

"Right." Janice ran a hand across her face as if she could rub off how tired she felt. "I showed Leslee already, earlier. If it's alright, Les?"

"Of course." Leslee squeezed the hand the woman offered. "Get some rest, love. We'll take care of it."

I followed the hedge witch around the side of the cottage to where the narrow path opened to a healthy garden. I noticed the dark wood we'd driven through from the airport was only a good jog away, putting it closer to Leslee's cottage than I'd initially considered. I couldn't say what, but *something* about those trees felt wrong. It had the night I cowered in the mud, and it did now as I stood staring out across the meadow between us and them. There was no comfort in the cheery warmth of the back porch light or in Leslee's hand in mine.

"Oh." Leslee let out a soft gasp before stomping a firm, booted foot on top of mine.

I yelped, glancing down to see tendrils of earth slinking away from where they'd started to climb my leg.

"'Oh' indeed."

"We have to get you sorted," Leslee said, tugging my arm so I followed her to the far side of the cottage.

"One monster problem at a time," I said.

"Speaking of." Leslee gestured to the wall in front of us. There was a single crank-open window set neatly above a small ledge. Flickering light from a screen danced on the walls inside, barely visible above the potted herbs pressed up against the inside of the window.

But it was the ugly gashes in the house itself that pulled and kept my attention.

They started at the ground and rose to the window as if some ghastly creature had clawed its way up for a peep. Wood chips littered the ledge, and I guessed the creature had to gain its balance more than once, gripping and regripping. The marks were far too big for a raccoon, and something about them nagged at the back of my mind—as if they were familiar.

"That's a bloody big raccoon," I said.

"Or a small ghoul." I met Leslee's gaze and saw the determination there, the set of her jaw. "Let's settle in."

To my absolute horror, Leslee dropped to all fours and crawled beneath the thick wall of hedges behind us.

"Leslee," I whispered, whirling around to watch the soles of her boots disappear. When she didn't respond, I hissed her name a second and third time until she thrust an impatient finger back out, crooking it in a "come hither" motion.

"I'm *not* crawling in $600—" Another hand shot from the hedge and gripped my shoulder, hauling me into the waiting branches before I could protest further. But instead of razor-like leaves and twigs, I felt the tell-tale whisper of magic on my skin.

I blinked, looking around at what appeared to be a tiny waiting room crafted from roots, with barely enough space for the bench that swirled up beneath Leslee. She perched lightly there, wearing a pair of camo-printed binoculars around her neck, cheekily patting the bundle of roots next to her.

"What is this?" I asked, sitting beside her and wincing at the invasion of knotted root against my backside. "And how long do we have to be here?"

"Don't tell me you've lived this long as a vampire and never hedged." She mocked an affronted look.

"That's not what the contortionist in Amsterdam called it." This time, when she smacked me, I caught her wrist, neatly flipping her palm open and planting a kiss in the middle. I held her gaze, drinking in her soft gasp of surprise, the widening of her eyes, my favorite flush blooming beneath her freckles. I could drink just that gentle pink and be satiated.

"This is a *stakeout*," Leslee said, breaking the tension and wiping her hand on her skirt, much to my mortification. "Stop trying to seduce me."

"Worried I'll distract you?"

"Don't be ridiculous." She lifted the binoculars to her eyes, clinking gently against her round-frame glasses before lifting those out of the way and trying again. "I'm not so easily distracted."

I could see her pulse leaping in her neck, could hear the thud of her heart between her ribs. It was all too easy to catch a human in a lie.

"That sounds like a challenge," I said, draping a lazy arm on the hedge roots behind where she sat and leaning in.

She straightened, and I didn't imagine the goosebumps prickling across her skin.

"It's not."

But when I ran a gentle finger down the back of her arm, I saw her eyes flutter closed and heard yet another soft gasp flutter free from her lips. Her pulse was so close I could feel it humming against me, singing its siren call. But blood wasn't what I wanted to sink my fangs into from this woman—not when there were more satisfying pursuits.

"A wager then," I said, leaning closer so that her hair ghosted with my breath. She shivered, and I half-smiled to myself. "I bet I can seduce you before the ghoul arrives."

"I already told the universe—"

"—you're not sleeping with me, yes," I said, venturing closer still. "Obviously, I respect all a lady's pacts with dynastic entities."

"Hard to seduce me with a pact in place." There was a playful thrill in her voice, a throaty joy that told me she'd be more willing to play my game than she was letting on.

"Seduction is not just about fucking, Miss Hawthorne." I leaned back now, careful to check in and survey the heated tension I was twisting between us. She turned, her glasses slipping back down her face as she removed the binoculars. Her face was flushed, her mouth half open, her eyes wide and bright in the dark as her gaze dropped to my lips. "It's about pageantry as much as it is connection. It's about all the ways I can tease, taste, and tempt you before you give in to me."

"Billy, that's—"

Footsteps.

Leslee's use of my first name flittered away before I could catch it. I held up a hand for silence, focusing entirely on the shuffling, dragging gait my vampiric hearing had picked up. Whoever they were, they were crossing the meadow—away from the woods, directly toward us. It was most certainly two feet, one dragging slightly more than the other, and as they drew closer, I didn't imagine the labored wheeze of their lungs or the crackling moan that pressed free with every other step.

"Is Ashbourne known for bipedal raccoons by chance?" Leslee fixed me with a look, and I shrugged. A ghoul it was, then.

"Close?" Leslee mouthed, her entire presence tightened to a breaking point as if stilling her molecules would improve the silence.

A scuttling sound near the creature drew my attention before I could answer—this one had four feet, claws, and a distinct chittering. *That* was a raccoon. The creature let out a huffed growl before I heard the distinct screech of an animal caught in the jaws of death and the tearing gore of teeth meeting flesh.

I shook my head, trying to bring my hearing back to a closer circumference, away from the ghoul and its noisy, vicious snack, but nothing I did would clear it. In fact, it got louder, as if I'd shoved a microphone at the creature's feet instead of relying on supernatural skills.

I clamped my hands over my ears, desperate to block out the screeches, the wet ripping, the dull thump of bones hitting the dirt as the thing finally died in the creature's hands. I was enveloped in the sound of teeth grinding, tongue slurping, wheezing breath rattling around it all, and still the creature made its shuffling way forward.

A tremor in the ground rattled my feet, and I snapped back to where my body was shaking lightly beneath Leslee's warm hands. She rubbed circles over my shoulders, standing over my huddled form, concern tight in her brow.

"Alright, then?"

I managed a nod. "It's still heading this way. It had to..." I swallowed down the bile in my throat. "Have a snack."

She nodded, tilting her head and closing her eyes as if she, too, could hear it.

"Vampire hearing," I said as if apologizing.

"Remind me not to tell secrets in a mile radius of you."

"I have to attune it," I said, rubbing the side of my head where I'd clenched my jaw to nearly splitting. "It's usually easier to control, but something about this place..."

Leslee fixed her bright eyes on me, face open and waiting for me to finish my thought.

"...makes it impossible to stay in control."

"Of your hearing?"

"Of anything." I couldn't help the way I was looking at her, gaze drifting down her profile, along her neck, lingering where her coat wrapped neatly over the porcelain flesh of her chest. It was amazing how she still inspired such lust in me even when seconds ago I'd been listening to a monster devour their appetizer.

When I finally hauled my eyes back up to her face, Leslee met my gaze with a matched intensity. I was surprised the air between us didn't catch into flames.

"If you lose it? Your control?"

"I would never hurt you."

"You couldn't if you tried." She flashed me a wicked half-smile to match the one creeping across my face. "I'm nasty with a trowel."

"Stop, I can only be turned on by so many strange things. Curly-headed women hefting gardening tools is making my list embarrassingly long."

"Awfully whiney for a man who was dead set on seducing me." It was my turn for goosebumps as her hand snaked from my shoulders to grip the back of my scalp. Leslee splayed her fingers through my hair, tugging lightly to tilt my face up. She stood over me and slid between my legs with a certain command that sent heat low in my stomach, and when she leaned down, I swore the branches around her followed suit, encasing us in trembling green. Her lips ghosted across mine as she whispered, "Not so sure of your bet, now, are you?"

A tiny moan slid from my mouth, and she swallowed it before it could slip free of our cover, slanting her mouth over mine. Our tongues met with the same ferocity sparked in our eyes, warring for territory either would have freely given. I gripped her hips, hauling her closer to me, desperate for any press of her I could get despite our winter coats. I groaned in frustration, ready to tear the damned garment from her in my search for that tender, warm skin, that pulse I could hear hammering in her body, everything flushed and taught and ready for—

A very wet, very loud thud landed just outside the hedge. We both whipped our heads in its direction. Despite our labored breathing, there was no mistaking the shuffling steps, and the wheezing groans outside.

The ghoul had arrived.

Chapter Twenty-Eight

Leslee

The blood in my veins slowed to a crawl, my heart holding its breath as I listened to the ghoul's shuffling steps on the other side of the hedge. The stench of rotting meat and disturbed dirt was enough to make me choke. I pressed my coat sleeve over my nose and mouth, turning to Billy and arching my eyebrows in what I hoped was a universal signal for "ready?"

It was not.

I leapt through the hedge, realizing too late that I was surprising a flesh-eating monster entirely alone.

It whipped around, claws still gauged into Janice's windowsill, rows of fangs bared and dripping with stinking saliva.

Up close, I could see the creature's pale flesh pulled taut across its bones. Fingers pushed into bony talons where they met the wooden sill, and its spine hunched over its shoulders, neck pushed forward from the deformation.

Its eyes were all black, yawning open in a skull-like face and reflecting the moonlight in a predatory flash as it whipped its head back and forth, taking in my frozen form. It had no nose, just two slits where it used to be, and its mouth hung open unnaturally wide, the blood red shocking against its pale flesh.

On instinct, I raised my arms above my head, spreading my legs wide as I let out a roar. The creature cocked its head before answering with a chilling scream.

"Hey, ugly!" Billy's voice came from over my shoulder. "I've got your dinner right here!"

The creature released its grip on the windowsill and took one shuffling step toward us, letting out another shriek. I sent out a silent prayer to the swaying trees in the wood that Janice wouldn't get too curious about what we were doing. I couldn't explain if I tried.

"No," Billy breathed behind me. I chanced a look over my shoulder to see his face pulled down in shock before it twisted into something more.

Before confusion could set in, the ghoul launched itself at Billy with a guttural scream that sounded more like rage than hunting. I blinked and the two were no more than a twisting collision of limbs and movement, each strike a blur.

The garden path where they struggled was narrow, and I had to press myself to the cottage wall to avoid a rogue talon. A shadow moving inside the house, flickering against the TV light made me reach for the hedge a second time.

"*Hide them*!" I called, splaying my fingers through the dirt and pushing my intent through the ground to the roots of the obedient bushes. I couldn't think about where they would take Billy and the ghoul—I didn't have time. As the hedges swallowed the feuding monsters like a great, green mouth, Janice swung open the bedroom window.

"What's all this?" she asked, squinting into the dark.

"Sorry, love," I said, trying not to sound as breathless as my body felt. Huge clumps of grass lay scattered across the garden, slick with dark blood. "Didn't mean to wake you."

"Never mind that, looks like you got the bastard." Janice nodded to the half-eaten raccoon lying in a pool of organs where the ghoul had dropped it. "A little extreme, your friend."

"That's Billy," I said, pressing a hand to my chest to steady my racing heart. "Does nothing by halves."

"I'd guess not. Have him send me the bill. I'm finally going to get some sleep." I took the hand she offered and accepted her friendly squeeze as all the thanks I needed. Janice didn't bother stifling her yawn as she sent me a half smile before swinging the window shut. The room went dark, and I stood in the silence, shaking, every nerve straining for sounds of Billy and the ghoul. Nothing but the soft breath of the breeze through the hedges.

I let loose a shuddering sigh, clenched and unclenched my hands, and wiped the sweat off my palms onto the folds of my skirt. My eyes landed on the half-eaten raccoon carcass.

"Of course," I groaned. Always a bit of bloody unfinished business—literally or otherwise—behind Mr. Barlow.

Kneeling gently next to the corpse, I pulled the collapsible trowel I kept tucked in my pockets for gardening emergencies.

"You're not exactly a misplanted mum," I said, setting to work in the dirt. "But we'll have you tucked in tighter than a tulip in no time."

Janice's garden was well cared for, and she'd clearly turned and replaced the dirt around the hedges in the spring. I didn't have to fight against stubborn, compacted dirt that had sat for several years like I often did for clients. In fact, the dirt yielded so easily that before I'd shoveled more than three times, a raccoon-sized grave yawned open next to me.

I spread my fingers across the ground and opened myself to messages.

RETURN.

I gasped, pulling my hand from the dirt as if it burned.

"Alright, then?" Billy stood over me, blood trickling down the side of his face, his fine linen button-up shredded across his taut torso. He met my gaze with concern, kneeling to take my face in soft hands sticky with blood. "Leslee, you look like you've seen a ghost."

"Something is very wrong," I managed, letting myself fall victim to his touch for just a moment longer.

"Given that ghoul bested me, I'm inclined to agree."

"Oh gods, of course, Billy," I shook out of my shock, brushing his hands away and inspecting him for injury. Aside from a small cut along his hairline, he seemed fine, but I didn't let that stop me from running my hands across his chest, along his neck, and over his shoulders. Just in case.

"You know, I won."

"You just said you didn't." I squinted at him, only vaguely aware that my hands were crawling over his biceps like a blind woman gifted her favorite book in braille.

"In the hedge." He shot me a mischievous grin.

I dropped my hands as if they'd been scorched. "I think *I* won, Mr. Barlow," I said, shoving my hands back in the dirt as if they could be cleansed. The universe had an unfair way of reminding me of my promise, and yet here she was, challenging me over and over again.

"Oh?"

"I saw your face when I grabbed you. I could've straddled you under my skirt like a turn-of-the-century harlot, and you would've let the ghoul ransack the village for a feast."

"Please stop describing my future dreams," Billy groaned.

I paused, staring at where the raccoon corpse had been. I pointed. "There was a body there when you got here, right?"

"Half of one."

Then I noticed the open grave that had all too eagerly opened despite my minimal effort was now closed. Stranger still, the earth writhed beneath our feet, slipping twisting tendrils over my boots as it reached questing fingers up for Billy.

I placed my palms over the grave, pressing what I hoped was finality into my touch. I clenched my jaw against the sensation of touching a hundred velvet earthworms at once and said the final parting blessing.

"A final rest for all those that have lived." I didn't wait to see if it helped the ravenous energy around us, shooting to my feet and wiping my hands on my skirt. "We have to go."

"That was kind of you." Billy looked at me with a misplaced tenderness—as if I'd buried his childhood dog and not a midnight ghoul snack. I didn't respond, gripping his wrist and hauling him after me. "The town must love your dedication. Explains the complete lack of roadkill."

"As a member of a druidic family, my life is tied to the natural cycle of life on this earth. That includes death." I stood, rubbing dirt across my now filthy skirt. "It's part of my calling as both partial druid and hedge witch to help those who cannot finish their cycle, including returning their bones to the ground."

I felt Billy's eyes boring into me, felt him shifting closer to me.

"What does that mean for you and me?"

Not for the first time, I felt the impact of his words settle heavy over my shoulders.

"Have you ever held back a thought before speaking it?" I asked, turning to see him watching me so intently that the question nearly died in the air between us.

"I am a literal member of the undead," he said, shoving his hands in his pockets. His shredded shirt looked ridiculous, fluttering in the breeze. "Are you not called to bury me?"

I pointed to the dirt probing tendrils across the top of his shoes. "I'm not, but something is."

"I'd rather it were you."

"Terribly romantic, aren't we? Is that how you woo women in New York?"

"I'd put an unconscionable number of miles on my jet if it meant you were burying me when I was ready."

I shrugged out of my coat, flinging it over his shoulders as if he were a damsel in distress. "Come on, I need a drink."

"You're deflecting." But he grinned, slipping easily into the purple wool that was one of my favorites. I made a mental note not to let him run off with it. "I love it when a woman emotionally denies me. Really builds tension."

I didn't respond until we were back on the softly lit main road, shadows dusting each cobblestone, the bubbling laughter from the pub spilling out into the night around us. I hauled Billy behind me, feet moving automatically toward the warm building that promised a pint and a little relief.

But first things first.

I stopped dead, whirling around to face Billy, immediately wishing I hadn't. He'd been so close behind me, we were now nose-to-nose under a streetlamp. Our breath ghosted up around us and it wasn't the cold, wet air that sent a shiver across my skin.

"Yes?" It was not so much a question as a breath across my lips.

"I forgot."

"Good," he said, and then he kissed me. But this was not the hungry, desperate kiss of someone giving in to temptation, nor the teasing kiss it had been before, the sort meant to draw me into a promised heat. This was relief given lips; a sigh turned physical, a gentle taste of reassurance that two people who cared for each other had survived something and yes, yes, *here.* Here they were in one piece.

When he pulled away, there was something new in his strange, crimson gaze, and as much as I wanted to sink into it and let it carry me away to shores unknown, I knew I couldn't.

Not yet.

"You need to tell me about the ghoul."

"Yes," he sighed. "I do."

Chapter Twenty-Nine

BILLY

"So, a ghoul is a snack mistake?" Leslee stared at me over the top of her second pint, frothy and bubbling as the pub's guests jostled around us. Neighbors called to one another, friends hugged, and someone's uproarious laughter drifted over the top like thunder in a storm.

"Are you sure this is the best place to have this conversation?" I glanced nervously at the ruddy-necked villagers, quickly shedding their coats and scarves as the room heated with bodies. "Shouldn't we go someplace more private?"

Leslee rolled her eyes as if I'd asked why water was wet. She jerked her head toward the table next to us, where two men played cards. Their faces were solemn, pulled down at the corners by grizzled grey beards, beady eyes peeking out from wool caps.

"That's Jim and John," she said. "They're brothers who come to play cards every night. Jim stole John's girl back in the day, so John gets his by sleeping with her still."

My face dropped, and I felt my stomach lurch. "Leslee, easy," I gasped. But she didn't so much as blush, lifting her pint and putting on an award-winning smile.

"Ah, John and Jim!" She nodded in their direction, lifting her glass higher. Only then did the two men glance up briefly, tipping their caps before returning to the game.

"Incredible." They couldn't be more than a foot away from us.

"Ashbourne is a place of habit." Leslee set her pint down, licking the foam from her top lip. "And no groove is worn deeper than the one that leads to the pub. If I were you, I'd be more worried about people seeing me with that drink than discussing ghoul science."

I let my fingers hover protectively around the mug of prosecco I'd been nursing. The bartender had managed to dig up a sparkling wine from the back, wiping a considerable amount of dust from the surface before popping the cork, looking confused, and dumping the contents into a mug I guessed was usually reserved for hot whiskeys.

"I told you, I'm a texture person."

Leslee flashed me a mischievous grin before pushing a rogue curl from her face and settling into her seat, leaning her arms on the table.

"So. Ghouls?"

I couldn't help the nervous glance over my shoulder, but it only confirmed what Leslee had demonstrated—we could've been on an island alone for all the attention we were getting.

"From what I can tell, a ghoul is created when a vampire doesn't drain a victim to death and doesn't offer them sire blood to change. They become some kind of in-between thing—immortal and bloodthirsty like a vampire, but animalistic. They're completely lost to their primal urges."

"Who made this one?"

I glanced away, unsure how to start or continue my story. The beginning seemed too painful, the end too short.

"When I asked if the ghoul was your problem, you said, 'It is, and it isn't.'" Leslee prompted. A round of cheers went up from the bar, and I noticed the single, tiny TV above the liquor shelf was playing a football game. Jim and John put their cards down and wandered closer, as did many other villagers in the room until some kind of gravitational pull had all warm bodies jostling each other for a view.

"What did you mean?"

Of course, a determined witch passionate about her village's safety wouldn't let this go. And why should she?

"I was there the night the ghoul was created," I said, choosing my words carefully. "But I was not the one who created it. I believe it was a mistake entirely, as the vampire who sired me had been on a mission that went wrong. I don't think he would've left the manor grounds so quickly if he thought Huxley was still alive."

Leslee's jaw dropped. "That *thing* is a Huxley?"

"Not a. *The*."

"That's impossible. He'd be—"

"200 years old," I said, spreading my arms out wide and grinning. "Death day twins."

Leslee took a long drink of her beer before crossing her arms and leaning back in her seat.

"So that's why it's your problem?"

"That's why it isn't."

Another round of cheers filled the pub, drowning us in sticky, sweaty joy. Someone's jostled beer sloshed onto our table, mixing with my mug of wine. I knew I was making a face as I shoved it away. Leslee's tinkling laughter was quickly swallowed by more cheering. I wished my hearing had the ability to isolate a track like a sound engineer just to pull her bell-like joy from the cacophony around us to be savored and cherished.

"So why is it?"

I shook my head, lost in the maze of freckles on her face.

"Hullo, Billy?" She waved a cheeky hand in front of my face. "Why is the ghoul your problem?"

"I came back, fifty years later, to get rid of it."

She arched her eyebrows, waiting.

The mausoleum.

"I didn't do a very good job."

"Well, yes, that's clear." She finished her pint, launching herself up from the table and into the throng of bodies. She returned mere moments later with a fresh pint. Resettling herself at the table, she took a sip before fixing her bright gaze back on me.

"And the boys, tell me what this has to do with them."

"You mean the fanglings?"

There again, her laughter, spilling from her mouth like fresh rain, and I couldn't quite hear it, swallowed by a very obscene conversation about the football ref's mother.

"That's what they're called? Fanglings?"

"Young vampires are, yes."

"When do they grow out of that phase?"

I shrugged. "My sire didn't stay through my fangling years, and I knew few other vampires to teach me anything. I don't know much about the details of vampirism other than my own experience."

"So, you don't know if the ghoul did anything to turn the boys?"

I shook my head solemnly. I didn't know anything about ghouls other than their accidental creation, and that was mostly due to Gabriel's rushed explanation that fateful night in the stables.

"I have someone I can ask." Though I hesitated to call Dies-well yet again. I wasn't in the mood to hear one of his antiquated insults or talk about that damned minivan.

"That's what gets me more than anything." Leslee leaned forward, one hand gripping her beer, the other jabbing the table for emphasis.

"Six boys! Boys! *Children*! Their lives will never continue the way they wanted, and they had no choice in the matter. Poor Alex..." She let the thought drop, staring down at the table as if an answer might appear there.

"You're close with them." It wasn't a question so much as a revelation.

"Janice has been my neighbor a long time." Leslee sighed. "Since she moved here from Glasgow. Not everyone in Ashbourne was nice to the family at first. I know what it's like to get shoved to the edges of a place like this. It's painfully lonely when everyone else is tight-knit, and you're still on the skein, waiting."

"Cause you're a witch."

She laughed, finally looking back up at me. She pulled her phone from her pocket and tapped a few times before showing me the screen. A stunning woman with long, straight black hair and porcelain skin radiated demurely at the camera. Her long, strong limbs were draped elegantly around a cartoonishly short, stout older man with a pronounced wart on his nose. He was smiling with yellowed teeth and a bristling salt-and-pepper mustache. They both looked radiantly happy.

"Because the entire village thought Dad married a hooker after he knocked her up. They refused to believe anything else was possible."

"They're...quite the pair."

"And I was the product of that supposed marriage of ill-repute. It wasn't until Tyler chose me for his football team at school that I had any friends."

"That's the guy who—"

"I don't want to talk about him." She wiped furiously at her face. I took her free hand in mine and ran my fingers across her knuckles. She squeezed back before tilting her head to the door.

I followed Leslee through the press of bodies, spilling out into the chill night air as if we'd been birthed and the pub was the too-small, too-warm womb.

Leslee stretched her arms and yawned wide.

"Well, that's it for me." She looped her arm through mine, falling into an easy step toward the hotel. "I've been Business Leslee until I was back to Witch Leslee, and now I am Sleepy Leslee. We'll have to figure out how to help you do a better job killing ghouls tomorrow."

"Leslee, you don't have to—"

"Don't," she sighed, leaning her head on my shoulder and squeezing my arm. "Let me change the subject. I'm exhausted."

I tilted my head so that it rested on the pillow of her curls.

"Whatever the lady wishes."

Back at the hotel, Leslee slid into bed still clothed. Her quiet snores came a moment later, and I settled into some of the work I'd promised Rye.

My phone vibrated, rattling the table like nails on a chalkboard and hauling me violently from the best focus I'd had in the last week.

I recognized the building lead's name as I answered, glancing at the clock to see it was barely 4:30 a.m.

"Sorry to bother you, Mr. Barlow." Something sounded off. "But I've been trying to reach you since yesterday."

"Is everything alright?"

He sighed heavily and that was when I realized there were no other sounds coming from his end of the line—no men yelling, no bulldozers beeping, no tumbling piles of rocks and dirt.

"'Fraid not, sir," he said. "Two of my men went missing yesterday."

"That's terrible," I said, slipping into the bathroom and clicking the door closed. "Have you alerted the police?"

"Yes, but they didn't have much to do," he said. "My team found their bodies last night. Looked like some wild animal mangled them."

The ghoul. Realization slid through my bones like an icy current, dragging a wave of guilt close behind it.

I pulled the phone from my ear and tapped across the screen, bringing up my call log and texts. Sure enough, there were several missed calls and a few terse texts from the man on the phone.

Had I been so absorbed in settling my own emotional turmoil that I hadn't heard the phone go off?

"I'm so sorry, Collin," I said, sure that the words wouldn't convey the truth of it. "I'd like to contact the families and ensure they're taken care of."

"That's kind of you sir, but it will only solve one of your problems."

"What do you mean?"

"No one will return to the manor," he said. "My men all quit immediately and—"

"I'll double their pay."

"—I'm afraid there's no amount of money could make them risk the same end."

I groaned loudly, clamping a hand over my mouth and listening for any movement on the other side of the door. Nothing.

"I understand," I said, running a hand over my face. "I'll need to meet with my team and regroup. I'd prefer to continue working with you if possible."

"Not much scares me these days," he said. "Except my wife, and she's with her sister for the winter."

"I'll see about hiring you a new team," I said.

"You'll have to pay for travel," he said. "I doubt anyone who lives nearby will take the offer."

"Of course, of course."

"And sir?" He hesitated before letting out another sigh. "You'll need to have a think about what you'll tell the town council."

"Yes, I suppose I will."

Chapter Thirty

INTERLUDE

Ashbourne, 1873

The manor sat empty. A thick layer of grime coated the flatware left out in the kitchen, abandoned mid-bite when the young stable hand had thrown open the back door and announced that the master of the house was dead. That same floor he had stumbled over, clutching hands over his ears as every pair of feet in the house seemed to thunder at once—down the stairs, across the creaking floorboards, slamming out the door and into the crisp night air. That same floor was rotting through, gaping holes revealing the dirt beneath. The ceilings that had echoed a few whoops of joy at the news the stable hand had delivered were now sagging and dangerous, threatening to drop at any moment.

There was no structure to echo how the stable hand had flinched as if everything was too loud for him—unnaturally loud.

No one had noticed how pale he seemed. No one had noticed the color shifting in his eyes from blue to deep red. No one had noticed the sharp cut of his teeth and the way his mouth looked freshly full of blood—as if he'd taken a blow to the mouth a moment prior.

No one except the housekeeper and the little girl she still cradled by the fire.

Of course, that was fifty years ago now, and the little girl was now an old woman—much older than her adoptive mother had been when she'd taken her hand and walked her out of the fine manor house, never to return.

No one else had the sense to shut and lock the front door behind them, but the housekeeper did. And then she had unhooked the key from her belt and flung it far into the dirt.

The little girl didn't remember much from that night except the way the housekeeper had never once looked over her shoulder as they left the only home she'd ever known.

So, she had followed suit, refusing to glance back.

It was strange to her, at the ripe age of fifty-four, that now was when she should find her mind wandering to the manor. She kept waking at the stroke of midnight, wandering to the window as if in a trance, and staring up the village's main road to where the gates bared their rusted teeth. The place remained empty for the past fifty years. No one wanted anything to do with cursed land formerly inhabited by a cruel madman.

The girl-now-woman would stare at those gates, imagining what the manor must look like now. Surely, the carpet would have mold, the fine patterns stained and destroyed by hungry little plants. She imagined mushrooms growing in the cracks of the walls, reaching up to the cobweb-strung chandeliers as if in praise, and she imagined peeling wallpaper and stained walls leading along the stairwell and hallway until she reached what she thought was her old bedroom.

And then her husband would call her from the bedroom— "Matilda, not again, come back to bed" —and her imaginings would vanish. She never remembered them after, which she thought was odd. It was as if they were inserted directly into her brain and just as easily removed.

Of course, she never told her husband that part.

Then, Matilda had a very strange night.

She woke at midnight, just as she had before, but this time something was different.

This time, a voice spoke to her. It beckoned her forward, past the hall window where she usually looked out at the moon and down the stairs. It pulled her out the front door and into the cold night, barefoot in her dressing gown.

The voice seemed familiar, but she couldn't place how she knew it. Had she dreamed the voice as well?

Before she could stop her feet from carrying her away, she stood at the entrance to the old manor grounds, looking up at the thick, overhanging branches of the oaks lining the drive. A soft wind whispered through them, hissing and laughing above her.

Matilda knew this place too well to feel any fear. She had been born in that house and felt it call to her every night of her life away from it. But she hesitated.

The housekeeper who raised her—a woman she simply called Mum—had warned her never to return.

"Some evils will only stay gone if left to rot," she'd said one night when it was just them two in front of the fire, nursing whiskey in teacups. "Leave well enough alone, and don't go getting nosey, or there'll be trouble for it."

The voice called again, and Matilda felt herself moving forward. There, in the flickering shadows, just at the edge of the trees, was a pinch-faced man in a fine suit.

"Papa?" she whispered. She'd never known her father other than a few blurry memories, but the voice whispered to her that, yes, she was right; this was her father. He'd come for her at last. Confusion, relief, and grief all welled up in her chest as she stumbled forward at a faster pace. The stones and freezing earth bit into the soft souls of her feet, but still, she began to run.

"Papa? Is that you? Finally?" All those days at school as a child, isolated and lonely because no one would befriend the cruel man's daughter. All those times as a young new bride, desperate for a sewing circle or someone to trade gardening tips with, only to find cold shoulders and hard stares in return. All for coming from a man she'd never known.

She'd had to answer for his sins while lacking the presence of a father of her own—a twofold punishment for a single innocent soul.

And still, she felt joy at this strange-faced, tight-lipped man standing at the end of the trees. He held his arms out to her, a slow smile spreading as she reached him.

Before he could fold her into his waiting embrace, a shot rang out. The man transformed before her eyes, lengthening, stretching, cracking, screaming. He became a gaunt ghoul with bleeding eyes and bat-like ears. His mouth hung open as if cracked and forgotten, drooping along his chest. Two monstrous fangs hung from his jaw, slick with saliva and a strange-smelling substance Matilda didn't want to know more about.

She screamed and stumbled back, unable to tear her gaze from the monster she'd nearly touched.

"You're supposed to be dead." A cool, calm voice called from over her shoulder. The monster flexed its many-jointed arms in rage and let loose another shriek. Matilda could see it was bleeding from its chest, the color a startling deep brown.

A second shot rang out, and Matilda screamed as it collided with the monster, sending a spray of dark brown blood all over her dressing gown. This time, the monster fled, sending out one final shriek before it was lost from sight.

Strong hands gripped her shoulders and turned her away from where the monster had been, leading her back down the path and onto the main village road. Once they were a safe distance away, the stranger stopped and turned Matilda to face him.

A strange sense of having been here before, of having seen this man before, washed over her. It was more than the trance she had been under, more than thinking she saw her father. This was undoubtedly real and not the result of a voice whispering in her mind.

She looked into the crimson eyes peering down kindly at her and whispered, "I know you."

The man nodded slowly, a strange look on his face. "You do," he said. "Though I'm surprised you remember."

"The horse man," she said.

He huffed a soft laugh, a half-smile cracking his handsome face. Matilda was suddenly very aware of standing in the street barefoot in her dressing gown with a strange man.

"Stable hand," he said. "But you called me the horse man."

"I need to sit down." Matilda swayed on her feet. The stable hand—Billy, his name was Billy—gripped her shoulders and gave her a light shake.

"I know it's a lot for you right now," he said. "But your father has turned into a ghoul. He won't stop coming after you until he is killed. I need your help to capture him so the village can be at peace."

Matilda nodded dumbly as she listened to Billy's instructions. Perhaps this was all another strange dream that she would wake from soon. And if that was the case, best to see where it all led.

After a short hour, Matilda returned home, roused her husband, and changed into warm clothes. Then, they gathered bricks from the garden and a few spare trowels, pushing their offering up the main road in a wheelbarrow.

Matilda's husband grumbled the entire time, but she'd promised if he did this, she'd never wake in the night again. At least, she hoped the monster had been the cause of all this strangeness.

They reached the old manor graveyard as the moon began to hang heavy in the sky, sinking slowly toward its setting point to make way for the sun. Billy was waiting, leaning casually on a large spade, his long coat fluttering in the wind. He looked like some kind of heroic graverobber, Matilda thought. What a story that would be.

Billy introduced himself to her husband with a firm handshake and some muttered manly greeting before explaining to them both how Matilda would need to lure the monster into the old mausoleum so Billy could chain him there. Then, the three would work quickly to brick him inside so he could never escape again.

It reminded Matilda too much of a poem she'd read in the paper not so long ago. It was dark and eerie, and she couldn't believe something so macabre would get printed.

Matilda wasn't eager to dangle herself like a worm on a hook, but she got no sympathy from her husband as he practically shoved her into the dark of the burial chamber.

"Don't worry," Billy said, though she wasn't sure how he ended up behind her. "I'm right here. I won't let anyone hurt you."

She thought it was strange, the way he said that—as if there was more than one threat that night. But she believed him, and she took comfort in knowing that he'd saved her from the monster once already in the same night. Surely, he could do it again.

It didn't take long for the shuffling steps of the monster to sound in the dead leaves outside. Matilda wondered where the creature had gone since she'd seen it last. For it to have appeared so suddenly would mean it couldn't have gone far. Or maybe it hadn't left at all, and had simply been watching them from the shadows.

She shuddered, a soft gasp escaping as she did so, and this seemed to draw the monster's attention.

The creature appeared in the doorway, silhouetted by the fading moonlight. Matilda could see that it was nothing but tendons and flesh, its lines stretched and exaggerated. She wondered if it hurt to exist so wrong.

Before she could ponder whether killing this monster was a mercy to it or the village, the creature moved like lightning. She threw her arms across her face instinctually, although she couldn't see the thing at all in the dark, and she screamed as its hot, fetid mouth hung barely an inch from her face. But that seemed to be all it was doing. It never got any closer.

It thrashed and screamed, and Matilda heard the rattling of chains and a loud grunt from Billy.

"*Go,*" he commanded, and she forced her legs to carry her from the burial chamber. Once outside, she motioned to her husband to bring the bricks. They began laying the ground layer, mixing up a thick mud and paste to layer on top before adding more bricks.

Matilda tried to block out the sound of the monster shrieking, of Billy's grunted cries of occasional pain and frustration. She kept glancing up to see if the moon would finally angle enough to let her know what was truly happening, but the light in the sky refused.

Finally, when the bricks were about waist high, Billy appeared in the doorway. He was bedraggled and sweating, his fine coat shredded in multiple places. A gash bled on his forehead, and a large bruise bloomed on his jaw.

"Wonderful work," he said with a clap of his hands. He pushed himself over the half-wall and landed lightly on his feet between the husband and wife. "I'm afraid those chains weren't as new as I thought, so we're going to need to speed this up."

He grabbed one of the trowels and began bricking at an almost inhuman speed—three laid for every one Matilda and her husband could finish. They finished hours of work in a matter of minutes.

Billy wiped his brow on the back of his sleeve and let out an exaggerated sigh, setting the trowel back in the wheelbarrow.

"Alright," he said, planting his hands on his hips and looking at the new wall like a proud gardener surveying his hedges. "That should do it."

He pointed two serious fingers at Matilda and her husband.

"Don't let anyone come here and mess with this. Tell no one what happened here tonight, and if anyone asks, things are bricked up for safety reasons. We don't need those interested in spirits and mayhem to accidentally let anything loose."

"Hey, you said—" Billy clapped a friendly hand aggressively to her husband's shoulder.

"Look at me, friend," he said, and Matilda watched her husband's face grow slack as he gazed into Billy's strange crimson eyes.

"Your wife is an angel sent to earth to love you," he said. "The earth is blessed for the touch of her step every morning, and you wish you could be the dirt she shovels. You worship her like she makes the sun rise and set each day, and you love her as if you would die if you didn't." When Billy let her husband go, he turned to her, slightly dazed. She waited, holding her breath, unsure what had just happened.

"Tildy, sweetheart," he said, using the nickname she hadn't heard since they were courting. "You must be freezing. Here." He shrugged out of his coat and wrapped it carefully around her shoulders. He put an arm around her as if he would guide her away from the strange scene they had created and back to the safety of their home. From the corner of her eye, she caught Billy striding off in the opposite direction.

"Wait!" she called, and Billy paused, turning to her with an arched eyebrow. The barest hint of dawn was beginning to tint the sky, and she noticed a tension in his body that hadn't been there prior. "Did you kill him? Or, uh, it, I guess?"

Billy shook his head. "No. He'll live in that tiny, empty stone box until he either breaks free or starves to death. And given how long his kind live, it'll take a long time to starve."

"That's so cruel," Matilda gasped, horrified. Not even a monster deserved such a fate.

Billy shrugged.

"He should've thought of that before he killed my fucking horse."

Chapter Thirty-One

Leslee

I woke up with a luxurious stretch, palms skimming across the soft sheets in a wide arc, the emptiness of the bed nudging the sleeping disappointment in my stomach. I turned my head, pushing a cascade of curls out of my face.

Oh, right. Of course he wasn't in bed with me. Not even a weekend spent ghoul hunting would change that. *You made a pact with the universe, you dumb git.*

Stretching across the plush blankets, I bent over the side, peering under the bed. As expected, there was the familiar white-blond hair sprouting from the dirt. I could smell the dampness of it and wondered if he'd brought in a fresh pile.

Pulled by curiosity, I crawled off the bed, landing as quietly as I could on the floor. I reached a questing hand beneath the bed, a spike of adrenaline chilling my system. A flash of a horror movie stilled my hand—raging eyes, bloody fangs, my wrist in their vise.

"It's not like the movies, Leslee," I whispered, pushing my hand further and dipping a curious finger into the dirt. Sure enough, it was cool and damp, as if it had come fresh from the forest floor—or the grave. I remembered what Mum had told me about vampires needing to sleep in their grave dirt every day, or they'd lose all their inhuman strength.

I rubbed a dirt clod between my finger and thumb, finding the texture not unpleasant, and wondered if Mum had made it back to the village. It had been a few days since we last spoke and she'd sounded ready to come home on the phone. Maybe she could help me get my business launch in line after this job, when Billy headed back to the states, and I could get my focus back from whatever we were doing.

Another cry from the coiled disappointment in my gut had me snatching my hand back and pushing off the floor in almost the same motion.

So what if Billy left—he was *always* going to leave. He'd made that quite clear. And he'd likely be leaving after the town council approved his plans—he didn't need to be on-site to manage the project. He had hired capable people for that, myself included.

"I'd put an unconscionable number of miles on my jet if it meant you were burying me when I was ready."

He'd said that—not so many hours ago.

"Stupid, stupid girl." I rubbed my eyes so the tears didn't fall. I'd let myself get wrapped up in loneliness and allowed a hot vampire to suck me into his orbit—even as his path was quickly diverting from mine.

Maybe Tyler had been right. Maybe I wasn't cut out to do this alone.

"Shut up," I hissed to no one. "If that's not enough to knock some sense into you, I don't know what is." I grabbed yesterday's clothes from where I'd left them thrown over the back of a chair and clicked the bathroom door shut behind me.

This would all be better after a scorching hot shower and a cup of tea.

Naturally, I didn't notice Billy's note until I was halfway out the door, only doubling back to the nightstand to look for an aquamarine necklace I'd forgotten.

The hotel stationary was folded into a small card so that it stood on the nightstand. Billy's loopy scrawl, in all caps, asked for my attention.

"LESLEE—DO NOT GO TO MANOR. WILL TALK LATER."

The manor hadn't been on my list for the day, but now it was. Errands and a supply run in town could wait.

But first, there absolutely needed to be tea.

At the kitchen's threshold, I paused, careful not to cross the entry lest I irk Reginald and be out tea altogether. I called out first a hello and then his name. A long-suffering sigh sounded behind me, and I jumped, whirling around to find the hall still empty.

But had that door always been there? And who had left it cracked open?

In a few bold steps, I threw the door open, expecting a janitor's closet and finding, instead, the ever-sour Reginald.

He was perched with his knees tucked into his chest, back pressed against the wall—as if he had been folded before being put away. Butting against his raised shins was a tiny wooden desk that had clearly been shoved in the space with brute strength—Ford, I guessed—given the massive gouges in the wall that fit the edge of the desk perfectly.

"Good morning," I said as brightly as I could muster.

"Is it?"

"Is what?"

He sighed again, rolling his eyes so hard I worried they'd break free of his wrinkled head.

"Is it a good morning?"

"It will be once you've made tea for us both," I said.

Another hissing sigh breathed life into my dormant anger.

I popped a hip, planting a firm hand on my waist, the other pressing a commanding wide arm into the door. I held that door handle like it was my victory flag, and I planted it into the battle mound.

"Reginald," I said, hoping my voice sounded imperious. I lifted my chin, attempting to stare down my nose at him and finding it wasn't sloped enough to provide much aim. "I will take my tea, *now*."

I held his gaze, willing his folded body to move, willing my power stance to intimidate him into action where my polite efforts had not been enough.

Slowly, like a sleeping spring waking after a long winter, a bubbling, hysterical sound burst from his mouth. His eyes crinkled at the edges and his yellow teeth flashed beneath his stained lips. It took several more seconds for me to realize he was *laughing* at me.

My shoulders drooped as I watched his laughter grow louder and more raucous until the entire closet shook around him, jostling his still-folded form loose so that he popped out like a stuck penny in a slot, landing on the carpet with a thud. With more giggling, his limbs shook loose until, finally, he was splayed at my feet like a disgusting gingerbread cookie.

"Are you quite finished?"

Unfortunately, this set off another round of raucous laughter, which he fought against, forcing himself onto all fours and crawling past me to the kitchen, where his continuing guffaws bounced off the laminate flooring.

Not the start to the day I wanted.

***

As I neared the manor, I noticed more and more people on the street, muttering to each other and pointing. My stomach sank when I saw the gates were completely blocked by police cars. Blue flashed in the overcast light, and I could see each puff of breath from the officers talking seriously with one another.

"Excuse me, what's happened?" I asked, running toward the front entrance. A thick-necked fellow with crooked teeth stopped me.

"Sorry, miss, no one is allowed onto the property. Police business," he said.

"Yes, I can see that. I'm working here and need through." Reginald's laughter echoed through my head as I tried my best to stick out my chin and straighten my shoulders.

"This is an active investigation," he said, shaking his head.

"Into what?" I tried to breathe royal haughtiness into my tone. I sounded constipated.

The officer simply shook his head and gestured for me to head back the other way.

I remembered Billy's note warning me away from the manor and wondered if he knew something about all this. Probably. And here I was, charging ahead as if I knew better.

I glanced over my shoulder at the sleek edges of the hotel rising above the thatched village rooftops.

No. I could get to the bottom of this myself—and peek at the back of the mansion landscape while I was at it. I remembered something about stables that were planned for demolition in the back, and I had a hunch that Billy wouldn't oppose any plans for their reuse.

I headed along the iron fence bordering the estate, trying not to glance at the wicked spiked bars scratching the sky. I made a mental note to find a less menacing replacement for the manor's future.

I followed the fence line, nodding to the second group of officers idly chatting with each other at the far end of the block from the main entrance. They nodded back and didn't seem to mind my purposeful gait as I turned the corner and slammed a hand over my mouth to keep from shouting in glee.

The fence line ended amid an impenetrable tangle of thick tree trunks and unruly bushes, the spiked blackberry vines bare and formidable this time of year. You'd need a chainsaw to get through—or a magic touch.

I practically sprinted to the massive linden tree casting an imposing shadow over the far side, thrusting my hand forward as if reaching for a long-awaited celebrity handshake. The bark bit into my palm, and I immediately felt the connection open. This linden, unlike the sleeping ancestors at the entryway, was awake and alert.

I need your help. I must pass by you to enter the grounds.

In answer, I heard the mighty groaning of hundreds of years of trunk and bark and growth bending and twisting. When I opened my eyes, the linden had pushed back from the fence line just enough to allow me to slip between it and the final iron bar. I did so without looking back and not a moment too soon. The second my feet landed on the manor grass, the trunk made a groaning return to its former position.

My hand had stayed firmly in place the entire time, so I bowed my head in thanks.

Careful, the Linden whispered as I dropped my palm.

The warning chilled me more than anything the Ancestors had said. Lindens were not guardians like oaks or providers like maples and walnuts. They often had little to say about their bipedal relatives. To receive a warning from a linden was to enter dangerous territory indeed.

I took a deep breath and turned my back to the fence. I made it to the other side—might as well do what I came for, regardless of the hairs on the back of my neck standing straight up.

From where I stood, I could see the rising swell of the hill that separated this side of the manor grounds from the main house. At the base was the family cemetery plot and beyond that were the Ancestors, standing still and silent. I could just make out the various uniforms flashing through the gaps in their trunks. The officers seemed to be searching intently for something, and it wasn't until I saw the unmistakable white bulk of a body bag winking through the dark wood that I realized it wasn't a "what" they were looking for but a "who."

"Maybe I *should* go," I whispered to myself. But the more stubborn part of me refused. I'd come to get work done—okay, and to satisfy the nosey need to know what Billy wasn't telling me. Tyler would've charmed his way through the police barricade in minutes in order to complete a project. I'd made it through on my own terms, and I wouldn't let a little potential murder make me turn back now.

"I might be insane," I muttered as I made my way toward the hill, dew from the grass collecting along the hem of my skirt. I imagined I was a general riding into a losing battle, ignoring all strategy and advice from his command and letting intuition carry me into the dangerous, unknowable fight before me.

This bolstered me for the fifteen minutes it took to arrive at the base of the hill. Not even my imagination could quell the cold tendrils of fear that yanked my stomach to my feet when I saw the mausoleum.

I am not squeamish when it comes to death. Death is a part of the natural order of things, and its machinations make for fantastic fertilizer. Nutrients and minerals give back to the earth so that something fresh and new may grow tall beneath the sun. So it wasn't the gravestones rising around me; some monuments taller than I was and cast in shadow despite the overcast day. It wasn't the bodies beneath my feet I could feel decomposing when I reached my sense out. It wasn't the very real, very recent death flashing white between the trunks of the Ancestors.

It was the mausoleum—or what was left of it anyway.

From where I stood, I could see toppled brick and stone, shattered and crushed as if something had exploded out from it. Carefully picking my way closer through the debris, I noticed more and more claw marks along the sides of the brickwork, as if a creature's desperation—not their tinderbox—had forced open the entry.

Stopping before the entrance, I realized the bricks destroyed around me starkly contrasted with the solemn grey marble the rest of the building was made of. A chilling thought nagged at me, and sure enough, when I peeked around the side of the monument, I saw the same brick as the entrance solidly and thoroughly pressed against any windows or decorative openings as if someone wanted to ensure *no one* could ever peek in.

Or no one could get out.

"What happened here?" I breathed, reaching a curious hand toward the shattered entry as if I could feel the history of the place by touching the air.

"Oh, duh," I smacked a hand to my forehead. The air couldn't tell me, but the trees could. I glanced around, spotting a bent, gnarled old tree, bereft of leaves so that its crooked branches scratched at the sky. It looked dead, but I knew how deep a tree's life could hide while waiting out hard times. Trees were known to bloom after forest fires, floods, earthquakes, famine—anything that would wipe humans off the planet, a tree would weather just fine by turning inward and waiting.

Mum always told me to take a leaf from a tree's patience in the face of chaos, but waiting had clearly never been my strong suit.

The not-dead-dead-looking tree had a clear view of the mausoleum, making it a perfect eyewitness. All I had to do was get it to talk.

I placed my palm on its bark, feeling the bumps and knots of abnormal growth periods pressing back against my skin. I closed my eyes and focused, pushing my energy into the tree.

Please, I need your help.

Before I could ask my question, I was plunged into a whistling darkness. Shadows whipped around me, pushing through me with icy screams before being swallowed by the dark. I tried to pull my hand away but couldn't. The tree had swallowed it, a pulsing, ashen bark now swallowing my fingers, climbing rapidly up my skin to my wrist. I tried to scream, but my voice died in my throat, my mouth clamping shut with someone else's power.

Watch, little one. The tree's voice in my head was bursting with rage, each word cut at the end with jagged teeth and a hiss.

A red light in the dark pulled my gaze away from my entrapped hand, and I saw the mausoleum—not as it was, I realized, but as it had been before the bricks. Shadowy figures came into the light, their features slowly materializing. A woman, dressed in simple clothes from long ago, worked feverishly to lay cement and bricks in a slowly stacking wall. Her sleeves were pushed up to her elbows, and her hair clung damp around her face. A man worked next to her, and I thought for a moment he was the officer who had stopped me at the entrance. A second look told me he must be an ancestor to that man—they had the same uninterested gaze, the same thick neck on square shoulders.

A blur of movement above both the shadowy workers caught my attention. It seemed to be laying bricks at an inhuman speed, flickering in and out of focus like a hummingbird in the spring. Finally, the blur stopped long enough to wipe its brow, and I recognized Billy immediately. He was dressed well for the time period but looked identical to his modern-day self—as if he hadn't aged a day.

Natural, for a vampire, but startling none the less.

As I watched, he and the others finished bricking up the front entry and continued the windows. Inhuman shrieks tore the air, scratching through any crack left unbricked. The woman and the man would pause and glance at each other in those moments, waiting for it to end. But Billy continued unphased.

When every hole was bricked over, they all stopped and stood back to survey their work. They seemed to be talking to each other, but I couldn't hear what was said. Billy clapped a hand good-naturedly on the man's shoulder and the man gave the woman his coat, the woman's stricken face never changing.

It dawned on me then, the realization as slow and horrifying as the torture I'd just seen enacted.

They'd bricked in a living creature to that mausoleum and then left it—to die, to wither, to suffer.

To wait, the tree hissed. *Now, it is free.*

The black swarmed, extinguishing the red light in a pulsating dark cloud and pushing my hand away from the trunk.

I stepped back into wet grass, the overcast morning blinding. I clutched my hand to my chest and stared at the tree, whirling over my shoulder to check that no screaming monsters were crawling from the destroyed mausoleum.

The ghoul had been left there to suffer.

And Billy was the one to leave it.

Chapter Thirty-Two

BILLY

"*What did you do?*"

I blinked up at the angry voice towering over me. I seemed to be flat on the floor, but I couldn't figure out why or how.

Rubbing my face, I sat up, giving in to the massive stretch and yawn that took over my entire body.

"What time is it?" I asked and immediately regretted it when the response was a resounding smack to the face.

"Time for answers."

I barely recognized the voice and was startled when I could finally focus on the figure.

"Why do you keep smacking me?" I asked Leslee, rubbing my sore cheek as I stood from my grave dirt. Best guess was she hauled it—and me—out from beneath the bed.

"Rule of threes," she snapped. Her arms were crossed over her chest, and her eyes blazed with a rage I'd never seen before. The set of her jaw and the intensity in her face were, unfortunately, a huge turn-on—she seemed more likely to punch me again than to accept any advances. Somehow, this made it hotter.

The nightstand clock said it was 10 a.m., which explained the drained feeling in my bones—I'd barely rested for a few hours.

"You know I'm technically a monster," I said, gesturing weakly to my chest and brushing against the royal blue satin pajamas I'd chosen that morning. "Waking me like this could result in your death."

"Is that a promise?" A muscle twitched in her jaw and I had to fight the urge to drop to my knees and do whatever she commanded next.

"A lot of women have been angry with me in my time, but you wear it the best of them all."

I caught her hand this time as it sang through the air.

"Leslee," I said, more seriously this time. "What is this about?'

"You tell me," she snarled as I caught her other hand mid-air. I made sure I was holding her firm but loose, careful not to sprain anything as she twisted in my grasp. "Does bricking a living creature into a tomb ring any bells?"

I dropped her arms and took a step back.

"You couldn't possibly know about that."

"But you don't deny it." Her shoulders heaved with each breath, eyes red and watery. She leveled a shaking finger at me. "You took this world's most sacred energy—a *living creature*—and you...you..."

A sob shook her as she covered her face. I deserved the shame that threatened to swallow me whole. I deserved the guilt pulling me down like an earth-bound black hole.

"Leslee, please," I pleaded. "You don't understand, that creature was evil. It was hurting people. And—"

"And you never have?" She thrust her hands down to her sides, fists clenched. Her normally joyous freckled face was stone cold despite the hot tears running down the sides. "In your 200 years as 'technically a monster,' you've never hurt anyone?"

"I've hurt countless, but please, just listen—"

"Then I guess I have to brick you into this hotel room by your own logic."

"You make it sound like some gothic horror story." I could feel my own frustration rising, pushing back against the guilt and shame and fear. She hadn't been there.

No one had been there.

I'd had no other choice.

"He terrorized the village as a monster the same way he terrorized it as a man," I snapped. "And no one did anything until I came back and put an end to it."

"But you didn't!" She threw her hands in the air, voice shrill. "You didn't. You just tortured another living creature for a century—"

"And a half," I conceded.

"Unbelievable," she spat. "Absolutely unbelievable."

"He was slaughtering the people who lived here, and he would've done it until there was no one left. He didn't give a shit who he bled dry in life, and nothing changed when he turned." I took a step toward her, but she echoed the space, stepping back. She shook her head.

"Leslee, please, he deserved what he got."

"No one—nothing—deserves to suffer when a natural end is waiting."

"Nothing about our end is natural."

"You're right," she said. She put her hands up in the air and then pushed them out like she was shoving away spirits in the air. They dropped to her sides again as she let loose a huge sigh, her shoulders drooping, her head tilting back. When she looked at me again, there was a sadness in her face that gutted me—it would've been less painful if she'd smacked me again.

"The least I can do is give you one painless ending," she said. And I couldn't think of anything but the screaming inside my head as she turned on her heel toward the door. I couldn't think of anything but the dirt at my feet suddenly reaching for me again—like it hadn't in the days I'd spent with her. I couldn't think of anything but the ripping sensation in my chest, and before her hand was on the knob, I was on her.

I gripped her shoulder and whirled her around, pulling her into my arms and pressing my mouth to hers. But unlike our first stolen kiss, this one continued.

She kissed me back, heat and rage and tears mixing on her tongue as it probed my mouth. I succumbed, parting my lips as she pushed her hands into my hair, fingernails raking along my scalp. Her tongue found my fangs, running along the edge, and I shuddered, heat running through my core like a thunderbolt.

I picked her up, pressing her into the wall by the door, and she wrapped her legs around my waist in response. The heat of her was directly against me as her skirt fell away, hitched up around her waist. I tasted along her neck, smelling the heat of her blood in her skin, my favorite temptation, a sacred denial.

Leveraging her against the wall, I reached one hand between her legs, knees nearly buckling when I felt the wet heat of her. She writhed against me, tugging on my hair and grinding into my hand. I worked her for a moment through her panties before slipping a questing finger past the fabric. The warmth of her made me groan, and she echoed me as I slid a finger along her cunt, circling the clit and savoring her gasp as she bucked against my hand.

She pulled my head back by the hair, angling her mouth over mine as I continued teasing her clit, flicking over it once as she pulled away.

"Worth it," she gasped out, eyes heavy with lust when she looked down at me. Her hair was a halo, pressed against the forest green of the wall, and a feverish blush kissed her skin beneath her glasses.

"Worth what?" I practically purred, pressing on her clit and sliding a finger in. Her cunt immediately clenched around me, hungry and ready. I was in pain, aching with the need to be inside her, but I wouldn't rush this.

"I don't fuck clients, remember?"

My mind was hazy with lust. I wasn't registering what she was saying as I slid in a second finger, curving it in a "come here" gesture that made her cry out.

"Seems like you're a rule breaker," I said, pressing my face back into her neck, lapping and sucking there, inhaling her heady scent, wishing I could freeze that moment full of sensations and desires.

"I'm not," she said between heavy breaths, clenching and unclenching around my fingers as I worked them in and out. She was hot and slick and driving me crazy. I felt myself grinding against her leg, desperate for some relief. "You won't be a client after this."

I disentangled myself from her neck and hair but continued working her cunt, taking in the full flush of her face, her eyes screwed shut in pleasure, mouth hanging slightly open as she let loose a satisfied sigh.

"You won't regret it?"

She opened her eyes, returning my stare, never breaking contact as she rode my hand harder. Another heated moment flashed across my eyes— *"I can't let you regret me."*

My life was too long to live with regret; to live with the shame and disappointment that I was someone's mistake. Some wounds were not healed with time—even an infinite amount.

"No," she said, voice sure and clear. "I won't regret my choice."

The words went straight to my cock, and it was more than I could take.

I slid my fingers free from her cunt and used a shaking hand to push my pants down, my cock springing free.

"Finally," she said, glancing down to eye me hungrily. Two-hundred years and more sexual partners than I could count, and *none* of them had ever made me blush—not just because it wasn't physically possible. But then I felt it. For the first time in centuries, a heat crept across my face, burning in my cheeks and up to the tips of my ears. Leslee noticed and immediately giggled, pressing a tender hand to the side of my face.

"Oh my gods," she teased, grinning wickedly. "How dainty." She considered me for a moment, cocking her head to the side. I stayed frozen in her bright gaze.

"And unexpected," she said, guiding my face to hers for a kiss that started gentle, teasing, and grew desperate, starved.

Tongues at war, her fist tangled in my hair, I lifted her against me again, turning us and stumbling to the couch. I laid her down gently, guiding her hips to rest on the arm of the couch so that her cunt was angled up to me but the rest of her could rest on the plush cushions.

I had not fed in days, unable to keep anything down that didn't immediately come back up clotted and foul. I could see the blood pulsing beneath her skin, thundering to her heartbeat's wild rhythm in her cunt. I barely held back a growl as I lowered myself between her legs, hooking a fang along her panties, not caring that they ripped immediately. I heard her breath hitch, felt her body clench as I carefully—but not too carefully—ran my bared fangs along her bare cunt. My instincts reared, pleading with me for just a taste of her sweet blood but I pushed them away. I would become a monster if my only taste of her was wasted as bile later. I would never return to my senses if I lost that to this strangeness that plagued me.

But...

"I have a thought," I said, planting quick kisses along her thighs. I was a man possessed, convinced that if I stopped touching her, she would vanish—this dream would end.

"I have a penny," she answered, pushing herself up on her elbows and cocking her head at me.

"Do you trust me?"

She gestured wordlessly to where I was practically snuggling her vagina, rubbing my face along her inner thigh like a seamstress who's just discovered velvet.

"My venom has an ecstasy effect," I said. "It will heighten your experience, if you like."

"Billy," she laughed. "Are you asking to suck my blood?"

"I'm asking to suck your cunt," I said, a wicked grin splitting my face. "I'm offering to get you high beforehand."

She considered me a moment and I watched the thoughts play across her face. My cock bobbed between my legs, desperate to continue our work.

"Alright," she said. "I'll try it. But if I don't like it..."

"It only lasts a few moments," I said. "If you're uncomfortable, say 'garlic' and we'll wait for the effects to wear off and check in."

"I love a man with a plan," she said, reaching up with one hand and pulling me across the couch arm to her. She kissed me ferociously and I nearly came from the contact of her dripping cunt against my bare cock. "But one condition," she said, words pressed against my waiting lips.

She could've asked for every penny in my bank account, my heart torn from my chest, my fangs in a jar, and I would've given it to her.

"Anything," I answered—a dangerous deal between magical folk.

"Don't suck me dry just yet," she said, nuzzling her nose against mine in what was surely a teasing gesture. "I still have to ride that glorious cock."

Am I in love?

Now was not the time for that question.

I could only nod, struck dumb by her request, and I watched her relax like a queen against the couch cushions, looking up at me with hungry, half-lidded eyes. I lowered myself to my knees, skimming my hands along her thighs until I found a good grip. I tried to force myself to savor the moment but the smell of her was more than I could resist and before I could think twice, my mouth was on her.

Chapter Thirty-Three

Leslee

I had expected it to hurt more when his teeth sunk into my thigh, but instead, a warm tingle climbed up my body, sparking in my cunt and my chest—as if he'd injected the stars into my veins and they were lighting up my body's sky.

I sighed, settling into the sensation, and watched as Billy's mouth worked up to my cunt, nipping and kissing at my inner thighs. Each kiss sent a fresh wave of starlight across me, growing brighter and brighter.

Holy shit, this is why people are obsessed with fucking vampires. It had to be.

My body arched, rising to meet Billy's ravenous mouth. He swirled, licked, sucked, and nipped at my cunt like a man who hasn't eaten in weeks and has been handed an entire roast chicken, steaming and hot from the oven. Every sweep of his tongue was a sensation tripled across my body, the pleasure so intense it was almost torturous.

It was all I could do to hold on, raking my nails across the upholstery as he flicked his tongue inside of me, his fangs raking lightly across the tender skin on either side. Heat built along my spine, the energy twisting and building until my bones shook, frantic for more.

Then, glancing up at me with eyes that seemed bigger than before, gaze entirely focused on my face, I felt a single fang glance across my clit with a delightful force that made me scream. The sharpness of it, the implied threat, the trust it took to enjoy all of this—it pushed me over the edge.

I came, white spots pinging across my vision like fairies from old cartoons. Once my eyes could focus again, I realized that I had both hands clamped to the back of Billy's head and was holding him in place between my legs.

"Oh, gods, sorry," I laughed, releasing him. He arched a wicked brow at me and licked his lips clean before grinning, fangs hanging low over his bottom lip. His red eyes, normally startling on a good day, were wider than normal, sucking in all the light in the room. I would fall into them if I wasn't careful.

When he stood, I could see his cock still standing straight, a throbbing vein bulging along the bottom. It made my mouth water, and I felt a fresh heat sweep through me before the feeling even returned to my legs. I was still full of delicious starlight and didn't want to move ever again if it meant shaking the night sky free of my limbs.

"Can you die from sex?" I asked.

"If I kill you, I can always bring you back." There was no joke in his voice, and a pleasant shiver ran through me. There were worse ways to go.

"But," he continued. "I'd much rather keep you alive. Take a moment, rest."

Before I realized what was happening, I found myself wrapped in bed, Billy tucked in next to me, his erection pressed into my thigh. It was as if, in one moment, he reached out to me, and instead of helping me up, he'd transported us.

"How the—"

"Vampire speed," he said, trailing his hands along my shoulders and up my neck to cup my face. "Human eyes can't process it."

"Or feel it," I said, enjoying his touch. I found myself trying to memorize every minute of this as if I could tuck away a perfect record of the way he was looking at me, the way he held me, so that when I walked away, at least I wouldn't leave entirely empty-handed.

I turned, rolling onto my side so I could see him, nose-to-nose, eye-to-eye.

"That bite must really be affecting me," I sighed, realizing a second too late I'd said it out loud. I really needed to stop talking to trees so much.

"Oh?" He brushed his thumb along my jaw.

Too late to back out now.

"I was just thinking how nice it would be if I didn't have to leave," I said. He tensed next to me, but his touch stayed gentle as ever, tracing lightly up and down the side of my face.

"You still don't have to," he said, the look in his eyes more than I could take.

"Yes, Billy, I do."

"You can't stay with me because of what I did." His voice was tight, his face pained. I wanted more than anything to soothe him, to wipe away that worry and guilt, to tell him I'd changed my mind.

"And because you'll leave at the end of this all anyway," I said. He seemed startled by the news, and a brief flash of hope buoyed me. "Right?"

He cleared his throat and looked at me thoughtfully. "If I'm able to, I will most likely return to my home in New York, yes." He picked his words carefully as if he were considering each one before placing them in front of me.

"Why wouldn't you be able to?"

He propped himself up on one elbow, looking down at me, something unreadable on his face. Those red, red eyes were luminous and soothing, like the open sign on a café when you've been caught in a downpour.

"For the first time in my long, long life, I may have met a woman I'm unable to let go."

I didn't know what to say. He meant it—I could see it in his face, read it in his voice. This vampire had been alive for centuries, and he was saying that I, Leslee the Perpetual Fuck Up, was enough to make him stay?

It was more than I could take in that moment, and I felt humor chasing me away from the weight of it, cornering me with a bad joke so that I could dampen the heavy thud of my heart in my chest.

"Women let you leave?" I gasped, pressing a hand to my chest in mock surprise. "Gods above and below, how have you coped this long?"

Billy grinned, his eyes crinkling at the corners in a way that made my heart thud louder, like a tsunami warning piercing through a crowd. He rolled over so that he was above me, forearms framing my head, and I found my fingers reaching up to weave through his before I could stop myself, my body arching up to meet the hard length of him as it pressed between my legs.

"I have my ways of soothing the pain," he said, nipping at my bottom lip and teasing me with one promising thrust. My eyes fluttered, and a moan slipped free.

I was wet at the thought of fucking him; gods help me. I ground myself against his cock, needy, hungry, my fingers clenching his in the pillows above my head. Everything was infuriatingly soft around me when all I wanted was to be spiked straight through until my heart stilled for just a blissful, silent moment.

Billy lowered his head, a wicked grin splitting his face, yet his eyes were still soft. His breath hot on my ear as he whispered my name. A delicious shudder ran through me at the sound of it, low and rough in his throat.

"Tell me what you want," he said.

Stay.

"Fuck me," I gasped.

It was like the horses had been unleashed from the gate.

Billy's hands were everywhere at once, smoothing along my body, pushing off my clothes, finding my clit, my nipple, the hollow of my throat in such rapid succession I could barely process every sensation as it came.

But what I wasn't going to do was fuck a man while he was still half-dressed.

"Hold on," I managed, sitting up and putting a palm to Billy's chest. He stopped, hands coming to rest on mine.

"Something wrong?" he asked, concern furrowing his brow. I pushed myself up and kissed the wrinkle there.

"You're still wearing your socks."

Billy glanced down, huffing a soft laugh and a half-smile.

"I get cold," he said.

I laughed, throwing my head fully back and letting the sound burst free.

"Isn't that the whole thing about being a vampire?"

"Doesn't mean I have to suffer," he said. He quirked a brow. "Unless that's what you're into?"

"Oh gods no," I said, laughter still ringing through me. "I just prefer to curl my toes against skin instead of wool dress socks."

Billy held his hands up in peace and scooted to the edge of the bed.

"The lady need not say more," he said, dramatically pulling off one sock and then the other before flinging them across the room. He leaned back toward me, but I stopped him again.

"And the shirt," I said, crossing my arms over my bare chest.

He looked like he might pout but sighed and carefully unbuttoned his shirt before flicking it to a chair. I noticed that it seemed to float through the air as if controlled by his hand.

I pointed to it mid-air, my mouth agape.

"How are you doing that?"

He shrugged. "Most vampires have basic control of levitation," he said as if he were explaining why he had ten fingers. I glanced from the shirt on the chair and back to him, horny, magical thoughts dancing wild.

"Not for the first time," he said, eyes darkening as they roved over me. "I need to feel you beneath me."

My poor heart stuttered. I didn't stand a chance against this man. He could've asked me to throw myself into the Atlantic, and I would've walked off and done it.

"Well, what're you waiting for?" I asked, sounding like an unfortunate carnival barker as I leaned back suggestively on the pillows and spread my arms out. I could cringe about that later, I decided, watching Billy's hard, naked form stretch up and over me.

"A friend of mine believes you shouldn't rush art," he said. Before I could tell him that was corny and I was entirely rethinking this interaction, he scraped a fang along the tight bud of my nipple, and I nearly came on the spot.

So what if he wanted to recite tired lines? Was that a crime?

He dragged the point of the fang in a circle along my breast before his tongue followed, first the sharp pressure, then the soft warmth of his mouth. I grabbed a fistful of his hair and pressed into him, desperate for more, fighting against the thought that was rising louder and louder in my mind.

"Bite it," I moaned.

Billy paused, looking up at me. "Are you sure?"

"Yes," I said, looking him directly in those red eyes. I hoped I gave off "unflinching" rather than "desperate, needy whore." Or maybe I preferred both. "Bite my tit, Billy."

"What the lady wants," he said, a half-smile making my heart clench.

He dragged his fangs teasingly against my breast again, and then, like before, there was a brief flash of pain that I leaned into. Before the starlight had a chance to sparkle through my veins, Billy's mouth was on the wound, kissing lightly, hand teasing my other breast so that the pain and the pleasure mixed into a warm heat pulsing through me.

This man was going to ruin me for all others after.

But what if he stays? I couldn't stop the thought as it rattled through me, chasing the thrill of our pleasure together as if it were a hunting dog and my heart was a rabbit.

Best to just run harder then, little bunny.

I pressed against Billy, pushing him up, and he followed my lead, arranging me as I settled over him so that my wet cunt slid deliciously against the shaft of his hard cock.

I reached down and repositioned him so that the head of his cock pushed lightly against my entrance.

"You should look at a lady when you enter her," I pretended to chide. His eyes shot wide, meeting mine. There was so much in his gaze that I almost broke my own rule—surprise, need, hunger, adoration.

I angled my hips and slid down, pushing onto him so that he filled me from wall to wall. We groaned in unison at the fit of us together. I could've subsisted on the small gasping moans he made as I rocked my hips, adjusting to him within me before gripping the headboard edge and giving into what my body wanted.

I rode him like a woman fleeing a cursed mansion in the dead of night, like a war messenger with news from the oncoming enemy—like a woman who may never see her true love again after this night. I rode him like my body wanted: desperate, primal, ravenous.

And Billy matched me, rising as I lowered so that his cock hit every inch of me, sparking against my core until the fire caught, grew, burned within me so hot and tight I was sure I'd combust.

We chased that impending explosion together, Billy pushing himself up and wrapping one strong arm around my waist to press himself closer to me. His cock angled up, sparking white heat at the edge of my vision with each thrust. I was going to pass out, hands still clutching the headboard like I'd die if I let go.

Finally, just on the cusp of the great fall, Billy's hand tightened on my back, raking at the skin, and I felt his fangs sink into my neck. The sharp pain from both points on my body sent me over the edge, and I came like a crack of lightning.

My orgasm shot through me like roots, bursting deep within me and seeking richer soil. I slumped into Billy's waiting arms, letting him guide me into the lush pillows and soft sheets. I closed my eyes, enjoying the remaining starlight in my veins, sighing contentedly at the flush of my orgasm as it loosened all my limbs.

Something warm and soothing pressed against my neck where Billy had bit me, and I peeked one eye open. Billy sat beside me, a warm cloth in his hand.

"Did I hurt you?" he asked.

"Only in the best way," I said. *Only like love ever could.*

Something flashed across his face, again, unreadable.

He administered the same warm cloth to my breast before snuggling against me, completely enveloping me in his arms and fitting his face to the crook of my neck.

I fell asleep like that, entirely unaware of what time it was, or what we needed to do. All that mattered was one hand snaked through his hair, the other twisted among his gentle fingers, pressed together and immobile for that precious, single moment.

Chapter Thirty-Four

Leslee

I was rounding the corner to my cottage when I saw smoke swirling from the chimney. Certain I'd left something smoldering for the last several days—it wouldn't have been the first time—I kicked into a sprint, flinging myself over the garden gate and through the front door in what felt like a single, breathless dash.

The front room was thick with incense and hot enough to rise dough, a hearty fire roaring in the stove. A tall, gorgeous woman with long raven hair cooed at my collection of Christmas cacti on the kitchen counter.

"Mum!" I rushed into her waiting arms, inhaling her woodland smell. She squeezed back, resting her chin on the top of my head.

"I hope you don't mind, Lessy honey, I borrowed your kitchen. You know how Dad hates it when I commune."

I also hated it—the stench of the incense, the heat of the room, the way the spirits were always knocking down picture frames and mirrors. But I was willing to let it go in favor of the comfort her presence provided.

"Can we talk?" I asked, wiping at the tears that already threatened to spill down my face. "And can we open a bloody window?"

"Of course, dear," she said, gesturing at the kitchen window. It flung itself open and I heard the cacti audibly sigh. "It seems I continue to be the only one who prefers a cozy atmosphere for spirit talks." She arched a perfect eyebrow at the succulents, who grew silent in response.

"Is it cozy if you've made a cactus uncomfortable?" I hung my coat on the hook, followed quickly by my scarf and hat. I kicked off my boots and peeled off the thick wool socks as well. Relieved of my layers, I opened the living room window as well, reaching an almost comfortable point as the room began to breathe.

Mum waved a dismissive hand and settled on the couch, patting the seat next to her.

"Some plants simply have a hard time remembering home, that's all. But never mind them. What's troubling you?"

I let myself flop onto the couch, taking the hand Mum offered.

"I think I'm in love," I started, my voice already quavering.

"Oh, Lessy, that's wonderful! Tell me everything—who are they? How did you meet?" She leaned in, dark eyes wide and glossy in the low light.

"It's not wonderful. It's horrible." I burst into tears, unable to stopper the dam anymore.

Mum clicked her tongue and squeezed my hand, rubbing my tears off my cheek with the sleeve of her sweater. "It's okay dear. Human marriages don't last that long these days; it's really just a matter of waiting it out."

"He's not human," I sobbed. "And he's not married."

"That complicates things a bit."

"Remember the vampire I called you about?"

"Even better! The undead are so..." Mum paused, rolling her eyes skyward as if the words she wanted were there. "Fascinating. But why does that have you distressed? Love is a wondrous event in our lives."

"It's over already." I let it all take control of me then—the harsh reality that had been hovering around our romantic bubble for the last several days. Billy would leave Ashbourne once the manor was settled, he would forget me once I was out of sight, and I'd be lucky to see him ever again. Did I even *want* to see him again? We still hadn't resolved the business with the ghoul and his cruel involvement.

Could I love someone—truly, for a long time—who could do such wicked things?

I folded over into Mum's lap, weeping into her soft leggings as she stroked my hair and made soothing noises. It was just like when I was little and, for a moment, I allowed myself to be comforted as if this were no worse than a skinned knee.

"Leslee, my sweet girl," Mum cooed as she lifted me upright by the shoulders. "I think it's best if you start at the beginning."

An hour and half a bottle of whiskey later, Mum and I were slouched into the sofa. Our legs comfortably intertwined, heads propped up on the pillows, a throw blanket tossed over us as the room chilled and the fire burned low.

"One more time, so I've got it right." Mum readjusted herself on the couch, pushing a little higher on her elbows. "Billy is the first client of your new solo landscaping and gardening business, but he's also incredibly hot and emotionally available so, naturally, you fell for him."

"Close enough." I sipped a little more whiskey, aware my speech was slurring.

"But it's also clearly evident he fell for you as well because he keeps saying painfully romantic things to you, including offering to keep coming back to this knee-pit of a village just to see you."

"Check up on the manor," I muttered.

Mum raised an eyebrow. "Sure. And despite this handsome, wealthy, supernatural gentleman practically crawling on his knees to you, you're sure things are over because he was mean to a nasty piece of—"

"*Mum.*"

"Alexander Huxley—the first one—was a nasty piece of work, and the world was better off when he was starving in a stone box."

"How can you say that?" I gasped, bolting upright and knocking my whiskey to the ground. "How can you be what you are and practice what you practice and think that torturing another living thing is justifiable?"

"Because nature may be straightforward, Lessy, my love, but humanity demands nuance." She took a dainty sip of whiskey before reaching for the bottle and refilling her cup. She didn't look so much as flushed. "And you'd learn that sooner if you'd allow for a little in your life."

"Humanity?" I squinted at the multiple versions of her in front of me.

"Nuance." She held up a finger as I opened my mouth to protest. "And before you start on about that 'as above so below' business, remember that everyone is responsible for their *own* input and output, so to speak. If Billy Barlow wronged the earth—and his own dirt in the process—by refusing to put down a ghoul, then it has to be Billy who makes it right and the earth who forgives him. Not you."

I snapped my mouth shut.

"But," Mum continued. "You will have to find it in your heart to forgive his past actions. Do you believe he'd do it again, here and now in the present?"

I thought of Billy insisting on changing the horse's shoes himself, of the gentle way he engaged with the fanglings, of his persistence in hiring local contractors despite the hassle of phone chains and voicemails.

"No," I whispered.

"Then I think you have some work to do for yourself, honey." Mum stood, untangling herself from my shaking legs, and stretched to the short ceiling. She let out a satisfied groan before helping me up. "And we have a town council meeting to attend."

I slapped a hand over my mouth, gripping Mum for stability. "That's *tonight*?"

"Yes, dear, it's Monday. Where have you been?"

Chapter Thirty-Five

BILLY

I rolled over, arm stretching across the cold mattress next to me. I sighed heavily into the pillow, opening one eye to confirm what I'd known the minute I stirred.

I was alone.

Sitting up, I ran my hands over my face, feeling the low throb of a headache at the base of my skull. Flashes of Leslee over me, her face contorted in pleasure, were rudely interrupted by the insistent chirping of my phone.

"What," I sighed.

"Don't be a princess; I've been trying to reach you for two hours." Rye's voice snapped through my door, echoing through my phone.

"Shit, what time is it."

The council meeting was tonight.

I shot out of bed, sprinting around the room to get dressed, fix my hair, fix the bed, hope it didn't smell like sex in here, and open the door for Rye. All in all, it took six seconds longer than I would've liked—what was super speed for if not moments like this?

Rye blinked twice when the door opened before hanging up the phone and quirking a brow.

"From your voice, I assumed you'd still be sleeping off whatever you do at all hours of the night, but you look..."

"Ravishing." I threw her a wink as she stepped inside.

"Less dead than usual."

"You flirt."

"It's weird."

As with most of the humans I employed to keep my endless life running smoothly, Rye did not know I was a vampire. But her keen eye and distaste for niceties meant she often edged a little closer to the truth than even she knew.

This was one of those moments where even I had to take a breath and remember she didn't mean it *literally* like she could.

"When is the meeting?" I asked, breaking the silence when I realized she was still staring at me.

"15 minutes," she said. "We'll go over what you need to say on the walk down."

"Walk?"

"It'll be faster than trying to get the hotel to call us a car, trust me."

I took her at her word, grabbing my Burberry coat from the ornate wood rack by the door.

"Lead the way, General."

Outside, the cold, damp air pushed against us as we walked, urging us back indoors, where it was warm, bright, and safe. But we trudged on, Rye's boots clicking sharply on the cobblestones, a kind of drumbeat beneath her clipped instructions.

"We mourn the loss to your community and will ensure the families are provided for."

I nodded.

"We believe the manor to be a priceless historic building and will work to ensure its continued reconstruction in a safe and timely manner."

I nodded.

"We will adhere to the council's ruling this evening and ask for grace and patience for future efforts."

I stopped.

"What if they take the manor back?"

Rye gripped my wrist and pulled me forward again, practically dragging me along.

"I'll handle any specific questions, comments, rulings, or arguments. It's what you hired me for, and you need to trust me. You are here to look authoritative and to give a pretty face to the name these people have been seeing on paperwork for the last however many years."

We were practically sprinting through the village now. Rye took a sharp turn and dragged me down a street that somehow seemed darker than the others, a looming church building squatting at its end. The bell tower stretched to the night sky like a single, desperate limb, and I tried not to shake at the sight of the massive cross atop it. The windows were ablaze, and condensation beaded on the glass from all the bodies packed inside.

Shit, a church.

"Rye, I can't go in there," I said without thinking.

"Don't worry, I'm an atheist. If anyone's going to burst into flames at the threshold, it's me."

"I wouldn't be so sure."

Before I could think of an excuse, Rye hauled me up the steps to the massive wooden doors. I watched in slow motion as she stepped across the threshold, and I braced myself as first my hand, then my arm, then—

It was like walking into an invisible wall. I yelped in surprise and reached up to rub my nose as if I had truly smacked into a surface. My headache had been building in intensity and range since leaving the hotel and was practically blinding me now. I had to squint to see Rye's face stretch into livid rage.

"You are making it *particularly* difficult to do my goddamn job, Billy."

"I'll come in, I promise," I said, frantically glancing around. "Just not through these doors."

"*What.*"

"It's um. Bad luck."

"If you don't come inside, I will quit *right now.*" She looked like she'd break my arm off and beat me with it. I knew very little of her history or experience—other than that she was a shark of a lawyer—but had heard whisperings of certain violent connections that made me take her seriously enough. Now was not the time to cross the line with her, but I had no choice.

I slipped back into the dark and around the corner of the building, Rye's hissing of my name floating in the damp air.

Whatever she dished out couldn't be worse than the crippling pain in my head or the dull ache where I'd slammed into the spiritual barrier at the door.

I needed another opening, one not so carefully warded or blessed. There had to have been at least one lazy priest in the last 200 years.

The silhouettes of bodies pressed into the meeting filled the windows, meaning I'd have to crawl over people even if the window were a viable option—which I was sure it wasn't. Finally, near the back of the building, I recognized a distinctive poof of curls.

I rapped sharply on the glass behind Leslee's head and held my breath as the screaming wood and glass cranked open. An attractive woman with an ageless face and a dark curtain of hair peered out at me. Her eyes were mossy green, and I wasn't sure I imagined the flash across her skin, not unlike the brilliant green veins of a leaf held up to the sun.

She looked me up and down, more curious than judgmental, before a sly smile played over her pert mouth.

"Oh, Lessy, baby," she cooed. "He's *very* handsome. I understand getting all tangled up in that."

"*Mom, stop.*" Leslee's flushed face appeared next to her mother's.

"Hello...Mrs...Hawthorne?" I could barely think for the sudden rush of relief Leslee's presence granted my headache.

The woman gave a soft chuckle like leaves in the wind and put a long-fingered hand over her heart. "You dear thing. That's so sweet. Did you hear what he called me?"

"The same thing *everyone* has been calling you since you married Dad." Leslee finally looked at me, her curls haloed by the yellow light behind her. She wasn't wearing as many crystals as usual, and her glasses were pushed up into her hair. Her eyes were red and puffy, and I realized the flush in her face might not be from embarrassment.

"I just think it's darling. They keep trying to name me," her mom said, the coo returning to her voice as if she were talking about a gaggle of kindergarteners and not an entire town.

"What are you doing out there?" Leslee asked.

"Have you been crying?" I sputtered.

"Gods," she groaned, running a hand over her face. "That isn't exactly your business."

"It is if I caused it," I said, tone growing sharp. "Leslee, it doesn't have to be like this, we could—"

"The priest's office at the back of the church hasn't finished renovations," she snapped, cutting me off. "It connects to the main hall." She swung the window shut with an inarguable finality, leaving me once again in the dark.

She *had* been crying. And I was stuck out here in the cold like an asshole—not that she was giving any sign I could comfort her once inside.

Our moments from that afternoon chased me around the back corner of the church, where I could see loose planks, abandoned tools, and a tarp across a wall that sighed slowly open, then closed.

"Did I hurt you?"

"Only in the best way." Only like love ever could.

I wasn't supposed to be able to hear a witch's thoughts—they were naturally warded against it.

But that thought blasted through like a cannonball through a pillow. It was as if she wanted me to hear it.

Only like love ever could.

And now she was tear-stained in a church with her mother.

"Good fucking job, Billy," I muttered, practically punching the tarp out of the way.

I could just stay. Sell the penthouse in New York, buy a cottage here, and settle into Ashbourne for however many too-short years Leslee and I would have together. But I couldn't just uproot my life for someone who fucked me and fled the scene.

A vampire can't go where he's not invited, and I couldn't let this be yet another regret.

I thought for the briefest moment of the sharp cut of Evelyn's jaw, the flash in her eyes, the desperation in her heart. She was with the love of her life now—the one she'd fought so hard for when we met.

I imagined her, safe at home on her couch, happily intertwined with her mershark boyfriend, occasionally flinching at the memory of me.

A sudden snap of air pulled me back to reality, and I turned to see Rye's outline in the office door. A cascade of chatter poured out from around her, muffling immediately as she slammed the door shut.

"I know you're not out here moping about ex-not-girlfriends when that whole meeting is waiting on you to start."

"Rye." I took a breath, shoving my hands in my pockets and fixing her with what I hoped was a serious stare. "I need you to tell me the absolute truth, no matter how insane it may sound."

"Billy, I'm going to punch you in the teeth, I swear to *god*."

"Can you read minds?"

The punch missed my mouth entirely but landed square on my jaw, snapping my head to the side. Any suspicions of Rye's violent ties were immediately confirmed as stars swam across my vision, and I touched a surprised, ashamed hand to the tender spot on my face.

Rye shook out her hand, face betraying nothing.

"That was a warning. You get *one*," she snarled.

I nodded, stunned.

"Now get in the fucking church."

When I hesitated, she turned on her heel with such force I expected the exposed concrete to crack beneath it.

"Fine," she seethed. "I cannot read minds, but any bitch with one working eye can tell you're moping over that Boston broad. Which is pissing me off more than usual because you've picked a helluva time to kick that shit off."

She took a step closer, and I flinched.

"If I had to guess, I'd say you're better at being tortured about love than receiving it."

My jaw dropped. Rye gently tapped it closed with a single, well-manicured finger.

"Leslee is in there staring a hole through the door, waiting for you to come through it. Don't be stupid."

"How—"

"I don't need *any* eyes to know the two of you are in deep," she called over her shoulder as she walked back to the office door. "It's a wonder I get any work done with you both sighing and moaning all the time."

The chatter washed over us again as the door opened. But Rye waited, arching a sharp eyebrow, her mouth turned down.

"What're you waiting for?" she asked, gesturing inside. "An invitation?"

Chapter Thirty-Six

BILLY

Inside, the whispers and murmurs rose to a clamoring level, pressing in on all sides as if the curiosity alone could pluck at my clothes, face, hair.

I made it as far as the threshold before finding the ward this time. I leaned against the doorframe and waved a hand at Rye. She rolled her eyes before stepping up to a raised dais to the left of where I stood.

She approached the group seated there, each elderly member in a metal folding chair, each looking more withered and ancient than the last.

Except for the man in the middle, who looked alarmingly familiar.

"We're ready," I heard Rye say politely before stepping back down to me.

The man in the middle stood, raising both arms for silence, and a hush fell almost immediately.

"We call to session this meeting of the Ashbourne council," he said in a clear, strong voice. "I thank you all for joining us tonight and we will ensure your concerns regarding the events at Huxley Manor are heard. But first, I believe Mr. Barlow has a statement prepared."

Every head in the room swiveled to me, and I immediately wished I'd spent more time with Rye preparing for this meeting.

I held up both hands in what I hoped was a peaceful greeting.

"Good evening," I said, pushing as much warmth into my voice as I could gather. "First, I want to say a hearty thank you to the village of Ashbourne and the endless hospitality I've enjoyed during my stay here."

Silence. *Maybe starting with a lie wasn't a good idea.* I heard Rye suck her teeth from my right.

"I have long awaited the restoration of Huxley Manor and the possibility of a new future birthed from a dark past. I am saddened and shocked by the loss of life on the property, and I will be personally ensuring the families of those devoted workers will be well provided for. I ask that those families meet with my representation at their earliest convenience." I gestured to Rye who immediately dropped the rage from her face and beamed a soft smile at the room.

"That said," I turned to the council. A flash of memory made me wince as I locked eyes with the man in the middle. It was uncanny the way genetics could stay unchanged through so many years. "I ask that Alexander Huxley the Fourth and the esteemed council grant me the opportunity to continue the restoration of Huxley Manor."

Murmurs sprouted, slow and steady, in a curling whip around the room.

Huxley Junior's face was ashen as he squinted at me from the dais.

"I don't believe we've had the pleasure," he said. "But if my family name precedes me, then you must know I, too, have a stake in the manor's fate. Although, I don't appreciate the implication of my family's supposed 'dark past.'"

"Alexander Huxley was known almost as much for his cruelty as he was for his rape of the village daughters and wives. I would not paint over that truth for all the lucrative property in the world."

Gasps joined the murmurs, inflating them to a louder chattering that threatened to swallow the rest of our conversation.

Huxley Junior's face grew tomato red, a vein bulging dangerously along his neck, eyes popping wide as he bared his teeth at me.

"You dare come here, tear apart our historical landmarks, endanger our residents, and malign my family history?"

"It is my property and my history as well," I said. "It deserves to see the light of truth."

"I don't know *what* you're implying—" the rest of Huxley Junior's spittled outrage was cut short by a blood-curdling scream from the audience.

"A monster!"

"I saw it too!"

"Outside!"

"My god!"

The church descended into a stampeding mass of bodies as people fought to reach the exits—or the windows for a better look. A woman with long blonde hair, bundled tightly in a wool coat and bright red scarf, barreled into me, and I caught her by the shoulders.

"Don't go running into its mouth," I said as she pushed against me.

The mausoleum. I hadn't gone. I hadn't addressed the nagging thought in the back of my mind—the warning, I realized. Icy dread dragged its nails down my back as I scanned the room. Rye was at the window with the others, her phone open to its camera as she waved it around, trying to get proof.

But I couldn't find Leslee and her mother. Panic gripped my limbs and pushed them forward until I was pressing against the invisible force of the ward so hard I looked like I'd chosen the most inopportune time to perform a mime act.

Before I could gather my senses, the front doors of the church were finally dragged open. A rush of freezing, wet air pushed in, and on it came the unmistakable scent of rotting flesh. There, beneath the moon, framed like a grotesque gothic portrait in the arches of the door, was Huxley Senior—Hurls—just as I last remembered him.

The moonlight flashed in his predatory eyes as he whipped his head back and forth taking in the trapped feast. He let loose an ear-splitting shriek, and the crowd descended into further chaos around me.

I did this. I refused to bring death where it was expected because I believed myself the judge of this man's sins. And now several families and an entire village were paying for it. I could feel the dirt beneath the church floorboards screaming up at me, and realization clicked into place like a key in its long-lost lock.

Dies-well and the Madame were wrong—It wasn't *my* grave dirt I had wronged. It was Huxley's. And the dirt didn't care which death-defying body it claimed so long as it got the bones it was promised.

I had to kill him.

I pushed with my will against the church door. It slammed shut, although the effect was like pressing bare palms against hot iron.

"Listen to me!" I called out across the loaded silence. It felt like I was getting ahead of one hundred lungs waiting to scream. "You are safe so long as you are inside the church. Do not leave until I return."

A tsunami of questions, chatter, concern, and tears broke over the room, crashing down upon me so entirely I would've drowned but for a fierce grip on my arm.

I turned to see Leslee's hazel gaze locking with mine as she pulled me through the back door.

"Mom is luring it back to the manor," she said, letting go of me once her feet touched the bare concrete of the half-finished office. I felt the absence of her touch, as if she'd pulled a chunk of my arm away with her hand.

"Leslee, I—"

"Don't." She cut me off with a wave of her hand, but I didn't miss the pain flash across her face. "We can't do this now."

"If not now, when?" What if the dirt claimed me tonight, and I never again saw her face, heard her voice, or felt her skin beneath my hands?

"After the thing is dead, we can talk until we lose our voices," she said.

"I'm holding you to that," I said. She simply nodded in response. We stood there a moment, fingers twitching, bodies swaying, eyes glancing from mouth to eyes to mouth again. Finally, when it was clear there wouldn't be a heroic final kiss between us, I sighed and flipped up the collar of my coat against the chill.

"Let's go kill a monster."

Chapter Thirty-Seven

Leslee

It was nearly impossible not to kiss him.

But I knew if I started again, I might never stop—and where would that leave me?

Alone all over again.

First my business partner then my client-former-client-not-boyfriend—lover? I shook my head to clear it, catching back up to Billy's clipped pace through the village.

"You know I have a private jet," he said.

"Bit late to be flexing your wealth, innit?"

"Vampires don't experience jet lag."

"Billy, don't—"

"Just listen, Leslee."

"There isn't time!" I was frustrated, heartbroken, and annoyed all at once. I wanted to kiss him and then drop-kick him out of my life. I wanted to tell him simultaneously that I hated him and was desperately in love with him..

"We don't have to end when this is over," he said. "Look, I didn't even slow my pace." He pointed to his still-moving feet as I stopped dead behind him.

"You can't do this!" He turned to face me, pausing mid-step. Something like hurt seemed to slide briefly across his face before it was replaced with a calm indifference.

"You can't just swoop into my life, give me work when no one else would, be so bloody charming and handsome, seduce me with mind-blowing sex, *and then also* not disappear into the night." I threw my arms into the air like my frustration could fly from my fingertips. "It isn't real! There is a catch or another shoe to drop or or or—"

Before I could come up with something grizzlier as a downside, Billy was in front of me, pressing his mouth gently to mine in that perfectly infuriating way. For a moment, I considered melting into his arms and letting the ghoul rampage through the village—everyone else be damned.

But then he pulled away, resting his forehead on mine, eyes closed. His hands rubbed slowly up and down my shoulders. I tried not to purr at the contact.

"At least stay with me long enough to finish the manor," he said, dazzling red eyes staring down at me. "And if you'll permit a visit or two in the future after that, I would do more than cross an ocean to see you again."

Had I accidentally swallowed climbing ivy, or was that my stomach trying to make sense of the romantic things he was saying?

"Obviously, I'm not going to quit before the job is done," I sighed, wishing I could slip my hands around him and enjoy the press of him against me. I crossed my arms to give them something to do, putting space between us. "That would be unprofessional."

"Professionalism be damned," he said, dipping his head as if he'd kiss me. I ducked. "We left those lines behind in the hotel." His face dropped, and he stepped away from me. "Though apparently not entirely."

I pointed a shaking finger at him.

"I haven't forgiven you," I said. "We're going to finish what you started, and then we're going to have a serious discussion about your ethics."

He held both hands up for peace, and I didn't miss the amused smirk twitching for freedom on his face. Billy got control and nodded, face serious, eyes alight.

We continued to the manor in silence. I wondered, briefly, what it would be like for us on any other night. We could be two lovers on a stroll, savoring the chill air before a heady intertwining in front of the fire. Maybe, if I permitted both of us the time—Billy to prove himself, me to forgive—that *could* be us.

But not tonight. Tonight, we were out to kill.

The ancestors stood large and dangerous, sharp limbs scratching at the night sky. We slipped through the gate, crime scene tape draping lazy fingers over our shoulders as we shrugged past.

Something was off. I felt it the moment I entered the shadow of the ancestors. The air felt heavier here—an oppressive weight I had to force out of my lungs before it pushed back in.

Billy's grip on my shoulders tightened, his mouth a grim line, a muscle ticking along his jaw. His eyes were trained on the trees as we walked beneath them.

"They don't like me, do they?"

I would've enjoyed his nerves in any other setting—it wasn't so unlike bringing a new boyfriend to meet all the aunts and uncles. But the slumbering giants around us were dangerous when threatened.

And there was no doubting the threat the ghoul presented.

A crack like lightning split the silent air, and we both leapt out of our skin, the identical flinching carrying us into the waiting arms of the ancestors. I felt the bark contort, twisting around my waist and pulling me away from Billy.

I watched, helpless, as panic clawed my throat and strangled anything I could say to the ancestors as they lifted the vampire into the air. His arms were pinned to his sides by the massive, twisted branches, and a threatening, angry shudder ran through the line of trees as they flipped him upside down.

He cried out once before a slithering band of leaves clamped over his mouth.

The sight of him, bound and gagged, sparked something in my gut, and I slammed my hands down against the branch that held me, pushing my connection to the trees around us out through my skin without waiting for an answering call.

"Put him down," I commanded, hoping the shake in my voice wasn't noticeable.

It is evil, little one. Another angry shake of leaves around me.

"He is not," I said. "He is the reason this place still stands—"

IT. SHOULD. NOT. This time, the very roots of the trees around us pushed up through the earth in rage, the tiny, localized earthquake forcing the dirt and paving stones into unnatural ripple forms.

"What do you—"

Evil was done here but never punished. Death walks where it should not. An unnatural creature will never die—a curse to the living to watch all else return to the earth when it will not.

I sighed. But in the back of my mind, things were clicking into place. I had an idea and could only hope Billy wouldn't be too squeamish.

"We will return the earth what it seeks." The whole time, I hadn't taken my eyes off Billy's face, returning the confused stare he was giving me. But now, his eyes widened, and I recognized the fear there. He began to thrash against his captors, but even a vampire was no match for centuries of ancient magic.

"But first, we must destroy the evil birthed here," I continued. "I need that creature you're throttling to do so."

Billy thudded to the ground with no warning, as if the trees had dropped a sack of coal.

With a great groaning and creaking, the branches set me gently back to my feet, receding to their former archway shapes. As the bark left my palms, a final whisper among the leaves came to my heart:

Be careful, little one. We are watching.

I knelt, running a soothing hand over Billy's back where he hunched on the ground.

"Are you alright?" As his shoulders began to shake. "I'm so sorry; I should've warned you. I just didn't think—"

Billy sat upright, thudding down to his ass and letting a barking laugh loose into the night. He pushed a hand to his face, laughter shaking his whole body now, eyes squinted tight.

"Billy, what—"

He waved me off, standing as the laughter receded and offering me a hand to join him.

"Sorry, it's just, I couldn't stop thinking about how much weirder meeting my future in-laws will be than I could have anticipated."

The ivy I swallowed seemed to have remembered how to climb again, but now was not the time to press on the realities of sweet talking.

I chose to keep walking, shoving aside the implied permanency of his joke. It couldn't freak me out if I wasn't entertaining it.

Yet.

Maybe I'd find it in myself to forgive his 150-year-old transgressions.

Maybe we'd get through this alive, and I could tease him about that being a weird way to propose—later.

Maybe I'd believe good things could stay and I deserved them after this was all over.

In the meantime, Billy caught up to me, face pinched and eyes wide.

"Leslee, that was absolutely a bad joke, I didn't mean—well, I did, actually, which is also confusing for me, but I don't want to freak you out or—"

"How attached are you to all your fingers?" I asked, cutting across his frazzled babbling before either of us drowned in it.

"I'd say ten times as they are to me."

"Make your peace with your least favorite." We left the shelter of the ancestors, the manor grounds sprawling before us under the moonlight. Stark black shadows pressed against the ground, giving everything the threatening possibility of hiding our ghoul. From the left, the manor stared at us, its empty windows so sad they almost seemed apologetic—as if the manor was sorry for the state of it.

"Are you going to cut off my finger?" Billy looked aghast. The war between soothing him and slicing his pinky off right then was all-consuming.

The Ancestors said the earth needed the bones and flesh it had been promised. But I wasn't ready for all of Billy to be taken from me. If my plan worked ...

A hair-raising shriek rent the air from the direction of the graveyard, and before I could breathe a word, Billy was gone, his form barely a blur in the night.

Sending up a silent prayer to the ancestors behind me, I followed.

Chapter Thirty-Eight

BILLY

I chased the ghoul's shriek as if I could snatch the notes from the air. Cresting the hill above the graveyard, I found Leslee's mother facing down the creature amid the headstones.

She was resplendent, hair flowing out in the air as if she were floating in water, her coat and scarf joining in the magic ripples. Her eyes were bright in the dark and I watched, stunned, as she flicked a hand and tendrils of creeping vines that had clenched around grave markers met her demand and wrapped around the ghoul. He was held in place by the very roots of the place he befouled.

That I befouled. I should've killed him when I had the chance and instead, I let petty revenge drive my hand.

"Time to go home, Hurls," I said, slipping from my Burberry and leaving it in the moon-drenched grass.

But my first step betrayed me, and I sank deep into the earth.

Dirt pressed into every part of me, my eyes, my nose, my mouth and ears. I couldn't move, couldn't breathe, couldn't think for all the panic and white-hot fear pulling me under.

Return. It was not so much a voice as a need, pounding through the earth in all directions around me. *Return.*

The earth would have the bones it had been denied—mine or the ghouls or both. As long as the ground had hungered, it was ravenous now. It hauled me deeper and deeper, swallowing me until the world above was a faint echo.

My lungs burned from the weight of the earth, my head growing faint by the second. I didn't know it was possible to bury a vampire alive.

My thoughts muddied, swirling together into a giddy fever dream. Flashes of New York lit up at night, of silk sheets and beautiful women, of lavish meals and smiling, agreeable faces as I paid each and every check, invoice, receipt. I plunged further into the dirt and thought that at least I had lived well with the extra time I'd been given.

But regret slipped in and there was Rye, tapping her foot and arching an eyebrow. There was Patrick, laughing in the candlelight of his guest room in Boston, refilling my glass and listening as I told him about my latest woes and exploits. There was Evelyn, but then, before the ache could seep in, Leslee was there.

Leslee, face bent over her work, bright eyes darting across the sketch pad. Leslee, streaked in dirt, hands on her hips, hollering at the work crew at the manor. Leslee, looking up at me, eyes half-lidded, face flushed, mouth plump.

There was Leslee, reminding me I wasn't done with this life.

Not yet. Not now. Not as long as she was alive.

And then, cutting through the grating sound of the dirt in my ears, silencing the sloughing of the worms and the chattering of the roaches, came a crystal-clear, familiar voice:

Give. Him. Back.

A thunderous rumbling from beneath my feet erupted into thick, gnarled roots. They wrapped around me, and I tried to fight against them before realizing we weren't going *down* anymore.

We were going up.

I broke through the grass, clawing my way up and forward, fistfuls of grass and dirt coming away in my hands as the roots pushed me up and completely free. When they released my legs, I scrambled away as fast as I could, heaving lungfuls of crisp night air in and out. A loud slurping sound came from not-so-far-away, and when I looked again, the place that swallowed me had disappeared.

Another shriek tore the air, snapping me to my senses as I climbed to my shaking feet. It was now Leslee and her mother against the ghoul, both druids in full force against the undead.

Leslee's magic radiated from her, turning the air around her hazy like the forest after a hard rain. My heart clenched, my stomach seized, and I realized seeing her like this—*all* of her, not just the human side—was pushing me past the cliff and into a freefall of new obsession.

Waiting for her next invite was going to be torture.

The ghoul advanced on the druids, spurring me into action. I collided with the frigid, damp flesh of the ghoul and screamed as he whipped around to meet my attack.

We hit the ground in slow motion, a tangle of fangs and limbs and creeping vines that snapped with the force of our clash.

Touching the creature made my insides flip and my blood chilled in my veins. Staring into those monstrous eyes as my muscles strained against his, I was reminded that only a matter of moments kept me from becoming him—a few mere seconds lost to an endless lifetime meant retaining what small piece of humanity kept me from mindlessly, endlessly feeding like the ghoul.

"You were a bigger asshole in your first life," I grunted, finally catching the ghoul off balance and shoving him to the ground. He landed with a shuddering thud, dazed. I pinned one clawed hand beneath my loafer, the other I awkwardly held down with my body while scrambling my free hand through the detritus surrounding us, fingers finally grasping a rusted piece of metal and driving it through the ghoul's wrist.

He shrieked and howled in pain, writhing beneath me as I leapt up to dodge his kicking feet. He'd be out of his misery soon enough—I hoped. Keeping my foot tight on his limb, I waved an exhausted arm at the creature, voice hoarse and breathless as I challenged the earth itself.

"Here are your bones," I yelled. "Here is the blood you were denied. Come and take it."

"Billy, *no!*" I heard Leslee just as the earth opened up beneath me, cracking and shaking like hell itself was rising.

Something slammed into me, carrying me away from the warm, wet, gaping hole just as it reached me. The ghoul was not so lucky. His screams echoed, bouncing off the damp walls of the chasm as he fell.

Frantic, I sat up, shoving Leslee off and scrambling back. The hole released hot breaths into the chill air over her shoulder, the ghoul's echoing screams filling the night. I couldn't look away. Something called to me from deep within the dark—something ancient and quiet beneath the noisy world around me. It offered relief, rest, silence in exchange for my weary life. It would be as simple as standing up and taking six steps and the exhaustion that coated my life would—

A slicing hot pain caught in my left hand and broke my trance. I looked down to see Leslee expertly wrapping the stump where my pinky had been. She brought it to the opposite shoulder, gently guiding my right hand to hold it in place.

"Sorry, Billy, it's the only way."

She stood, my bloody pinky in one hand, in the other, a pair of small gardening shears, the sharp, tiny blades dripping with my blood.

I watched in shocked silence as she walked to the edge of the hell hole and dropped my pinky in without ceremony.

"*There* is your blood and your bones," Leslee said. She knelt in the dirt, placing both palms flat to the ground, head bent in reverence. Movement in the corner of my eye told me her mother was doing the same.

I tried to adjust my position to join them, but a wave of nausea and spots in my vision told me to sit back down. I watched Leslee's silent form as the minutes dragged by. The ghoul's screams continued, coming from further and further away, scraping against my soul to the point of madness. How was this better than imprisonment?

The hole sealed itself in silence, not even making a satisfying squelch as it closed. It was as if it had never been there at all. Leslee turned to her mother and nodded before slowly standing. When I glanced over to see Mrs. Hawthorne's actions, she was nowhere to be seen.

Another tackle by Leslee had me flat on the ground, wrapped entirely in her arms, her hair, her mouth.

"We did it," she breathed when she stopped kissing me long enough to speak.

"I didn't do anything," I said, pulling her mouth back to mine.

"You delivered the corpse the earth was promised," she said, pulling back and leaning over me on her elbows. Her pupils were huge, her mouth plumped from kissing, a delectable flush glowing beneath her freckles. "And so did I."

"You mean my pinky was dessert for that big earth mouth?"

She hummed against my mouth and slid questing hands beneath my shirt, raking fingers over my skin. Goosebumps rose, and my cock twitched beneath her.

"Don't complain, I could've picked something far more sensitive to offer up," she said, those curious hands sliding down my waist and into my pants. I arched against her, groaning and pushing into her hands with need.

"Don't you mean 'heftier?' Or 'bigger?' I'd even accept 'girthier.'"

She wrapped her hand fully around my shaft, and I yelped in surprise.

"Wait, are we really doing this?" I asked, sitting up and testing my weight on my elbows. The world still shifted around me, but Leslee didn't waiver.

"You did the hard thing," she said. "The *right* thing. Even if it took you a long time. You brought a life to its natural completion in the face of its unnatural existence, and that takes a special kind of person."

"Vampire," I corrected. Something tugged at me, threatening to pull me away from flush, panting, ready-and-willing Leslee. "Let me show you something."

Before I could try and stand, Leslee shoved me back down, hands firmly on my chest as she flung a leg wide to straddle me.

"Fuck me first, emotional reveals second."

"I bet you're wild at funerals," I laughed, surrendering to her next questing kiss. A lance of pain and reality shot through me as I tried to push myself up to meet her. I *had* just lost a finger.

"Hold on, darling," I said, wincing as I sat up. "I'll need a few moments, unfortunately. And we *really* should talk."

Leslee peered down at my hand, eyebrows knit in concern.

"I thought vampires could heal in moments. I wouldn't have cut off anything if I'd thought it would cause problems."

"Were you not *just* livid with me?" I asked, sighing. It physically pained me to divert from her current focus, but if I wanted there to be a next time, I needed to know where she stood.

I stood, careful of the weight I put on my still-shaking legs. She looked up at me from the ground, skirt splayed out around her like one giant fallen petal from an inhuman rose, eyes huge and inviting. It was all I could do to offer her a hand up instead of falling on her right then.

"I'd like to show you something," I said. "I think it will help."

I led the druid witch with my heart in her hands to the one place I'd never taken anyone else—the only place on the Manor grounds that was left off any drawings or plans. My empty grave, my blank marker, my yearning echo in the earth waited for us in its usual place. But this time, as we approached, the lone oak that had been so content to ignore me on my last visit seemed to shake in anticipation of our arrival.

"Hullo, darling," Leslee said to the tree, breaking our hands to place both of hers on the trunk. She gasped immediately, turning to me with a stricken look on her face. "Oh, Billy."

I would've felt less exposed if I'd been standing there naked.

"I had no idea," she said, patting the tree lightly before dropping her hands. The branches leaned in toward her, one draping over her shoulder like an old friend. "No one should have to bury themselves—much less alone."

"I had no one else," I said, trying not to sound too pathetic. But it was—immortality wasn't everything if you had no one. And I'd set out into my new, unusual life full of bravado to smooth over how entirely alone I was. I didn't even need to leave Ashbourne as fast as I had—there was no one to mourn my human death. But, just like any other young man, I'd been eager to make my way and didn't want the trappings of my past to hinder me, so I'd buried who I'd once been, unable to afford more than a stolen blank grave marker.

"We can't bury ourselves, Billy." Leslee knelt at my grave, folding her hands respectfully and bowing her head. I shuddered involuntarily. "The version we shove down always rises back up."

Unbidden, the image of The Colonel waiting for me at the end of the stables rose in my mind. I had been so tired, then, maybe even more so than now despite the added weight of the earth trying to swallow me. Despite the parade of pretty young women in and out of my bed every night, my only true companionship had been The Colonel.

"I was lonely," I whispered, uncertain who I needed to say it to. "And I didn't ever want to be again."

"You can't smother the need for connection," Leslee said, gently tugging me down to her. I knelt beside her, feeling the ground beginning to writhe beneath me. "Even immortals need friends."

"I'm sorry, Leslee," I said. "I'm sorry for the monstrous things I've done. I was so angry and so alone. I had no idea what I was or wasn't supposed to do, and the only thing I could think when I heard there was a ghoul in Ashbourne was that the fucker killed my only friend and I was going to make him pay."

"I don't think it's me you have to apologize to," she said. She guided my hand to the ground next to the marker and pressed it there. For the first time, the dirt sighed but did not attempt to swallow me—like it was waiting.

"I'll be by the mausoleum when you're ready," she said, dusting off as she stood.

"Wait, Leslee, I don't—" Panic rose up in my throat, threatening to close it.

"You do," she said, firm but comforting. "You absolutely do."

Before I could protest further, she was gone. The oak shivered, folding its branches around me to create a makeshift haven. The leaves shook with invisible wind, and I heard a distinct, "*Go on*," from somewhere above me.

There's no arguing with a tree.

I took a deep, shuddering breath and placed both hands over my grave as if I were going to give it chest compressions. I closed my eyes and pulled from the part of myself I so often shoved down.

"I'm sorry," I said. "I'm sorry you were so alone. I'm sorry you were so scared. I'm sorry you felt you had no other choice but to act from those fears."

I thought about The Colonel again, how my last memory of him was his slowly cooling corpse in the dark. I wished desperately that vampires could cry.

"I'm sorry about your friend," I sighed, voice tight and shaking. "He was a good, kind creature who didn't deserve the end he got. And I'm sorry I never let you feel your grief. You deserved that much."

The ground rippled, pressing against my palms.

"And I'm sorry it took me this long to get here," I said. My face was hot, my vision blurry. My stomach flipped, and whatever deities were watching were surely laughing at the desperate release I would never receive. Tears had never seemed important before. "I'm sorry I didn't let you—us—grieve, or feel, or truly fall in love because we were afraid of the potential for carrying a mistake through our long life. Because that's how this all started—it was all one big fuck up.

"But you are not. *We* are not. We are more than how we started, more than what was made of us against our will, more than the grief we hold. It's time I started acting like it."

The ground rippled a final time, roiling beneath me before settling with a final long sigh. The whispered voice rang out above me as the branches opened to the brilliant moonlit night.

"*Good.*"

Chapter Thirty-Nine

Leslee

"Oh, Lessy honey, morals are a human problem." Mum was perched elegantly on a tombstone, chin in her hand as she listened to me rant. I hadn't been able to stop pacing since I'd come back from Billy's grave.

"Well, I'm human, Mum," I said with a sigh. "And I don't know how to move on from Billy torturing another living creature."

"Technically, it was an undead creature—"

"Mum!"

She held her hands up in apology. "I'm only suggesting that maybe what he did in the past doesn't have to be so bad with the right framing." Her voice was light and nonchalant. Druids were always painted as serious protectors of nature, but those caricatures had clearly not been drawn from my yoga-loving, we're-all-one, what's-done-is-done Mum.

"As above, so below, Mum," I said, ignoring how she mouthed it along with me. "You taught me that. All things we do have consequences."

"Yes, dear," she sighed, rolling her eyes. "And your Billy has paid the price ten-fold by now. Look at him." She gestured over my shoulder, and my breath caught in my chest at the pitiful, beaten, exhausted man shuffling toward us. There was no more swagger, no more polish, no more bravado at a world that needed to be set to rights. Which meant one thing.

"Holy shit, he did it."

"What a man," Mum sighed from behind me. I waved a frantic hand at her, not bothering to turn around to know she had folded into the wind.

My heart clenched as Billy closed the last few staggering steps between us. He leaned down, swaying lightly, and pressed his forehead to mine. His eyes were closed and there was a fresh pain on his face.

"If you hate me for the rest of your life, I'll understand," he said, voice rough. "But please understand that if you ask me to leave you, I will die again every day we are apart."

Holy shit.

"I have lived my entire immortal life sure I had no regrets, but I was lying to myself and to the earth I defy," he continued. His breath was a whisper in my hair. He smelled of sweat and dirt and blood. I wanted to sink my teeth into him, to lick his wounds clean, to roll him in mud and bury him again to sprout something new and holy together. I clenched my hands at my side. "You helped me realize that. I could not possibly be more grateful to you, or more in awe of your empathy than I already am. And although the very thought of you consumes me, I will go if that's what you ask."

Holy SHIT.

A breathy gasp came from behind a nearby tombstone.

"*MUM.*" I seethed.

"Darling if you don't take him, I will."

"*GO.*"

A ghost of smile crossed Billy's somber face. My stomach fluttered and my hands broke free of my will, sliding between his blood encrusted fingers.

"I thought your mum left?"

"She was waiting for a traditional funeral orgy," I said, hoping he thought I was joking.

"That would certainly explain why you're so much fun around death." His smile grew, pulling my heart up with it. But just as soon as it appeared, it vanished. His brows pinched together, his face grew paler than usual, and he dropped to his knees, sagging over at the waist.

"Billy!" I cried out in alarm, dropping to meet him and tilting his face up to mine. His crimson eyes were glossy and unfocused.

"I haven't fed properly in days," he said. "Now this business with my grave dirt is resolved, I'm starving. I don't think I've ever been this hungry. I need to get back to the hotel."

He started to slump over again, and I barely caught him.

"You're not going to make it that far," I said. "Feed on me."

The offer escaped me before I could think about what I was offering. But then I remembered the ecstasy of it, the starlight in my veins, the floating high of the orgasm his venom offered.

"And maybe, if you're feeling better, we could go back to where we were before your emotional turmoil kicked in?"

"Is your Mum still here?"

"She better not be!" I yelled over my shoulder. Turning back to a weary Billy, I felt my heart soften, and I felt my human morals recognize a man who was trying his best in a world that had done its worst. "All seriousness, please feed, and we can go from there. If you need to rest, then—"

His hand found my cheek, pulled me gently to his mouth and kissed me once.

"Did you not hear all the desperately romantic things I said just now?"

"I did. And I'd like to say some back—I'm in love with you, Billy. Even if I hate the things you've done and may never be able to forgive them, it tears my heart apart to think about saying goodbye to you permanently. It goes against everything I've learned and practiced to this point, but I can't give you up, and I can't just bury my feelings for you. There isn't a hole deep enough to keep them."

"There isn't a hole deep enough to keep me either," Billy said, voice thick, jaw clenched. "And I love you, too. If I hadn't made that entirely—" I crushed my mouth to his, swallowing whatever smart-ass thing he'd say next, relieved, overjoyed, comforted by the press of him against me, by the tangling of our lips, teeth, tongues.

Mischief reared its head, and I scooted away from him, shimmying out of my skirt and knickers. I let my thighs drop open, baring my cunt in the grass.

"May I offer you a snack until other appetites are sated?"

If this vampire didn't feed off me so he could fuck me properly I was going to open the earth back up and throw myself in. After everything we'd been through that evening, Billy was hot in my veins like a drug I couldn't flush out, no matter how much tea or water I drank.

I wasn't going to make it through however many hours it took his hand to heal on its own without combusting like Billy had done on my porch. And I didn't think burnt pubic hair was a turn on.

"Are you sure?" he asked, eyes trained on my pussy like it might disappear if he blinked.

"Don't turn me into another ghoul, one was more than enough, thank you." I swallowed and then continued. "And don't turn me into a vampire either. You can do that right?"

He nodded slowly, before finally tearing his gaze away to find my face.

"I trust you," I said, whipping off my blouse so now I was fully naked, sprawled out on the grass in the middle of the graveyard.

And it was true. Something new had blossomed between us since leaving the church. It was a glorious, renewed comfort—the knowledge that we could mess up and still have one another. Hell, the man had just killed a ghoul and lost a finger to make things right.

Whatever this new feeling was, it was only serving to bolster the need rapidly building between my legs.

I let my other knee drop, supporting myself on my elbows. I barely had time to arch an eyebrow in question before Billy was on me, good hand skimming across my soft stomach to tweak a nipple, mouth licking lazy strokes through my cunt. I let my head drop back, eyes closed, as he worked my clit.

I pushed my hands deeper into the grass, each stiff blade a sharp sensation contrasting the soft pleasure Billy sent through my core. The night air whispered across my skin, pebbling my nipples along with Billy's fingers.

"Please, Billy," I moaned. I needed him to have his full strength. I needed him to heal. I needed to know he would fully take what I offered him with an open heart—that I wouldn't be left alone in the cold.

Slowly, carefully, Billy rose from between my legs, covering my body with the warmth of his still-clothed chest. I'd have to do something about that in a moment.

He pressed a gentle kiss to my mouth, pulling away enough to let me look into his eyes but not so far as to let the cold get to me.

"You're sure?"

"Absolutely," I said. "Bite me, Billy." I laughed a little at how ridiculous it sounded, but I meant it.

He kissed me again, tender, careful—loving. Instead of questioning it, I folded into it, letting the kiss sweep me up and away. He nudged his nose along the side of my face, trailing it along my jaw until he found a sensitive place on my neck that had me arching into his touch.

His fangs scraped my throat as he opened his mouth, and at the gentle press of his good hand against my check, I felt him hesitate.

"Please, Billy," I breathed. "Take me."

This bite was different than the ones before. Although the euphoric starlight swept through my veins, there was the unique sensation of something caught beneath my skin where I knew his fangs were doing their work. I tried to ignore it, letting the starlight simmer in my core, but then he shifted, sinking his fangs deeper, and everything in me lit up like a sunrise on fast-forward.

I'd feared catching on fire from want. Now desire was an all-encompassing flame. I was engulfed, and all I could do was cling to Billy for dear life as he took what he needed—what I offered.

Finally, the pressure in my neck gave way to gentle kisses and Billy's warm breath. He said something to me in a low murmur, arms wrapped entirely around me as the brilliance in my body dimmed to a manageable voltage.

"You're alright," he said, over and over again. "You're alright, you have to be alright."

"I'm better than alright," I wheezed. "I might actually be a supernova."

"I'll give you a moment to catch your breath."

"Don't you *dare.*" I pushed myself up and over him, thrilled at the hard length of his cock through his pants as it rested against my bare cunt.

Before I could tug on his belt, I felt myself lifted off the ground despite Billy's hands busying themselves running across my body.

More levitation.

The sensation flipped my stomach and sent a whooshing feeling through my limbs, but it also granted me better access to undo Billy's pants. His cock sprang free, erect and ready, a small bead of pre-cum dripping down the side.

"So you're also fun at funerals?" I grinned down at him. He smiled back up at me, something earnest and tender mixed in with the mischief.

"I've been known to keep a few sexy tricks up my sleeve," he said and rose to meet me in the air, securing an arm around my waist as we rose still higher together. I took the opportunity to free him of his shirt, smoothing greedy hands over the hard plane of his chest and stomach.

"Ready?" he asked, and I nodded, probably too eager and wanton, too far gone with lust and need to care.

I let Billy brace my back with one hand, following the guide of his other to lay down mid-air. I met resistance where I would've thought there'd be nothing and comfortably pressed my weight against it. Wrapping my legs around his waist, I hauled him to me, shaking as the head of his cock pressed at my opening.

"If you don't fuck me right now, I'm going to light you on fire again," I hissed as he circled his hips tauntingly.

"You haven't let me finish my trick yet," he smirked, flashing both hands out at his side and waggling his fingers like a magician on a stage. "Ta-dah! No hands."

"No pinky, at least."

"For now," he said, taking a fake bow. "Thanks to my airborne nubile queen, I'll be back to two pinky business soon enough."

I flailed a leg at him in an attempt to kick him, but he caught my ankle, nipping lightly at the arch of my foot.

I shrieked and wiggled my foot free, returning it to the back of his waist and digging my heel in. He lurched forward, catching himself over me and laughing.

I caught his mouth, kissing him hard enough to bruise, raking my teeth across his bottom lip.

Finally, he answered my need, returning the rough kiss and pressing a hand along my lower back to lift me slightly, notching his cock against my entrance. He didn't make me wait as he pressed in, filling me completely. We both sighed as he seated himself fully within me, hips grinding against my hips.

Slowly, he pumped in and out, picking up speed as I dug my nails into his back, desperate for the tight coil of my orgasm to release me from its insanity-inducing grip. Without anything else to grip, I had only Billy, mid-air, and I was sure I was drawing blood.

"Let go," he said, more gentle coaxing than a command. I immediately released my death grip on his skin, letting his hands take mine and guide them above my head. The invisible force holding me up suddenly dropped from behind my head.

I yelped but realized it wasn't unlike hanging my head over the edge of the bed to see upside-down.

"Let go," Billy said again, and this time, I listened, letting my neck take the full weight of my dangling head.

From this vantage, I saw the ground beneath us, whole and sealed, bathed in moonlight. The trees were still in the breeze—no more sinister whispers or warning shudders. And the wind played through my hair, teasing my curls one way and then the other.

"Ready?" he asked. I barely said yes before he slid out almost entirely and slammed in hard to the hilt, pressing a thumb to my clit at the exact moment his hips made impact. The effect was like pushing the dimmer switch all the way up again, the starlight in my veins bursting back to life. He repeated the action again and again, swirling and flicking and teasing my clit as he did until the heat in my core was a tight twist along my spine.

I was going to snap in half.

Then, on a final deep thrust and well-placed grinding along my clit, the stars exploded. I came, screaming like a wild creature in the night and clenching my legs around Billy to ensure I could hang on as he thrust through my clenching pussy. My head swam with warmth and hazy pleasure, my entire body pulsing with the rapid beating of my heart. After only a few moments, Billy cried out, slamming home a final time before slumping over me.

Carefully, as if we were on a mechanical platform, we lowered to the ground and splayed out in the cool grass, gasping for breath.

After a moment of silent bliss, Billy started laughing his whole-hearted, unprotected, real laugh. He was practically chortling.

"Yes?" I asked, grinning despite myself.

"Please tell me druid funerals aren't a family affair."

"We ensure orgies avoid incest if that's what you're asking," I said, giggles bubbling around the words.

He rolled onto his side, gazing down at me and tracing a soft finger along my cheek.

"You're a strange, wonderful being," he said. "But my dick is very cold, and I would like a cup of tea."

"You're not staying for the orgy?" I pretended to pout.

"Will your mother be joining?" He waggled his eyebrows at me as he sat up. I threw a dirt clod at his back.

We dressed in laughter, wrapped in flirtation and relief. I let him take my hand and guide me away from the manor, let him drape his expensive coat over my shoulders, let him tell me about "next times" that he had already been planning.

And maybe it was a trick of the stark moonlight washing the world around us, or maybe it was the promise of new love pushing through the dirt, but even the manor looked less sad as we crossed the gate and left it behind for a life that looked forward.

Chapter Forty

EPILOGUE

Ashbourne, 2 months later

"Given the state of things, what I'm offering you is more than fair." I gestured to the dilapidated horse shelter that threatened to collapse into a rusted water trough. Three more bare-bones, ill-shod, tired horses—two mares and a gelding—wandered the dirt enclosure.

"And I'm saying it's not." The breeder was a foot shorter than me and about three times as wide. He had tiny black eyes that peered out from under a wool cap and a ruddy complexion out of place for the weather—as if he'd been sweating in the frost. He was the type of slimy man who would take one look at my fine clothes and posh accent and decide I had more money to offer than I was letting on.

"No one else is going to buy these animals off you, much less the entire operation," I said, frustration clipping my words.

"And yet here you are." He crossed his arms and let out a puff of smoke from the side of his mouth. I hadn't even noticed the soggy cigarette until that moment. A distressed whinny came from the far end of the enclosure. One of the mares was trying to bend to drink, shifting her weight from one side to the other, and clearly in pain.

I could make him give me these horses. It wouldn't be the first time I'd relied on hypnosis to sway a deal. But I'd promised Leslee I'd not be driven by my baser urges going forward, and I couldn't start my new chapter by forcing someone's hand—even if they wouldn't know I'd forced it.

"You can't possibly expect me to pay you anymore for this mess of an operation," I snapped. "Look at them!"

The breeder shrugged, letting loose another stream of smoke.

I'm going to tear your throat out and make you swallow that—

"Mister Barlow!" A familiar voice rang out from down the street. Richard appeared one moment a few blocks away, and in the next stood directly in front of me, not even winded. "Mail, sir! An invitation from the looks of it. I had to practically wrestle the twins to keep them from opening it, and you know how strong they are these days, what with being well-fed and—"

"*Richard*," I hissed, throwing a glance at the breeder.

"Oh, don't worry about him, sir," Richard laughed. "We already made him believe we're just really athletic types. He won't bat an eye at anything I say. Watch."

Before I could stop him, Richard nodded to the breeder in acknowledgement and flashed him a fanged smile.

"I had a bag of lukewarm blood for breakfast," he said.

If I had a heart, it would've stopped cold.

But the breeder simply shrugged again.

"Must be good for your heart and joints," he said. "Like raw eggs for muscle."

"What the *fuck*, Richard." I was aghast even if I was also amused.

"He doesn't have much going on upstairs, so it doesn't take much to convince him of anything," Richard said, leaning in conspiratorially and waggling his eyebrows. "I'm not even sure we actually hypnotized him if I'm being honest."

I rubbed a hand over my face. "He's not convinced I'm paying him fairly for the stables and everything in them."

"Why would you want to buy this place?" Richard jerked a thumb over his shoulder at the miserable scene. "Those beasts'll make a better dinner than carriage pullers."

I shot the fangling a look, desperate not to lose my cool. Thankfully, my prior chronic migraines had gone the way of the ghoul—buried and gone with a past made peaceful. But damn it all to hell if these fanglings didn't try to reinstate my pain.

"Right, well, I'm sure you have your reasons, Mister Barlow, allow me." Richard sketched an obnoxiously deep bow before turning to the breeder. He fixed him with a deep stare and waved his hands fluidly through the air as if he were conjuring a spirit. "You'll give Mister Barlow everything he wants for free, even if it's the pants off your bottom." He added a high-pitched, wavering "woooo" and then dropped his hands.

"Your mail, sir," he said, handing me a small purple envelope. I stopped him before he could sprint back to the hotel, catching him by the shoulder.

"Does that work?" I asked him under my breath.

"Try him, sir."

To the breeder, I raised my voice. "I'll be taking these horses and your breeding operation so you can retire and never work with horses again. Sound good?"

The breeder shrugged.

"Dunno why you think I'd argue."

I let my shoulders loose in relief but grabbed Richard again as he started to step away.

"How many people in town have you done this to?"

"Just the bad ones, sir."

"Richard..."

"I don't have a missus to keep me on the straight and narrow, sir." He pantomimed, making a long, straight line with his arm. "Or a sire." I didn't miss the puppy dog eyes he gave me.

"I'll see you at the hotel, Richard," I said, letting him go and trying not to sound as annoyed as I felt. This was another lesson I would have to impart on the fanglings before my trip back to New York. And I had a feeling they'd need plenty more instruction on my next return.

After arranging transport of the remaining three horses to the new stables by the hotel, I assured the breeder I did not need any of the clothes he was currently wearing, and my only other desire was that he never so much as look at another horse again.

He pulled his hat over his eyes and stumbled away as I headed back to the hotel, taking my time through the dimly lit cobblestone streets.

I stopped beneath a lamp to look closer at the letter Richard had delivered. My name was written across the front in silver ink, each spindly letter done with care. The return address gave me pause.

Without another thought, I ripped open the envelope and went stone still at the wedding invitation in my hands.

"Caoimhe Ryan and Leith Riordan request your presence at the celebration of their marriage in Boston, Massachusetts, USA, on the 27th of May. Dinner and reception to follow."

Beneath the tasteful watercolor flowers intertwined with four-leaf clovers was a space to check yes or no, put my dining preferences, and...

"A plus one?" My eyebrows nearly left my forehead. That was generous, given my limited interactions with the leprechaun and the mershark. Although Will's relationship with them was intimate, they may have placed me in higher regard than I thought, given the help I'd offered in locating him while he was cursed.

But that would mean seeing the woman who had entranced me into helping in the first place.

"Oh, Evelyn." I shoved the invitation into my jacket pocket. "This is going to be weird."

Back at the hotel, I was relieved to hear Leslee's voice coming through the closed door. We'd taken to alternating between her cottage and my room over the last month, though our cozy pseudo-living arrangement would come to a close with my flight to the States.

"And another thing, you gormless tosser," Leslee seethed into the phone. "If you don't lose my number, I'll give you reason to be *truly* sorry rather than these approximations you keep calling me with."

"That's my girl!" I threw a fist in the air and received a rude gesture back as I closed the door behind me. I hung my coat in the closet just in time to hear Leslee end her tirade.

"Does this sound like we can still be friends? Bloody sod the hell off!"

The phone whizzed past my shoulder, landing with a clatter in the bathroom.

Leslee let loose a wild, feral roar before flopping onto the bed.

"Was that too mean?" she asked without breaking her stare at the ceiling.

"Probably not mean enough," I said, settling down beside her. "You didn't threaten his manhood once."

"He grew up gay in Ashbourne, that doesn't scare him anymore."

"Fair."

"You know what would cheer me up?"

"More levitating sex and then a cheeky little blow job in the shower?" The punch was expected but still painful. I flinched when she sat up, leaning over me.

"A moonlit ride on horseback with a stunningly handsome man." She smiled down at me, and I wondered if I'd ever miss the sun again.

"I think that can be arranged," I said, smiling back.

THANKS

This was a weird story to chase down and it wouldn't even exist if it weren't for adamant readers screaming at me "WHAT ABOUT BILLY?" I wrote this book in hotel rooms across the country, talking through plot snags in casino bars while at 20Books Vegas and drafting chapters in Air BnB kitchens while swatting away curious friends and family members—thanks everyone who shared a room with me and my lapop the last year. I owe a massive thanks to Britta and Molly for talking my ear off about turn-of-the-century gun models, emotional arcs, vampire lore, and what to name a hotel run by teen fanglings. This book wouldn't exist without either of you and writing together continues to bring much-needed joy to my dirt pile. More thanks to Kourtney, Billy's biggest ride-or-die. I wasn't kidding—this one's for you. And to my sisters, Amber and Jac, who read everything I write with endless joy and enthusiasm. Thanks to every reader who has found me and my unhinged crew of characters, and who took a chance on this story. And finally, thanks to my husband, Rohan, for always digging me up when I am swallowed.

About the Author

Kel Bruem is a Bay Area-based indie monster romance author. Her Unusualities series include WHAT'S LUCK GOT TO DO WITH IT, EVERY BITE YOU TAKE, and NEVER GONNA DIG YOU UP. She is also an editor for the annual monster romance anthology TAILS, TRYSTS, and TENTACLES. When she's not writing, Kel trains her pit bull to be less stupid, explores new restaurants with her husband, and catches flights to her Sagittarian heart's content. You can find her online everywhere @kelbruem.

ALSO BY KEL BRUEM

What's Luck Got to Do With It

rumpy/Sunshine, He Falls First, Hidden Identities, Forbidden Love, He Has How Many Eggplants?!, Meddling Best Friends, Secret Societies, Boston in the Fall

Caiomhe Ryan is the luckiest girl in Boston—she has a great job, a cute apartment, and a ride-or-die best friend. All her ancestral luck as a leprechaun doesn't hurt either. When she takes a chance on an urgent client, the mysterious man at the heart of a scandal has her wondering how much longer she can keep herself a secret.

Leith Riordan just wants to drive boats by day and turn back into a merman at night—as simple as that. All his plans are destroyed, however, when a single lost temper lands him in a viral social media storm—and on Caiomhe Ryan's client roster. He knows his life can't go back to being simple. After all, it's not easy to tell a beautiful woman you're actually a merman.

Sparks fly and porridge burns when these two magical beings in the heart of Boston must decide if they can hide their real identity from the public while still being true to one another—and themselves.

Get your copy here!

Every Bite You Take

Bad Boy With a Heart of Gold, Woman In-Charge, Call Me a Good Girl, Caught in Public, Monster Romance, He Has How Many Eggplants?!, Whoops the Vampire is Hot, Woman Can't Choose So Tries Both, Fantasy Romance, Paranormal Romance

Evelyn Sharp thinks she's found her happy ending until a mysterious sea witch from Will's past appears and ruins everything.

Will Burleigh thought he'd found the key to breaking his curse—love and forgiveness from a human in the sexy and hilarious Evelyn. But his dark past quickly catches up to him when memories of his new life are erased, and he's returned to his dangerous, monstrous, former self.

Now, he must rely on his love to save him from future nightmares.

Dark truths are dragged into the light as two lovers learn to reconcile who they were with who they want to be. They say true love never runs smoothly, but is it supposed to be this bumpy?

Get your copy here!

www.ingramcontent.com/pod-product-compliance
Lightning Source LLC
Chambersburg PA
CBHW071354300726
48976CB00006B/1872

* 9 7 9 8 9 8 7 8 7 8 5 4 5 *